BABOUC'S VISION

ACORN BOOKS

Glenn Searfoss

Babouc's Vision

Originally published in 2000 by
1st Books

This revised edition published in 2021 by
Acorn Books
www.acornbooks.co.uk

Acorn Books is an imprint of
Andrews UK Limited
www.andrewsuk.com

For my wife, Cynthia, without whose support I would never have finished this book. And for my parents, Bill and Polly, who never lived to see its completion.

Contents

BABOUC'S VISION

Prologue: Customer Service

'Babouc's Appliance Repair'

The neon words glowed faintly through the shop window; their brightness dimmed to a lavender haze by the glare of a brutal, late-summer sun.

Murial Caffree wedged her face between the window bars. Even with her hands blocking the glare, she could discern little of the shop's interior save for the shimmer of overhead lights and dark mountains of indefinable objects stacked around the floor.

With a muffled, "Humph," she rocked back on her heels. A worn, podgy face with double chins and a cap of tangled, mousy hair frowned back at her from the window.

"My gawd," Murial snorted and tossed her hair. "Wouldja lookit that." The reflection flashed a snaggle-toothed grin.

Still grinning, Murial squatted and snatched up the strap of her lumpy canvas carryall. Lopsided with the weight, she wrestled the bag along the sidewalk to the shop's narrow doorway. Deftly, she flicked the door wide and propped it open with her left foot. A warning buzzer sounded as she wrenched her carryall sideways over the sill. With an awkward lunge, she tumbled after the bag. The door swung closed behind her, and the buzzing stopped.

Immediately, the odor of scorched circuitry prickled her nostrils. Murial inhaled deeply. "A-h-h," she smacked her lips, savoring the tangy air as it flowed over her tongue. "Filtered air. Such a treat."

With a contented sigh, she dragged a rumpled square of damp, yellow cloth from her brassiere and gently blotted sweat from her face. Each pat of the rough weave brought a stinging ache from the red, sun-chafed skin. A final, careful dab at her nose saw the cloth refolded and tucked back into its berth beneath her left cup.

"There," she patted her breast. "Now let's see…" Eagerly, she scanned the room.

The shop looked much the same as it had the week before. Racks of steel shelving crammed with tagged appliances hunched against the walls. Whipsaw benches mounded with electronic bric-a-brac occupied every foot of available floor space. Beneath the benches, coils of fiber optic cable fought for space with stacks of dusty, pink storage bins.

Everything appeared as she expected, except... Murial gnawed the raw insides of her cheeks. "Where is that man?"

An irregular passage zigzagged through the benches. Its winding path led to a glass service counter at the far end of the room. *He might be in back doing busy work or he might be... someone might have...*

She peered anxiously along the corridor, craning her neck to see around the jagged turns, examining the shadows for a moving... or still form.

"Yoo hoo," she called softly, "Mr. Babouc?"

There was no response.

Behind the counter, an archway trimmed with blue and white striped curtains screened the shop's work area and private living quarters. A faint clink of metal against metal sounded behind the striped folds.

Murial's eyes flashed at the sound. "Mr. Babouc!" Her voice detonated through the shop. "Mr. Babouc are you there?"

A loud thump sounded from the backroom and was immediately followed by a string of muffled profanity. Grinning delightedly, Murial hoisted the carryall to her left hip, and waddled to the counter.

"Sonofa..." Harl Babouc rubbed his knee where he had cracked it against the workbench. Acrid, white smoke curled from a thin gash in the Sump casing clamped to his workbench. Startled by Murial's shout, he had twitched the beam of his hand-held laser welder and sliced a three-centimeter furrow across the casing's metal surface.

Muttering a soft string of profanity, he dragged a hand along the back of his neck, smoothing the bristle of greasy black hair. There was nothing to do but repair it before carbon residuals obscured the gash.

"Just a minute!" He swiped his nose and eyes with a grimy coverall sleeve. "I'll be right there!"

Hands flying, Harl daubed metal flux into the fresh incision. Adjusting the torch optics to broadband FL, he swiveled the bench-mounted welding shield before his face and played the torch's crimson beam back and forth across the slit. An oily, smudge dulled the metal surface as he prodded melting flux through the crevice.

With a practiced flick of his wrist, he snapped the torch off and returned it to its wall-mount bracket. Twisting the shield aside, he rapped the casing with a dun hammer. Black slag chipped away, revealing a smooth, shiny blue surface. Grunting in satisfaction, Harl tossed the hammer onto the bench and hurried to the front counter.

Murial had just inflated her lungs for another bellow when he burst through the curtains. "Mr. Ba— Oh there you are!" She dimpled and extended a limp hand.

"Why Mrs. Caffree." Harl took her fingers and squeezed. Moist, putty-soft skin oozed in his grasp, and he fought to keep his smile intact. He liked his customers, he really did, but he never enjoyed shaking their hands. It always left him feeling queasy and needing to wash.

Oblivious, Murial Caffree grinned back, sunburned cheeks bulging, her eyes twinkling with delight. Harl released her hand and nonchalantly dragged his palm across his chest. "It's wonderful to see you again. I'm sorry to have kept you waiting, but as you can see," he swept a lanky arm at the banks of gutted appliances stacked around the room, "business is piling up."

She nodded enthusiastically. "I can tell."

"Now," Harl smiled, "what can I do for you?"

"What's that smell?" Murial leaned over the counter, her nostrils twitching at the prickling odor of scorched metal wafting from the back room. "You know," she strained to see around Harl's shoulders, "I was saying just the other day to Earl…"

"I see you've been out collecting?" Harl clumped a hand against the carryall, interrupting what he knew would be a long tirade on safety in the workplace and shouldn't he be more careful—God knows the place could burn down—if only he would apply a little common sense— you hear about it all the time what happens when people don't use common sense—why just the other day-

"Oh yes indeed!" Murial chuckled and shook the bag. There was a rustle of fabric and the muffled clank of metal against metal. "Had terrific luck too. Found a stash behind Mallows and another down the alley at Third and Pierce. Had to beat off a couple rummage rats for that one." She brandished a deceptively flabby arm that, Harl knew, could heave his own thin frame across the room.

"Seems everywhere I turned there was something." Murial opened the bag and poked her nose over the lip. "Got some aluminum and steel cans, a few copper and brass fittings, a couple bundles of plasti-film that're still in one piece. Even," she jerked a wad of crumpled, yellow pages from the bag and waved them beneath Harl's nose, "real paper."

The lingering scent of urine invaded Harl's sinuses and stung his eyes. He eased back, careful to keep his distaste from showing.

"Eh? Eh?" Her eyes glittered with excitement. "Nice?" The recycle center don't give nuthin for static sheets, but these...," she cradled the soiled sheets lovingly against her cheek before tucking them back into the bag and re-rolling the top shut, "these should bring a couple few credits, don't you think?"

"At least." Harl laughed, pleased his evasion had worked. Getting Mrs. Caffree to talk of her exploits was the easiest way to sidetrack her. "It's a nice haul that's for sure." He hefted the bag, his eyes widening in surprise at the weight. It *was* a good haul, and he nodded respectfully.

Mrs. Caffree was an inveterate scavenger and rightly proud of her triumphs. Like most of the neighborhood, it was how she stretched her family's means—successful foraging often being the difference between eating today or going hungry until tomorrow.

"I even got something for you." Grinning broadly, she dragged a fistful of spaghetti wire from her dress pocket. Lint and plastic fragments sprayed across the counter as she shoved the wadded mass into his hands.

"Why that's awfully nice of you." Harl turned the clump over in his hands. "Industrial grade." Holding it to the light, he noted the frayed ends. It was obvious the wire had been ripped from its moorings. He stretched it across the counter. *A good two and a half feet.* Stooping close, he examined the insulation. *No obvious breaks. I'll run a conductivity test later.* Without a word, he wrapped and tagged the bundle.

"Where's the Mr.?" he asked, stuffing the wire beneath the counter. "Thought he'd be with you."

Murial's hands fluttered nervously to her nest of bristling hair. After a flurry of needless primps, they dropped to her worn collar, tugging it first one way, then back again. "Not today." She picked at the frayed edges of her sleeve cuffs. "Earls at home sick."

"Ah." Harl glanced away. "Of course."

Forcing cheerfulness into his voice, he rubbed his hands together and leaned over the counter. "Well then, I hope he gets to feeling better. Now, what can I do for you?"

"I come for Earl's...I mean, my Tingler." Murial's lips quivered, trying to decide between a smile and a frown. The smile won, as Harl knew it would. "You said you'd have it fixed in a week." She checked her wristwatch, then glanced at the calendar display behind Harl's shoulder. "It's been seven days as of today."

"Finished it yesterday." Harl rapped a knuckle on the countertop. "Got it up front here, tagged and ready. Won't be but a sec." He turned and pawed through several dusty shelves, then stepped back scratching his head.

"Now where did I put it." He frowned at the mishmash of appliances, their laser-code tags glowing whitely along the shelf edges. "I know it's here somewhere. Hold on."

He retrieved a hand scanner from its wall mount and shook it beside his face. "What's the use of having technology if you don't use it, eh?" Murial chuckled in agreement as Harl keyed a code sequence into the scanner's handle. With an exaggerated flourish, he began flashing its beam over the wall of items.

He'd barely completed the first sweep when a gentle cough sounded behind his back. He cringed inwardly but kept scanning. The cough sounded again, louder this time, more insistent. He grimaced. *Here it comes.*

"Oh, I just don't know," Murial sighed. Her voice, muffled by the shop's crowded racks, sounded tiny and alone. "Earl just about had a heart attack when it stopped working."

"Is that right?" Harl shifted a container aside for easier access. With short, rapid movements, he waved the scanner across the visible tags. The device remained silent. Scowling, he continued along the racks.

"You know," she glanced apprehensively over her shoulder, "and don't tell him I said this, but I think he's addicted to the damn thing. Why just the other day he threatened to go out and buy a new one if this one wasn't ready. Imagine, buying a new one of all things! And us barely able to afford what we got! Well, you can bet I told him to just hold his horses. That man! I swear, some days I could wring his neck!" She giggled nervously at her boldness.

Harl bobbed his head in sympathy. He had never acquired a taste for tinglers; the hangovers were too vicious. But Earl Caffree loved them.

Nearly every night the man blustered about the neighborhood; his blanched face soaked with thick, oily sweat; his temples swollen angry red from overstimulation. Jacked high, he was impervious to pain and lashed out at anybody and anything that obstructed his path. Once, he shattered his knuckles beating a brick wall. If a passing CitySec patrol hadn't dragged him away, he would have continued until either his hands or the wall had given way.

Most folks prudently crossed the street when they saw him coming.

And Mrs. Caffree… sharing meals every day… a bed every night… He had seen the swollen eyes and the angry, half-concealed bruises on her arms and throat, and could not for the life of him understand why she stayed. *Maybe she's one of those people who prefer it to loneliness.*

The scanner beeped as its beam passed over a tag projecting from the top of a crowded rack. "Found it," he called.

Pulling a Johnny-step close, Harl retrieved a flat, ovoid device from the dusty shelf. Lap-sized and half a handbreadth thick, the unit weighed just under 400 grams. A pair of dermal induction leads coiled from either side of its featureless, flesh-toned surface. An on/off toggle and a recessed, pulse-intensity slide were the only controls. To repair it, he'd violated warranty guidelines by splitting the casing—though to be honest, the unit was so old he doubted a warranty still existed. After replacing a fused processor with one salvaged from a scraped vid-com unit, he'd melded the halves back together.

"Sorry to keep you waiting." He set the unit on the counter. "One of the loop processors overloaded. I replaced it with one spec'd for twice the capacity. Should work good as new, probably better."

"Oh Mr. Babouc," Murial burbled, "you're a godsend that's what you are, a godsend." She trailed a gnawed fingernail along the Tingler's newly re-melded seam. The line of epoxy slashed blood red against the compact housing. "If it weren't for the color, I couldn't tell you'd done a thing."

"You've got a good piece of equipment there. A bit out of date, but top shelf." Harl hesitated, waiting to see if the quip registered. When she didn't comment, he shrugged and patted his breast pockets.

"Now where did I put the credit pad?" His voice trailed off as he rummaged through one pocket, then another. Finding nothing, he began rooting among the piles of miscellany cluttering the countertop. He located the Creditor beneath a parts box and tugged it free.

"You know," Harl offered, keying the transaction, "most folks toss stuff like that rather than fix it."

Snorting, Murial twisted her waist purse to one side, letting her stomach sag comfortably over the narrow bellyband. "That may be," she drew an Omni card from the purse, "but Earl and me, we can't afford to be buying new stuff every time something breaks." She lightly rapped the card on the countertop, tat-tat-tat-tat-tat, waiting for Harl to finish the billing. "Used to be things were made to last, nowadays everything seems to bust soon as you get it home."

"You're right there," Harl agreed. "They sure don't make appliances like they used to." He passed her the credit pad. "That'll be 5 Cr, minus 3.27 for the wire." He winked. "No need to tell the tax man."

"No sirree Bob!" Murial spat vehemently. "Those blood suckers hit up Earl and me with a tardy-tab ten years back that we're still paying on!" She slipped the card along a slot at the top of the pad, then pressed her thumb alongside the display. "Any time I get a chance to gouge 'em, you bet I do it."

Harl nodded and poised a finger over the scanner's display. "Do you want a print copy, or an electronic statement sent to your Web code?"

"Print!" Murial demanded. "I don't trust the mail. There're too many peepers out there."

The handheld gave a short beep as the transaction verified and an invoice rolled from the bottom. The electronic copy, cached into the pad's permanent memory, belonged to the shop. Harl tore the strip of static film from the pad base and handed it to her along with the repaired unit. "There you go Mrs. Caffree. Now keep this invoice in your pocket; too much sunlight for too long and it will degrade, like your last one. You have a nice day now." He smiled. "And do come back."

"Oh, I will. I will." Hugging the Tingler to her ample bosom, Murial Caffree hurried away. She had only taken a few steps before Harl called out, "Don't forget your bag!" He thumped the carryall.

"Oh!" She giggled and minced back to the counter. "I swear, I'd forget my head if it weren't attached."

She wrapped a free arm tightly around the bag and trundled for the door. As she wedged it open, a wall of blistering summer heat rolled over the sill. "Thank you!" Murial called over her shoulder and pushed through onto the sidewalk. She paused a moment, her legs braced firmly apart, and squinted carefully up and down the sunlit street. Without warning she uttered an ear piercing "Yoo hoo!"

Even through the closed door, its volume startled. Flinching behind the counter, Harl thanked God it was directed at some invisible recipient and not himself. The unfortunate victim must have tried running because, much to Harl's amazement, Mrs. Caffree leapt several inches into the air and immediately disappeared from view.

He stared at the doorjamb, listening as the squealing sounds of pursuit faded down the street.

The shop grew still.

Craning his neck, Harl peered carefully into the dim recesses of the shop's front room. Silence always seemed unnatural after a visit from Mrs. Caffree. He could almost hear it rustling in the shadowy niches, peeping timorously around the corners. Is she gone? Is she really gone?

He sighed and wearily massaged the back of his neck. Stiff, knotted muscles rolled beneath his fingers. All morning a persistent ache had spread upwards from his shoulders, inching towards the base of his skull. The wall clock read 11:30, but he felt exhausted. "I need a break."

Slipping his fingers beneath the counter edge, he pressed a concealed button. Bolts chunked into place along the front door frame and sharp clacking sounds rattled from the backroom windows. The shop window display flared briefly then settled into a shimmering clock face with its hands set to 2:00. The words "Back at" glowed above the clock.

Rising on tiptoe, Harl stretched his arms high overhead, gave a low moan, then staggered through the heavy drapes into the back room.

Eidolon

Harl's head lolled to one side. A thin ribbon of drool trickled from the corner of his mouth and spread damply along his collar. Gentle gusts of moist air brushed his cheek and stirred his hair.

He smiled. The sea breeze felt good. It had been a long while since the last blue advisory permitted open windows. His sagging eyelids fluttered, then snapped wide in alarm. *Open windows! How in hell did they get open?*

Dust motes shivered as a severe, gray-suited figure flowed through the shafts of golden sunlight angling through the windows. Stopping before the recliner, it reached forward and drew a finger lightly across Harl's brow.

With a bleat, Harl leapt from the chair and crouched behind it. Heart pounding, shoulders braced against the wall, he twisted the lounger between himself and the intruder. Blinking madly into the haze, he received a fleeting impression of flat features, pinched, bloodless lips, tailor-cut lines, and razor-edged creases.

"Who…," Harl's voice cracked. He swallowed hard around the sharp edges and tried again. "Who the hell are you?" he finally managed. "Who are you? And how did you get past my security locks?"

"I am Ithuriel." There was a pause, as the tall, dour faced visitor waited for Harl to gather himself. "And how I got here," a cadaverous hand waved towards the open windows, "why I simply arrived."

"Now," the intruder extracted a sheaf of documents from his breast pocket. Close-set eyes examined the sheets. "You are Harl Babouc?" Without waiting for confirmation, he refolded the papers and returned them to his jacket. "We have business to discuss."

Half listening, Harl readied himself for a mad dash towards the exit. He leaned forward, toes flexing inside his shoes, when a silver badge on the figure's jacket lapel drew his attention: I.C.A. The initials stood bold and black across the badge's triangular surface.

"An auditor!" Harl choked, struggling to keep suddenly watery knees beneath him. "You're an I.C.A. auditor!"

"I'm not really-," the stranger began.

"You're an auditor!" Harl's lips quivered uncontrollably, and his fingers clutched at the chair's back. The I.C.A. was the government's tax revenue enforcement bureau with the authority and the means to enter any place, anywhere, at anytime. If they decided to audit you or your business, you were as good as dead.

He shivered at the intruder's impassive features. His face was like the caricature sketches done by sidewalk artists in LoDo—all sharp angles, heavy lines, and of exaggerated proportions. Lonely wisps of gray hair swirled neatly about a shiny, pink scalp. Cropped sidewalls and jug-handle ears gave the head a narrow, pointed appearance. The slit mouth worked soundlessly, open… closed… open… closed. No teeth were visible. Clear, expressionless eyes stared unblinking from beneath a single, bushy brow.

"I'm being audited!" Sobbing, nearly in tears, Harl lurched around the chair. "But I've done nothing wrong. My books are in order. I file on time." He gulped a short breath and dared an inch closer.

"Look," he fawned, "I'm a small businessman. I have to barter to stay alive. It helps my customers. It helps me. It even helps you in the long run. Why would you want to close me down?" he wailed, crawling forward on his knees.

"You see," Ithuriel gazed heavenward, his hands lifted in supplication, "this typifies our problem. Because so many have forgotten, we thought a familiar authority figure would receive easier acceptance. Well," he shrugged resignedly, "you see how it is. They've become more terrified of themselves than us."

A small, bewildered voice drifted upwards from the floor. "You mean you're not an auditor?"

Ithuriel sadly shook his head. "I'm sorry this guise frightens you tinker. Here." He bent low. "Let me."

Harl stared transfixed as an ashen hand reached towards his face. Fat, blue sparks leapt from the outstretched fingertips and snapped painfully against his skin. With a yowl, he fell back clutching his cheek.

"That," Ithuriel smiled brightly, "was to focus your attention. Now…"

The gray suit expanded into a scintillating ball of white light that stung Harl's eyes. The glare settled into a translucent, childlike face that peered serenely from atop a ruffled collar. Golden ringlets cascaded across the shoulders, blending with folds of alabaster cloth that flowed gently to the floor. The robe seemed alive, billowing with each breath of air that coursed through the windows.

"There." Ithuriel's mantle rustled as he rolled his shoulders. "That's better."

"What… What…" Harl's jaw swung limply, and his eyes bulged. A bit of drool stretched from the corner of his mouth. It grew longer and longer, then snapped in half—one length spattering on the floor, the other recoiling to his lips.

"What do you think?" Ithuriel turned in a slow circle. "This is closer to my true form. You may call me a Genie, an Angel, a higher level of consciousness, even," his voice acquired an amused tone, "an extraterrestrial. Whichever concept works best for you."

Harl gaped at the tall, white-robed image. As a child, his father dragged him to the local church every Sunday morning. Installed on an uncomfortable pew, he'd been dutifully awed by the grand scenes of angelic hosts that filled the apse. Growing older and more learned, he'd come to consider such imagery the fantasies of cloistered minds; fanciful impressions of divine existence; ecclesiastic phantasms relegated to Christmas cards and stained-glass windows.

But now… He drew a trembling hand across his face. Here it was. It couldn't be, and yet here it was. His mind struggled to grasp the implications. "You're an angel?"

Delicate, milk-white hands folded themselves before the golden sash girding the Ithuriel's waist. "As you wish." His reply reverberated through the room.

Lips moving silently, Harl bowed his head. Of all the events in his universe this was one he'd never considered. Day-to-day survival was difficult enough, but to receive a visitation, a true manifestation from heaven of all places. He recalled the Sunday school tales of unfortunate souls pressed into service by these powerful, now suddenly real beings. "And what…," Harl swallowed uneasily, "what do you want from me?"

Ithuriel struck a regal pose. Chest swelling, fists planted on hips, his presence filled the room. "Harl Babouc," he intoned, "you have been chosen to perform a solemn duty of grave importance. We require an envoy to enter your city and report faithfully to us its nature. From your account we will decide its fate. We—"

"Fascinating." The angel's attention veered suddenly to the devices scattered around the room. The abrupt shift left Harl's mind scrambling for balance.

"Such an eclectic assortment. Do you really repair all of these?" Ithuriel extracted a micro-googol drive from an assortment of drives stacked on top of a chest refrigerator. It seemed like a tiny silver coin nestled in his palm.

"I fix whatever comes through," Harl whispered, staring blankly at the wall. A spasm ran through his body and his head snapped around. "What do you mean, fate?"

"Hum?" Ithuriel glanced over his shoulder. He'd been toying with the optical pad of an event scaler. "Oh," he flicked a dismissive hand, "over the years tales of your city's degeneration has grown so horrifying that we have decided to either chasten it or destroy it."

"But... but," Harl stammered, "how can you destroy an entire city?" He fought to keep himself and his voice steady. "I thought angels are supposed to be good; the things they do, good."

Shrugging blithely, Ithuriel traced colored markings on the pad's display. "I suppose that depends if you define good by intent or by result."

Harl shook his head. The words, the concepts refused to register.

"It is like this," the angel explained. "Which is better, a good action that harms or a bad action that benefits?"

Harl stared helplessly from his position on the floor. He was distantly aware of numbness creeping through his legs and a painful aching in his knees. "I... I don't know," he managed.

"You have heard of the road to hell?" Ithuriel returned his attention to the optical pad. He didn't wait for a reply. "Well, the road to heaven is paved in a similar fashion. It is impossible to judge any course of action as good or bad without first determining its ultimate result or," the angel turned and stared fully into Harl's eyes, "its supreme intent."

Harl buried his face in both hands attempting, without noticeable results, to stop a sudden fit of shaking. Dampness slicked his palms, and it took several tries before he could swallow. *Don't get drawn into this! I can't be drawn into this!*

"Why pick on me?" he croaked from behind clenched hands. "Surely your kind are better suited to the job. Isn't your view supposed to be all encompassing?"

Ithuriel lifted slightly into the air and peered idly out a window. "Therein lies our dilemma. Omnipotence limits our ability to comprehend subtleties. It is our nature to perceive the whole, not the fractional."

"You see," he drifted back to the floor, "all angels are of like mind, and so are equally biased. We ensure objectivity by employing a disinterested third party, such as yourself, to evaluate the particulars of a situation before we take action." The angel twitched his chin upwards. "It is an old custom."

"But I live here!" Babouc wailed. "How can I be unbiased! It's impossible!"

"Live here?" Ithuriel snorted derisively. "According to our records you inherited this fix-it shop after your father's death fifteen years ago. Since then, you have not left its walls except to purchase necessities. You know nothing of your city except what you see on the vid or read over your electronic mail. You do not live here; you exist here!"

There was a moment of silence as Ithuriel brushed and straightened his robe. "This is a dream, right!" Harl blurted, his voice quavering higher with each word. "It's gotta be, right! Any second now I'm gonna wake up here in this chair, right!"

He scrunched his eyes tight, then snapped them open. The room appeared the same. The windows stood open, and a moist, salty breeze blew in over the sill. He was still on his knees and the angel still hovered before him.

"Maybe if I…" His gaze darted wildly around the room. "Yeah! Yeah!" Scrabbling across the floor, he snatched a needle punch from his tool bench and jabbed it into the back of his hand. Fiery pain lanced up his arm and he stared in horror as dark, red blood welled from the wound. With a strangled cry, he brought his hand quickly to his lips.

Across the room Ithuriel carefully buffed his fingernails against his robe. "No tinker," he murmured. "No dream."

Not a dream. Harl clutched his hand to his chest. *Not a dream.*

Sunlight throbbed in rhythm with the pulse crashing through his temples. Hard edges softened and blurred. The room contracted to a point. Harl stared fixedly at a fragment of opti-fiber lying near the toe of his right shoe. *I can use that*, he thought inanely. *It's perfect for the casting array on Joe Wheeler's voice module. I'll just splice the ends to-*

The hem of Ithuriel's cloak drifted into view. The room snapped back into focus. This… all of it, was real. Really real. "Get someone else!" Harl shouted. "I've too much to do."

"That is at least one thing we got right," Ithuriel glowered. "Your selfishness. Sorry to inconvenience you tinker," he spat, "but we need help, and you are it."

The angel held up a hand as Harl began to protest. "Do not ask," he warned. "Our reasons for selecting you would only confuse. Suffice to say," his upper lip curled into a sneer, "you are the best of a jaded lot. Now," Ithuriel tucked his hands into his sleeves, "you have two choices: aid us or don't aid us."

A thrill ran up Harl's spine. He started to speak, but the angel's commanding glare brought a muting tightness to his throat.

"If you accept the trust, your life goes on as it always has, no tangible rewards, no punishments. But if you choose not to assist, I can ensure your being audited by the real I.C.A. by," Ithuriel grinned nastily, "how does this afternoon sound."

Harl hunched into himself. The angel stood before the curtained doorway, strategically blocking the exit. Escape meant a wrestling match, that Harl knew from his queasy stomach, he wasn't capable of winning. He was trapped and knew it. Though desperate to refuse, experience had taught him the wisdom of his father's earthy advice.

"Always keep this in mind boy. When the foot that's doing the kicking is big, it doesn't matter how narrow your ass or how well it's covered."

Harl glanced ruefully at the angel's feet. Shrouded by the spreading white robe, he imagined hobnailed behemoths filling the concealed space.

Reluctantly, he nodded his head.

"Wonderful." Ithuriel chuckled at Harl's tight features. "You need not worry tinker. Your needs will be provided; your passage safe." Leaning close, he brushed a finger lightly along Harl's cheek. There was a tingling crackle at the touch. "You can trust me," he purred.

Mumbling his sincere hope that it was so, Harl excused himself. He gestured weakly towards the curtains, "I've got to get my coat."

Ithuriel smiled and stepped aside. "Of course."

Inching sideways, Harl slid past the angel and through the curtains.

Omnipotent, he snorted, dragging his jacket from beneath the counter. Mrs. Caffree's wire bundle tumbled from the shelf. Harl glared at it for several seconds before savagely kicking it across the floor. The bundle skittered through the dust and crashed heavily against a bench leg. A trio of wafer cards clattered to the floor.

Know all! He jammed his arms through the sleeves.

See all! He shrugged the jacket around his shoulders.

Harl breathed deeply, trying to still the quivering inside. His hand throbbed from the puncture wound, but that didn't matter. That pain he could bear. It was just…, his eyes heated, and a hitch caught in his throat, he was afraid to leave.

Closing his eyes, he sensed the comfort of the stacked shelves and cluttered tables. The musty scent of dust and plastic were old familiar friends. He had worked here all his life. He belonged here, not running off on some fool's errand. Certainly not on one whose final decision might result in the city's destruction. A tear trickled down his cheek as he thought of Mrs. Caffree and how, right now, he'd relish the feel of her handshake.

But the angel promised his acceptance meant business would go on as before, that he would be safe, and all his needs provided. It was either that or an audit, and Harl had no doubt that the angel could and would arrange one. He really had no choice but to go through with the mission.

Harl snorted. He may have a guardian angel, but precautions were never unwarranted. Quietly, he retrieved an Omni card from an emergency lockbox beneath the counter and slipped it into his pants pocket. *There.* He patted his pocket. *At least I'll have that.* Glancing once more around the shop, he sighed and pushed back through the curtains.

Ithuriel's instructions were brief.

"Harl Babouc, you will enter the city and examine all you encounter. Upon your return, you will report your findings. We will use this report to decide the city's fate."

"During your journey you will be as a wraith," the angel counseled, "undetectable, and invulnerable. However, the successful completion of your task requires two essential abilities. First is a proficiency in idioms, so…"

Ithuriel pressed a thumb to Harl's forehead, and his mind exploded with bursts of multicolored light. Staggering backwards, Harl shook his head, trying to clear the dazzle. Before he could regain his balance, he felt pressure again between his eyes.

"Since few things are as they appear, you will also need the gift of discernment. This faculty allows perception beyond the surface." Again, Harl experienced an explosion, but not as brilliant this time. Instead of staggering, he wobbled slightly.

Ithuriel paused as Harl fought to maintain his equilibrium. "On this journey you will encounter circumstances which at first may make little or no sense. The tools I have provided will promote your understanding of these situations, but to successfully use them you must guard against quick judgments. Be prepared," he cautioned, "to ponder eventualities."

He speared Harl with a bleak stare. "I can provide only this. To give more will imperil your objectivity." His colorless eyes bored deep into Harl's own. "Are you ready tinker?"

Fingers trembling, Harl snapped his jacket at the waist. He felt inexorably thrust along some dark, endless tunnel, his feet moving without his volition. This wasn't a situation he was ready for, or ever would be. His stomach gurgled and sweat misted his brow. With a sharp nod, he steeled himself.

Ithuriel raised an arm.

Descent

"C'mon you piece of crap!" Joey rammed his foot hard against the accelerator. "Move it!" The electric turbine rose to a scream and the tram bolted forward. The reflective tips of highway markers winked in the periphery of his vision as he sped through the foothills toward town.

"Piece of-!" He growled and slammed his fist against the dash. The faded Vynex warped, absorbing the impact, then slowly reformed to its original smooth green surface.

"Damn!" Joey rubbed his knuckles against the light fuzz of his jaw. Then again softly, "Damn."

Joy Jacking was supposed to be simple. Everybody understood the rules. You flash your strap and tell the citizen to get out. They get out. You drive it to Bouli's. He pays you fifty, maybe a hundred for the ride. You get the credits – you're happy. The citizen lives – they're happy. It's that simple.

But sometimes… Joey shook his head. "Stupid bitch," he muttered.

The driver looked decent enough: single-fit teasers cut high below and low above, shaggy brown hair styled to look windblown on a still day, nice tits, …but not too bright. Not only was she in the wrong place at the wrong time, but instead of getting out of the tram like he told her to, she cowered against the passenger door and whimpered.

"Well, if you want to stay," Joey grinned and licked his lips "how 'bout we take a little ride." He wriggled his eyebrows. "A little privacy." Hell, he hadn't been to the hills since, well, since the last time. It would be fun. "I know just the spot."

Her answer was a soft, rhythmic mewling.

The drive was unremarkable. He took Bay Shore to Waverly, then hopped onto Brighton just after the Pelmont intersection. He scanned for CitySec buzzers as the rooftops of the Banyon Reclamation District faded into the summer haze. When they passed the first rebar community, he leered at his passenger. She moaned and cringed deeper into the space between the seat and the passenger door.

The rest of the ride was silent except when he slid his hand up her leg and tugged at her panties - smooth, silky black, and o-o-o what's this here? He nestled a finger in a furrow and wriggled it back and forth. She howled and tried to push his hand away. He backhanded her, scraping a thin gash across her cheek with his ring. "We gonna have us a good time," he chuckled.

The tram climbed into the sun-scorched hillsides overlooking Sarong Bay. They followed a stony ribbon that snaked through a series of progressively higher hills, appearing and disappearing among brown mountain meadows. Fields dotted with boulders and tufts of scrub oak stretched upwards towards a serrated line of white-capped mountain peaks.

He selected a turn out, parked and climbed from the tram, hauling his passenger with him. She tried to pull away, digging her heels into the veneer of pea gravel that spread beneath their feet. "You ain't going nowhere bitch," he slapped and shook her hard until she quit struggling. "Not 'til I say."

They stood on the shoulder of an empty, slate-gray highway, the tallest objects for miles around. Ears straining, he swiveled his head, first one way and then the other. There was no sound except the constant whisper of rushing wind and the steady whimpering of his passenger.

To their left, the gravel melted into wiry grasses desiccated by the ferocious late-August sun. Nestled amid the dried blades, wild rose hips bobbed in the steady breeze. Joey hawked and spat a mass of yellowish phlegm. It clung to a blood red bulb, bending it toward the ground. He grinned and forced the woman onto the rough grass. "Looks like we're here."

....

Joey gripped the steering wheel hard and flexed his wrists forward, then back. "Man," he hissed through gritted teeth, "it didn't have to go that way."

He ran a finger along the bloody welt below his right eye. He might have let her live if she hadn't done that. But he taught her. Yeah. Joey licked his finger and touched the welt again. It hurt a little less this time. The stupid bitch had it coming. Now she was in a ditch waiting for whatever else would come. He knew some retreads that would like her, even now.

The roadway plunged through the course of low hills before angling into a sprawling gridwork of streets and buildings. From the high grade, Joey tried to spot his neighborhood, but the lack of detail frustrated his attempt. At this distance buildings were indistinguishable rectangles and the intersections too numerous to decipher. Still, he could make out the massive geometric fortifications of rebar communities spotted along the front range. Reserved and patrolled, their barbed perimeter walls surrounded houses regimented into neat, defensive rows.

Deeper into the city proper, lines fell away, and shapes disappeared—eclipsed by an opaque lens of murky brown haze. Squatting over the metropolis, its bulging center slumped against the greenish body of Sarong Bay. Megascrapers rose above the dense canopy, their peaks poking from its roiling surface. They were well over 200 stories. Their seeming insignificance the betrayal of distance.

Joey took a breath and tried to swallow. The air inside the tram was getting close. He jiggled the filter control, but the fan failed to come on. "What is this," he thumped the console. The tram was one of last year's models. It shouldn't be breaking down now. It had at least seven more months before that happened. He tried the filter control again. Still nothing. "P.O.S.", he snorted.

Joey punched the driver-side window key on the console. There was a faint hum as the window slid down. A gust of hot, damp air slapped his face and snatched at the open collar of his black shirt. He drew a deep breath and nearly buckled against the steering wheel. Searing pain ignited his lungs. Sharp, involuntary coughs exploded from his chest.

Horns blared from all sides as the tram slew sharp left, then right. Traffic backed away, giving space to the wildly careening vehicle. Throat burning, eyes streaming, Joey fought to keep the vehicle straight. With a tremendous effort that threatened to rupture his diaphragm, he suppressed the desire to cough. It took several tries, before he could sit straight.

"Christ!" he hissed between tightly clamped teeth. "I don't remember it ever being this bad. Wow!" He blew his nose with two fingers and flicked the snot onto the floor. "That's nasty!" Wiping his eyes, he scanned the sky and road for CitySec patrols. His antics were certain to draw their attention.

"Gotta get off," he sang. "Gotta get off…now!"

The tram swerved onto the 3rd street exit without slowing, traveled two blocks, then veered south onto Pelmont. Bouli's was over five miles away. If he was lucky, he'd make it through the Wiggers turf without being noticed. "I knew I should of dumped the bitch," he grumbled. "But no. I had to go and have me a party. Stupid! Stupid! Stupid!"

Joey slowed the tram to 10K over the speed limit. Any faster would alert the CitySec patrols. Any slower and somebody could grab ahold and hang on. *Well, they can't hang on*, he gunned past a cab with a no-hurry fare, *but they'll shoot if they make me*. He laughed, keeping his face turned slightly to the interior. "I make this, and I'll be the man. Yeah!"

The tram wound its way down the block, cutting through slower traffic and drawing curses from startled pedestrians as they dodged aside. A man in a black jumpsuit jerked a blond-haired woman out of its path. Joey glanced at the rearview and grinned. The black jumpsuit stood on the curb impotently shaking his fist.

"Fucking Uptowner," Joey chuckled. "Go back to your hole!" he bawled and laughed harder. His laughter ended abruptly as a tremor shuddered through the tram.

"What the hell?" Near the midpoint of the block, the tram shuddered, lurched, then the turbine cut off. Silently the two-seater coasted down the street. Jerking the wheel hard right, Joey slid the tram up to the curb beside an alley mouth.

Tossing the drive stick into park, he flicked the start switch back and forth. A light flickered from the console, then faded away. "Dead!" Joey stared at the blank console in disbelief. "The damn thing's dead!"

"Shit!" He slammed his fist repeatedly against the dash. "Shit! Shit! Shit!" The Vynex coating warped, then splintered into a spider web of cracks that spiraled outward from his fist.

"Ah-h-h man." Joey ran his hand lightly over the dashboard. The shattered surface snagged the skin of his palm. "That's all I need. Bouli's is gonna clip me good for this." He slumped back in the seat, disgusted with himself. A ripple of blue reflected in the rearview mirror caught his attention. His breath hitched.

Three youths in baggy, acid-washed blues peeled themselves from a doorway overlooking the alley and moved toward the tram.

"No!" Joey jerked open the door. "No!" He leapt from the tram and raced down the street with three faded blue figures in pursuit.

Waiting Room

April's heels clicked a staccato beat as she hastened along the polished, jade-stone floor. "Hurry up," she beckoned impatiently to the stocky, balding man trailing in her wake. "The office is right up here."

"I'm coming. I'm coming." Tom quickened his stiff-legged gait. With each step his styrene jump suit, already riding high in the buttocks, began pinching at the crotch.

"I knew I should have worn the other one," he grumbled, pulling at the crowding inseam. "But no, she says. The black one looks more professional, she says. As if it makes any difference."

With a final painful stride, he joined her before a textured-glass door. A brass plaque, inlaid with onyx lettering, hung at eye-level beside the doorway.

GENCON Associates

Dr. Alan K. Jerome M.D., G.I.C.

April examined her reflection in the plaque's burnished finish. With swift practiced movements, she primped and patted her pixie blond hair; a change, Tom noted, from her normal shoulder-length indigo. Giving her jacket waist a firm tug, she turned and uttered an exasperated, "Oh Tom!"

"Huh? What?" He stared blankly at her.

"Your shoulder pads. You didn't seal them in place like I told you to."

"Well, I thought..." Tom twisted his head to look. The pads had shifted giving his shoulders a hunched forward appearance. Working his fingers under the fabric, he tried pushing them back into place.

"Stop!" April slapped his hands away. "Let me do it!"

Tom stood helplessly, arms dangling by his sides, as April loosened the pads, shoved them into their proper position, and reattached them with a quick pat.

"There!" She briskly brushed his shoulders and sleeves, then straightened his collar with a series of sharp jerks that wrenched his entire body.

She took a deep breath and slowly released it. "I guess this is it. Are you ready?"

Tom Wyman licked his lips and nodded slightly. A drum thundered wildly in his ears and threatened to explode from his chest. Swallowing hard, he tried willing his heart into a slow easy rhythm, but each time he thought of what lay ahead it pounded harder.

It's not that big of a deal, he counseled himself. This is just standard procedure—nothing to it. They've run the tests. Just go in and find out the results. If there had been any problems, they would have cropped up at the start. Just take it slow.

Forcing a smile, he took April's arm and together they pushed through the office door.

....

The waiting room spread before them, sterile and silent, its walls glowing with soothing pink light. Warm breezes murmured from concealed vents high overhead—a baby's breath that gently caressed their cheeks and tickled the hair along their arms.

With chin lifted and lips set in a determined line, April charged forward. Her quick, precise steps sent ripples of molten fire coursing along the silver brocade of her silk jacket.

Tom followed, moving slowly, his eyes darting from side-to-side. The room made him uneasy. Maybe it was the smell. He hated the stink of a doctor's office, had since he was a kid. He recalled the hordes of screaming five- and six-year-olds waiting for testing. The long, white smocks of harried nurses and doctors. The stomach-knotting terror as his turn came. Surgical tubing cinched about his upper arm. White-faced, heart hammering, he looked away when they pressed the needle into a bulging vein and filled several vials with blood—his blood. Afterwards, the antiseptic, or whatever it was they used for sterilization, seemed overpowering. Yeah. Tom drew deeper into himself. He hated doctor's offices.

They passed a split row of contoured poly carbon benches. A low, triangular table covered with static news sheets and E-magazines nestled between them. As Tom sidestepped the table's jutting point, a holo-poster hanging at eye-level on the opposite wall caught his attention. Flickering 3-D text declared: *In-vitro: The viable choice. Northwest Regional Sperm Center - Member F.H.I.C.* Over the caption a wriggling sperm lustily burrowed into an ovum.

He paused, staring transfixed until an urgent tug from April broke the spell. Muttering a quick apology, he hastened to her side at the admission station.

Shielded by blast-proof crystal, a receptionist with blue-black hair and chalky skin guarded the inner office. Installed in a crash recliner, she appeared oblivious to their approach—her attention focused on a console display. A tarnished, silver badge pinned to her white uniform blouse read: *Ann Leeland R.N.*

"I thought you said this was a private enterprise," Tom hissed, "not an APM!"

"It's supposed to be." April whispered.

"Then why that?" Tom gestured sharply at the unmoving figure. The receptionist appeared artificial, like the mannequins behind the receiving windows of All-Public Medical establishments. Cleverly crafted of latex polymers, their benign features exuded comfort and encouraged visitor trust.

"I don't know," whined April. "There wasn't one at the other office."

"Well," Tom tripped the office com, "there's one here." He expected a taped greeting. Instead, a hushed, barely audible vibration coursed through the air. Mechanically, the receptionist's hand, index finger extended, lifted from the station desk.

"O-o-o-o-o-o-o look," April crooned, "it's alive."

"Yeah," Tom grumbled, "but not very responsive."

When no further movement occurred, he began grinding his teeth. It was just his luck. This must be one of the older, pulse-activated models designed for limited interaction. After several long moments, he pressed the com key again. Once more they received the finger.

"Of all the crap we've had to deal with, now this!" His exclamation came as a soft explosion. He began turning away when April nudged him in the ribs.

"Look." She jerked her chin as the receptionist's face underwent a series of convulsions. Lips twitched. The Adam's apple bobbed. Wrinkles and furrows appeared and disappeared as muscle groups strained beneath the skin.

"What the..." Tom stared at the figure. "You don't mean...?"

Lips clamped into a quivering frown; April managed several weak nods before exploding with laughter.

"No-o-o. Can't be." Bending close, Tom's face split into a wide grin. "Well, I'll be damned."

Giggling helplessly, they fell against one another.

Slowly, deliberately, the receptionist's eyes climbed to meet theirs, briefly acknowledged their presence, then dropped back to the screen.

"Oh god," Tom snorted, wiping tears from his eyes, "that's just too much."

Still sniggering, April tugged his collar. Tom leaned close, as she whispered into his ear. Nodding, he rapped loudly on the crystal barrier. His hand fell away as the receptionist blinked, stretched, and leaned forward actuating an office interlink.

"Sorry," she croaked, massaging her throat. "Needed to finish processing before I could stop. I just received my implant and haven't mastered subvocalization." Her voice rasped from hidden speakers and as she spoke, deeply scored fissures bracketed her mouth.

Look at those lines, Tom chuckled silently. A near gerrie for sure. I wonder how she got this job.

"Whisper talk takes practice… Ann," snickered April. "You should have seen me when I got mine. I was four and…"

"You may address me," the voice burred, "as Nurse Leeland. Now what can we do for you?"

"Whoa," Tom hugged himself from an imaginary chill, "ice city." Turning to the desk, his grin collapsed under Nurse Leeland's steady glare. "Uh-h-h… a-hem… uh-h-h… Wyman and Langston to see Dr. Jerome. We've a 1:30 appointment."

Flat, gray eyes hardened into bright slits. "You're early."

"Our activity agenda is full and… well," April smiled impishly and winked, "we thought if we got here early, Dr. Jerome could see us early."

"Appointment times may not be altered." It was a flat statement leaving no room for argument. "Now, if you'll confirm the information on the screen to your left, we'll start the processing." As the nurse spoke, a wafer LED built into the blast shielding came alive with columns of data.

April glanced at the display. "Isn't this on the Web?"

"Regulations require preliminary client verification." A pale hand gestured impatiently at the screen. "Please confirm its accuracy."

With annoyed grumbles, they reviewed their respective statistics: name, age, residence, cellular number, Web code. Everything appeared in order.

"All correct," said Tom.

"Mine too," added April.

Nurse Leeland murmured to herself, and the screen blanked. "Step into the center of the silver square located to your right. Miss Langston first."

Feeling foolish, April positioned herself with toes pointing forward. "Is this necessary?" she complained. "I mean really, we're not here to kill anyone. Surely that's obvious even to you."

"A weapons check," came the brusque reply, "is standard procedure for all visitors."

April cursed silently to herself as the detector field tingled up her legs and over her head. She was readying another outburst when a chalky finger waved her away. "Now Mr. Wyman." After scanning the console screen, Nurse Leeland reclined in her chair. "Thank you. Be seated. You'll be called when Dr. Jerome is ready."

"But..." April began to protest. An icy glare silenced her.

"You'll be called when Dr. Jerome is ready. Now please" the ice formed in full force, "be seated."

They huddled uncertainly for a moment before approaching the benches and selecting a seat. Knees popping, Tom dropped the last inch onto the formed surface. He rolled his shoulders experimentally, surprised at the comfort.

"What a bitch huh?" He leaned sideways and kissed April's ear. "Something to read?"

"God no. This preliminary nonsense has me too anxious. You go ahead." She patted his knee. "I'll sit here and realign."

Squeezing April's hand, Tom turned and examined the available reading material. Static news sheets and E-magazines littered the table: *In-vitro Today*, *CynCity Globe*, *Newsday*, *Nutricise*. From the holo-cover of *Fortune International* a three-inch figure of Huang-Wu, China's premier business leader stood beaming.

Selecting an E-magazine at random, he scanned through a copy of *You-genics*; the magazine, so its subtitle claimed, for informed readers. He had nearly skimmed its entire contents when a historical article caught his eye.

A Brief Chronicle of Clinical Cytogenetics

by: Allison Merrill Allison

"It has become increasingly evident that many diseases result from an accumulation of inherited and environmentally induced mutations in the genome."

—Geneticist X, 1992

For centuries, the concept of genetics has been considered a divine Chimera, able to transform life while its essence remained indecipherable and unalterable by human industry.

In this the sages were correct, but they misapprehended the allure of a mystery. There exist those for whom a puzzle, any puzzle, is a challenge that must be solved.

Throughout history, scientists like Mendel, Lamark, Hoyle, Bergeman, and many others, groped with the rudiments of heredity. Chasing clues, charging down blind alleys, they struggled to define what could only be guessed. Few realized where their research would lead, how others would build on their findings, and how these new discoveries would impact human society. For them solving the puzzle was all important.

Then Watson and Crick built their Nobel Prize winning model of the DNA helix and the oyster opened. The pearl was glimpsed at long last.

Clinical Cytogenetics was born.

Since its inception in the early 1960's, the field of Clinical Cytogenetics has undergone dramatic transformations. During its early period, DNA analysis was limited to counting chromosomes, roughly identifying them by size and centromere location, and assigning them to groups A, G, T, P. These broad categorizations allowed associations with only a few syndromes, such as Down's Syndrome in individuals with three copies of a G group chromosome.

In 1970, use of innovative chemical and enzyme treatments produced characteristic light and dark bands, or patterns, along chromosome arms. It was a staggering breakthrough—for the first-time chromosome abnormalities could be detected through direct comparison of homolog bands. Over the next twenty years, development of high-resolution analysis techniques allowed observation of ever more subtle chromosome abnormalities and their verifiable associations with a growing library of diseases and syndromes.

Imagine that. Tom picked thoughtfully at his nose. *They barely knew anything about chromosomes.* He quickly scanned the rest of the article, reading an occasional paragraph, and looking at pictures of political and scientific giants.

... By 1995 genetic testing and disease correlation had become a routine part of every medical practice. However, most clinicians found it virtually impossible to keep up with advances in the field. This changed in 2021, with a molecular cytogenetic breakthrough in nano microscopy of Prometaphase banding. Dubbed the Millennial Explosion by newspapers, this high-resolution gene mapping technique resulted in development of the Hanifan Test Series (HTS). Finally, medical science had a reliable system for determining an individual's statistical genetic predisposition for specific diseases.

Plate 014: The failed promise of gene editing as a health care solution. Early techniques in gene editing, such as SPLICR-Nuc8, delivered hybridized guide RNA (hgRNA) into a cell to cut the cell's genome at a desired location, allowing existing genes to be removed and/or new ones added. Touted as a treatment to correct inherited genetic diseases and somatic mutations, its application occasionally gave rise to the expression of previously suppressed genetic abnormalities. Faced with burgeoning costs from the appearance of these unintentional genetic disorders, the insurance industry looked elsewhere for a solution to their financial crisis and found it in HTS.

"Not long before I was born," he murmured.

"Tom!" Alice whispered from the corner of her mouth. "You're mumbling."

"Oh, sorry. But I found…" He caught the brittle gleam of a squinted eye and smiled tentatively.

The eyelid scrunched tight. "Just stop it!"

Hunching his shoulders, he turned back to the article.

… Implementation of HTS, while complex, is relatively straight forward. Using multivariate analysis, three predictor variables: heredity, genotype, and environment, are correlated to determine genetic cofactors. This makes it possible to cross-reference diseases, mental illnesses, and genetic defects with specific genetic abnormalities.

Plate 015: Professor Andre Willerton, a victim of Cystic Fibrosis, delivers a speech on Gene Mapping at the World Genetic Counsel.

Tom glanced sideways at April's calm features. He silently wiped sticky palms along his pant legs and swiped to the next page.

… By the year 2030, the public found itself reeling from soaring medical costs, poor quality health services, and upwardly spiraling insurance rates. Failure by private sector interests in providing reliable, cost-effective health care and limiting inflationary trends in insurance coverage, resulted in a public mandate for Federal regulation of the health care and insurance industries.

Plate 023: "Working for our future": Senator Willard Lechter, N-Kansas, stands on a lectern at the UCC National Convention, his arms raised in victory.

A soft buzz from the admissions desk hummed through the room. Tom looked up, a sharp pang knifing through his groin. April stirred slightly, shifting her legs to a more comfortable lotus position, but her eyes remained closed. Nurse Leeland's hand appeared above the console and the sound stopped.

… In 2034, politicians, riding the wave of public dissent, exhorted President, William (Big Bill) Preston to sign into law the first eugenics-based Universal Health Care Regulations (UHCR).

UHCR instituted compulsory HTS testing of all citizenries and under its directive each citizen, regardless their health insurance carrier, received basic coverage for physical trauma. Beyond this, individuals below 55 years of age received full, basic, or restricted health care as determined by their HTS scores. Persons aged 55 and older were guaranteed full coverage "... *until such time as it becomes practical to address the entire population under identical protocols." (This excerpt is quoted from Attorney General Elizabeth Dodson's 2034 speech to the Presidential Oversight Committee on Health and Welfare.)*

Opponents branded the regulations not only dehumanizing, but a political gambit aimed at appeasing the senior voting public, over 60% according to census figures.

Advocates touted the law a paragon of equality, insisting feasible implementation required transitional underwriting.

Plate 034: President William (Big Bill) Preston in the oval office signing into law the first federally mandated genetic health care/insurance bill.

To oversee UHCR's broad-spectrum implementation, Congress established a new regulatory commission: The Federal Health and Insurance Commission (F.H.I.C.). This led to...

"We've come a long way." Chuckling softly, Tom tossed the E-magazine onto the table and reached for a copy of *Tabloid Today*. Crossing his legs, he settled back and flipped through the static sheets. Mars colonists had sighted Elvis for the sixth time this year and Nixon's ghost was seen strolling the moonlit beaches of San Clemente.

Bedside Manner

Advertisements looped for the seventh time. Bright cheerful enticements offered a multitude of on-line products and services that Nora couldn't afford. She blinked and rubbed her swollen eyes. The flashing seven-second spots were giving her a headache.

She tried making herself more comfortable by shifting into a new position, but the action sent bright needles of pain shooting along her thighs. Nora quickly dug her thumbs into the knotted muscles and kneaded, nearly touching the bone. She was grateful for the diversion. It took her mind off her troubles.

Dig… push… dig… push. The rhythm had become a physical litany in her life. It seemed she'd been massaging her legs more and more lately. And now her arms and shoulders were having problems. Nothing moved as it used to, especially in the mornings. There were muscle spasms, aches and pains, swelling and stiffness in the joints. It had gotten to the point where it was all she could do to climb in and out of bed or her chair.

"It's like jump-starting an old car," Nora muttered. The thought brought a dull ache to her breast, and she dug deeper, attempting to obliterate the sensation. Once the pain abated and she could move freely again, Nora glanced back to the screen. Advertisements were still cycling. She recognized the dark-haired boy with a cranial-com feed. Next came the blurb for OptiServ: the right light in communications offering a starter package with over five petabytes of no-wait connections. And after that…

She stared into her lap. Her cheeks sagged in loose, dry, folds that nearly reached the bony chin resting on a thin birdlike chest. Watery brown eyes focused through cataract haze at the gnarled, blue-veined hands folded in her lap.

It was useless. No one was going to answer. They were going to leave her hanging on-line until she quit. They showed no interest in helping, just draining what little savings she had. And now that her nest egg was nearly gone, they wanted her to go away, to die so they wouldn't have to deal with her anymore.

She wanted to disconnect and end this terminal hold. *But I won't give them the satisfaction.* Her thoughts flared with an ancient, nearly extinguished fire. *They will talk with me.* Her tongue rasped nervously across dry lips. *They have to.*

The vid-com issued a series of beeps, boops, and pops, then made connection. It had happened so often without going through that Nora nearly jumped from her chair when an automated voice rasped from the receiver.

"Thank you for your patience. The counselor will speak with you now. Please hold while your call is being transferred."

Her screen flickered as the system traced and locked her signal. For several cycles a bright blue test pattern blipped across the screen. The display flickered then a rugged face appeared.

"Hello. This is Alan Jerome. How may I be of service?"

"Hello, Dr. Jerome. This is Nora Abernathy."

Alan Jerome leaned closer, his bronze face nearly filling the screen. He squinted, trying to place the matted, wiry gray hair and wizened features. His mouth pursed in thought, then lit the screen with a dazzling smile. "Mrs. Abernathy. Of course."

Pale blue eyes twinkled in recognition as he folded his hands on the desktop. "It's so very nice to see you. How may we be of service?"

Pulling a worn shawl tight around her shoulders, Nora forced herself erect and gently cleared her throat. "I've called concerning my tests." She fought to keep her voice strong and steady. "You said they'd be ready this week."

"Your tests!" Alan Jerome slapped his forehead. "Of course! I don't know what I was thinking." He turned from the screen to his desk station. "Let me access your General Medical file, won't take but a second."

Head bobbing to a tuneless humming, he made several rapid movements over his console. There was a sharp beep and the humming stopped. "Ah, here we go."

Nora watched as he stretched a hand towards a slave panel partially obscured by his body. She tried but couldn't read its display.

"Vanderkopf Laboratories concluded your testing at 1400 hours on 9-17-2041. That was yesterday afternoon, so the results should be posted."

He tapped several more keys. "Ah yes. Here they are. Now let's see..." Nodding slightly, he scanned the report.

Nora twisted a corner of her shawl first one way then the other as she watched Dr. Jerome's back. Atop the broad expanse of white jacket, his stiff, collar length blond hair swept backwards from the crown. The tight, precise locks curled and intertwined before thinning to wisps of carefully groomed threads that barely concealed a patch of gleaming, pink scalp.

I wouldn't have thought he was balding. She watched the fleshy spot bounce with each roll of his shoulders. *He looks so virile from the front.* Nora shook her head sadly. *And he has such nice teeth too.*

Alan Jerome took his time swiveling around. He stared fixedly from the screen and when he spoke it was with a flat, neutral tone. "I'm sorry Mrs. Abernathy. The biopsy results are conclusive." He paused, chewed thoughtfully on his lower lip, then continued.

"Mrs. Abernathy, you've malignant lymphogranulomatosis. That's a hundred credit word for breast cancer. An immediate radical mastectomy is advised."

Nora's stomach clenched at the words, making it difficult for her to breathe. She tried to speak, but her mouth had gone dry and all she could manage was a faint wheeze. Lifting a hand to her trembling lips, she stared hard at the screen, fighting an urge to vomit.

Dr. Jerome calmly stroked his chin and continued. "Your G&G report indicates hypodiploid abnormalities, probably inherited from a maternal source. Since these tests indicate a genetic predisposition, your insurance carrier is exempted from covering treatment. That leaves personal funding. You must produce the money for the operation yourself. One moment please."

He touched a finger to his ear and concentrated, listening to an inaudible voice. "Excuse me Mrs. Abernathy, I've a call on another line. Will you hold."

Before she could speak, the vid-com blinked to a screen saver pattern that dripped and rolled across her display. A mishmash of muzak accompanied the image and after several seconds of random discordance Nora's headache returned in full force. She began massaging her temples when the cacophony ceased, and Alan Jerome reappeared.

"I've placed the call on hold, so we'll try to make this brief. Now where were we?" He absently fingered the service key clipped on his sleeve cuff that linked to the Com unit built into his desk. "Oh yes. Tertiary melanomas may develop as the cancer pressures your system. They're a side issue that can be dealt with later. It's the lymphatic cancer we have to worry about."

Nora swallowed hard, forcing saliva down her throat. "What are my chances?" she managed.

"The same as we discussed during your preliminary testing last week. If left untreated," he shrugged, "you have six months, maybe ten."

A sudden chill coursed through the room, shriveling the skin of Nora's crotch and stomach. She gripped the chair arms. Sharp twinges in her armpits made her wince. "And you say," she whispered, "surgery's my only option?"

"That's correct. This cancer does not respond readily to alternative treatments. It's so far advanced that only radical mastectomy is recommended. There's a 90% chance of survival with this procedure, however you must cover the costs out of pocket."

"What about my insurance?" Nora looked bewildered. "Shouldn't that pay for it. I've always had full coverage. Always!" she insisted. "I've never let a premium lag."

Alan Jerome took a deep breath. *Old ladies*, he thought. *Somebody's gotta love em*. "It's as I just explained, your insurance will not cover an operation nor alternative treatments because HTS testing indicates this cancer stems from a genetic predisposition. I'm afraid there's no outside source of funding I can recommend."

Gathering the shawl tight about her throat, Nora leaned forward, nearly bumping the screen with her nose. "But there must be some mistake." Her eyes darted along the vid-com's left edge, vainly attempting to read the test results on Dr. Jerome's just visible slave panel. "There must be."

Swiveling idly in his chair, Alan Jerome carefully examined his coat lapels. Frowning, he plucked a loose thread from a buttonhole before looking back through the screen. "There's no mistake." He tossed the tread aside. "All cross checks came up positive."

"But I'm covered for this!" Nora pounded her fist against the screen, her voice nearly cracking. "Full coverage!"

Flinching at the sudden movement, Alan Jerome shifted slightly and crossed his legs. "I understand your anxiety, but I'm afraid you're not covered. Six months ago, the Federal Health and Insurance Commission issued new guidelines canceling all grandfathered policies which, unfortunately, included yours. At that time, you were restructured into the new system."

"They never told me!" Her voice rose in a thin quavering whine that threatened to end in hysteria. "Nobody said a word!"

"I'm sorry," Alan shrugged, his expression bland, "but you were automatically informed of your status change."

"What!" Nora's eyes grew wide, and her lower jaw trembled. Bits of foamy, white spittle flecked her lips. "I never received notification. Never I tell you! Never!" Her mouth continued opening and closing, but no sound emerged.

A fish. She's gulping like a fish. Suppressing an urge to laugh, Alan Jerome leaned forward, his face filling the screen. "Mrs. Abernathy," a compassionate smile slithered over his features, "may I call you Nora?"

"No, you may not!" she yelled and looked away.

He rolled his eyes. *Maybe I should have laughed. It might have knocked some sense into the old bird.* "All right then... Mrs. Abernathy. I've taken the liberty of checking your E-COM service records. You did receive it."

"E-COM!" Nora snorted. "Don't get me started. They switched my carrier without telling me. Different carrier—different system. I liked my old one. That one I could understand. Now with all the protocol changes I get lost so easily..." Her voice trailed away, and tears welled in her eyes.

"I'm sorry you find your new system confusing," Alan Jerome purred, "but the fact remains you received notification. It was your responsibility to read it and take the proper measures." *Not that it would have changed things*, he thought. *Just gotten you off my back sooner.*

"I didn't know." She buried her face in her hands. "How could I if I couldn't find it?" Nora's body heaved with muffled sobs. "What," she whimpered between her fingers, "what happens to me now?"

"FHIC rulings are very clear on this matter." Alan Jerome spoke carefully. "New provisions state that the only aid you are eligible to receive for this affliction consists of palliative care benefits."

"How can they do this?" Nora bawled. "I don't understand." Reaching into a box near her side, she gathered a fistful of tissues and dabbed them to her eyes. "There must be something wrong. Isn't there anything you can do?"

Silently, Alan Jerome cursed the government provisions that required 10% of his clientele be low income. "Look Mrs. Abernathy I'm just a G.I.C., not your primary care provider. As your genetic insurance counselor, I can only determine what treatments are covered under federal health insurance guidelines."

"But this is unfair!" Nora wailed. "I deserve better." Tears streamed from red swollen eyes. Her cheeks glistened, their pale wrinkles showing bright and deep.

Alan Jerome stared woodenly at the apparition on his screen. *There's nothing more pitiful than a sniveling gerrie.* He shook his head and sat up in his chair. *Let's get this over with.*

"I'm sorry Mrs. Abernathy, but rules are rules." His hands moved busily about his desk, arranging notes, and punching pad keys. "Your P.C.P. will be automatically notified of your test results. It is their responsibility to provide treatment as prescribed under FHIC Ruling 34-9851. Now," he reached forward, "I really must go." With a pop the screen blanked.

Nora gazed vacantly at the empty display, its harsh, blue light throwing the deeply etched lines of her face into ghostly relief. There were no thoughts, only the grim realization that her life had been switched off.

Mantra Blues

Tom slumped in his seat. His arms were folded across his stomach and his jaws worked rhythmically from side-to-side. April flashed an irritated glance in his direction. *I wish he'd stop. It's a wonder he has any teeth left.*

Shuddering at the steady rasp of grinding molars, she closed her eyes, attempting to ignore the grating sounds. *Focus on the mantra. Focus.*

"Hum-m-m-m-owm-m-m-naowm-m-m-m"

"Skir-ir-ir-itz-z-z!" The stentorian blast cut through the gentle waves of her formula.

Eyes popping open, she fired an annoyed look at Tom's sagging form. *Now he's snoring*! She nudged his shoulder, inducing a brief respite before the rumbles returned—softer this time, but still abrasive. She considered shoving him onto the floor, but in their three years together she learned he snored in any position.

April unfolded her legs, ceasing all pretense of meditation. She glared a moment at Tom, then reached over and nudged his head into a more comfortable position. *He's been awful jumpy lately. It's a wonder he fell asleep.*

They'd talked of having a baby for the last two years. Finally, with her promotion and Tom receiving junior status at his corporation, the time seemed right. She felt excited and knew Tom did too, but ever since her pregnancy test registered positive he seemed, well… anxious. She'd had to nearly drag him in for the Gen-G verification. *He's probably spooked like me.* She rocked slowly back-and-forth. *This baby will be a major change in both our lives.*

April restlessly tapped a foot against the bench leg—thump… thump… thump… She frowned and glanced around the room. *There's no one else here. What could be taking so long.* Leaning forward in her seat, she stretched her neck to see over the edge of the admission desk.

Nurse Leeland reclined in the cubicle chair; her attention focused on the console. April fumed silently. Good old Ann what's-her-face. The counselor is probably free right now, but she's just making us wait.

Glancing at her wristwatch, April crossed her arms and grimaced. "Damn!" she hissed. "Looks like I'll miss Reverend Rimblaugh's aerobics class. This will probably take all day."

With a resigned sigh, she shifted position and slumped deeper into the bench. "All this just for an approval."

Voyeurs on 3rd and Pelmont

"I tell ya Ed I just don't know what kids are coming to these days." Marta drained her drink at a gulp and mixed another of straight grain and synthetic limeade. She took a long swallow and set it down.

"Every day it's the same thing. I see 'em going back and forth all day long. First one building then the other. You'd think they'd come up with something else to do? But no. Just back-and-forth, back-and-forth."

Reaching over, she tugged Edna's sleeve. "I tell ya they're gangsters. Every one of the sons-a-buggers."

"Oh, for Christ's sake!" Edna slurped her drink. Tiny beads of alcohol glistened in the dark hairs along her upper lip. "They could be delivering messages for all you know."

"I told ya how I know!" Marta rapped a knuckle on the yellowed, Formica tabletop. Their mixing teaspoon jumped with a jingling clatter. "I watch 'em! Everyday!"

"Yeah, right," Edna snorted and guzzled the remaining half of her drink. Slamming it down, she wiped her mouth before brushing a snarl of mousy hair back from her face.

Lips twisting in anger, Marta rose unsteadily to her feet. "You don't believe me? By the Jesus, C'mere and I'll show ya!" Chair and table legs squawked along chipped, tile flooring as she wriggled through the narrow space between the table and kitchen counter.

Her efforts tumbled several plastic containers from the countertop. Hitting the floor, they burst open, spattering the cabinet and surrounding tiles with flecks of two-day old food. A dollop of bright yellow mustard smeared the hem of Marta's faded, print dress. Her shoes made squishing tracks as she lurched across the floor. Edna hollered about the mess she was making, but Marta ignored her and grabbed her arm. Dragging her to the window, she yanked the soiled curtains aside, and jabbed a weaving finger at the figures walking along the street. Blues, reds, browns, purples, the sidewalks pulsed with a rainbow of multicolored pedestrians.

"See that guy there." She indicated a watch-capped youth clad in loose, black shirt and baggy, black pants. "There's one."

The boy stopped and dug a hand between his butt cheeks. Standing on his toes, he scratched vigorously for a moment then continued on his way. "Just look at him." She nudged Edna's shoulder. "Sure is something, ain't he."

"Yeah, he's a piece of work all right," Edna agreed sourly. "So what?"

"Well look at him." She nudged Edna's shoulder again. "See how he's dressed?"

Edna rolled her eyes. "Yeah, so?"

"Well, it's black I tell ya." Marta shook a scolding finger. "And you know what black means."

"Oh, fer Christ's sake! Leave off with it, will ya Mart!" Edna turned and shuffled back to the table. Marta followed still pointing at the window. "Lots of kids wear black. Arnie and me, we see 'em all the time tramping around. In fact, we got neighbor kids dress like that and they don't bother nobody."

Plopping into her chair, Edna pushed a flaccid arm along the table. Snagging the Everclear, she upended the bottle and shook vigorously. A thin drizzle trickled from its neck, quickly slowing to a few lethargic drops. "Hey!" she announced. "We're out. What we gonna do?"

"No problem." Marta swiped playfully at her nose. "Got a little something special hid away. Now where did I stick it."

Frowning, she scratched vigorously at her rat nest of matted, silver hair. Several locks exploded from the loosely knotted bun atop her head and snaked down the sides of her face. Weaving back and forth, she suddenly brightened. "I 'member now."

Meandering across the kitchen, Marta dropped to her knees. Scorched pans and half-melted plastic bowls clattered onto the floor as she rummaged through the sink cupboard. "Stashed it in here somewheres," her voice echoed from the cabinet confines. "Ah, there you are. Come to Mama." With a soft grunt, she dragged a gallon glass jar from behind the gooseneck drain.

"Wait till...," Marta gasped, climbing to her feet. "Just wait'll you taste this." After several tries, she managed to loop an arm over the sink edge and haul herself to a standing position.

"Be right there." Cradling the jug gently in her arms, she tottered slowly across the floor. Waves of cloudy, beige liquid sloshed back and forth in the jar, threatening to upset her already precarious balance.

"You need help over there?" Edna called from the table.

"Nope." Eyebrows twisting in anxious concentration, Marta sidestepped several patches of spilled food. "I'm all right."

Reaching the table, she plunked the jar down and thumped heavily into her chair. "Prune jack!" she announced after catching her breath. "Made it myself."

Brown-speckled foam floated on the liquid's surface and clung to the jar's insides. Air hissed as she twisted off the lid. Like a warm spring breeze, the yeasty tang of newly fermented alcohol spread through the kitchenette. Eyes closed, Marta inhaled deeply and smiled. "Ain't it grand."

"Got lucky at the grocers. Old Tuong Win was throwing out a couple three pounds of spoiled fruit and I kotched him before he got to the recycler. Let me have the lot at a third price."

Laboriously, she filled their glasses to the brim then set the jar aside. "It mixed up nice and sweet. Been working for a week now, so it should be real good." Marta sniffed the concoction and lifted her glass.

"To your health," she crowed and drained the contents.

"Yours too." Edna peered warily at the dark liquid, shrugged, and took a large swallow. Smacking her lips, she tilted the glass back, belched once and set it aside, empty.

"Nice ain't it?" Grinning happily, Marta reached for the jug.

"Sure is." Edna used a fingernail to dig a piece of brown flotsam from between her teeth. She carefully examined the morsel before licking it from her fingertip. "Even gives you something to chew afterwards."

"That's the secret of prune jack. All the good stuff ain't settled out." Marta winked and twitched the jar. "Another hit?"

Head bobbing in a circle, Edna lifted her hand, thumb and forefinger nearly touching. "Just a tibble." With every nod, the fingers drew wider and wider apart.

Cackling, Marta refilled her glass.

A beam of afternoon sunlight knifed through a tear in the drawn window curtains, striking the tumbler a glancing blow. Focused by the glass, the light pooled muddy amber across the table. Eyes bleary, chin resting heavily on her fists, Edna stared transfixed at the brown particles floating in the liquid.

"I tell ya Mart," she mumbled, "ya gotta get out more. Meet some people. It ain't healthy staying cooped up in here alla time."

"I'm happy right where I am." Marta took a long slurp and dragged her wrist across her lips. "Ever since Dwight died I ain't felt like going nowheres." She upended her drink, but only a trickle of liquid wet her tongue. Frowning, she puzzled at the empty glass.

Her lips pouched in and out several times before splitting wide with short, barking laughter. "Ah! Ah! Ah!" She slapped the table. "Ed did you see that… Ah! Ah! Ah!… I just went and… Ah! Ah! Ah!"

"Huh? What?" Edna's sagging face panned slowly around.

"Ne'er mind." Grinning sloppily, Marta snagged the jug and poured herself another. Swigging deep, she set her glass aside and stared sullenly at the floor. The chipped black and white tiles rippled with each movement of her eyes and her feet seemed very far away. She tried wiggling her toes. There. She could just feel them twitching inside her battered jellies.

"Mart, there's a whole world out there." Edna slapped the table with her palm. Glasses jumped with the impact and the mixing spoon jangled to the floor. "And ya just can't act like it don't exist."

Eyebrows working, Marta glared from her seat, straining to bring her friend into focus. After several tries, she settled for the broken veins on Edna's bulbous nose; the rest of her features refused to emerge from the blur. "You a crazy penny. I tell ya Ed, I see stuff happen out there. Stuff I don't talk about."

Her knuckles grew white around her glass. "There's folks out there, ya see 'em and just get away from the window." Liquid sloshed over the rim as she lifted the drink to her lips. "It's gotten so as I only dare go out when it rains or when it's cold. There ain't so many folks around then."

Head sagging, Edna fluttered her hand. "You're getting buggy. Arnie and me, we go out all a time and ain't never been bothered. Course he packs his old service piece." She took a messy gulp at her drink, slopping some onto the table. Grunting, she sopped up the brown puddle with her sleeve. "What you need is protection."

Marta dismissed her with a low belch. "I can't afford none a that. Damned things cost too much."

"I ain't only talking about weapons. What about the Samaritan Squad or Citizen's Watch? They'll escort ya."

"Oh no! Oh no!" Marta got up and staggered nervously around the room. "Last spring, I saw our neighborhood S.S. get banged up by some of them black devils. The fight ran right past my window. A couple bullets busted my neighbor's window twenty, maybe twenty-five feet away from here. I don't want to take no chances being caught in that. No sir!" Her head shook violently. "I'll stick to my rainy days."

Edna rubbed her face. Her lips felt thick, and her palm registered only as pressure against the skin. "Ok, so you won't do that. How 'bout bodyguards."

"Have you gone dim." Marta leaned against the windowsill for support. "I just toldja I can't afford no weapons and that includes burly boys."

"Oh pish," Edna snorted. "I know some neighbor kids, nice boys. They'll escort you around and it won't cost a thing, just a place for them to hang. They'd be tickled pink to have a spot to get off the streets. Of course, I haven't seen 'em in a while, but next time I do I'll invite 'em over for a drink. You'd like 'em if you met 'em."

"Oh, I don't know." Marta teetered slowly to her chair, collapsing into its seat. "It might be nice to get out once in a while," she mumbled. "I haven't been to the beach in such a long time. I miss the sound of the waves. The last time was when Dwight took me there." She smiled, recalling the feel of his arms around her waist, his lips against her neck.

"Come on Mart," Edna cajoled. "You even knew their mothers. Now this...," she waggled an unsteady finger, "you'll get a kick out of this. Remember Karmine Jones and Annie Bolger?"

Marta furrowed her brow. The names sounded familiar.

"Come on. You remember. The old rec. center down at 5th and Ridge. They useta flounce around the weight room in Day-Glo spandex."

Marta's eyes grew wide, and she began to sputter. "Oh God. Not Smarmin Karmin and Annie-the-Fannie."

"That's them." Edna's lips canted into a lopsided leer. "They're the boy's mothers."

"By the jumpin Jesus," Marta gasped. "Now there's a pair. The way those two prowled you'd have thought they were cats in heat. Surprised they never kotched the big A."

"You and me both," Edna agreed, sucking a mouthful of prune jack. She sloshed it meditatively between her cheeks before swallowing. It was a surprise. Odds were, they should be dead. Nearly half of their childhood friends had died from some virus, or fungus, or one of the super germs that had ravaged the country; she shuddered and scratched a pustule scar on the back of her hand. Those who survived faced the general wear and tear of life. Yeah, it was amazing. Edna snorted and took another pull at her drink.

Marta shook her head. "God, Karmine and Annie. And they got kids you say." She chuckled again. "I don't suppose you know who the fathers are?"

Edna shrugged without looking up from her glass.

"Didn't think so. Not that it matters anyway. All right we'll have 'em over, but they gotta bring a bottle to pass."

"Great!" The grin returned to Edna's face. "They'll be so surprised," she murmured, cradling her head in her arms. "They're nice boys. You'll see."

Street Value

"This all you got?" The shadow riffled a small, stack of green debit cards.

Clarence scuffed his feet along the hallway floor and nodded uneasily. Moldy fragments of dry-rotted carpet flaked away, coating his grimy, blue sneakers with greenish black flecks. "I know it ain't much, but there'll be more next time. I swear."

"There'd better be," the dark voice warned. "I need at least twice this to make it worth our while."

A wave of sour cinnamon assailed Clarence's nostrils. Coughing slightly, he forced himself to stand firm. "But that's all the personal ones I was able to snag."

He tugged fitfully at his pants, dragging them to his waist then letting them sag back over the jutting bones of his hips. The sharp exclamation of his butt-crack peeped above the waistband.

"There ain't as many marks roaming as there was," he whined. "The regular walkers see me and dodge away. And what with fall coming on, the gerries are holing up. All that leaves are the dinges and they ain't got nothin."

Jaundice-eyes bored down from above rows of flashing, white teeth. "You know our straits probie. You want in, you gotta produce. We give you 2%. Them's the rules. You make swag, we let you in and your cut jumps to 10%." The brilliant teeth twisted into a sharp, wide grin. "But I'll tell you right now, you're a long way from it."

Shuffling his feet, Clarence glanced over his shoulder at the sunlit lobby. A murmur of busy traffic drifted in with the warm sunshine, reaching towards his shadowed niche. He took a half step towards the light before stopping. This was his one chance, and he wasn't going to blow it by running. Dragging a snot-crusted sleeve along his raw nose, he turned back.

"I produce. You know I do. Haven't I brung you good stuff regular like." His hazel eyes peeped from beneath locks of wispy blond hair. "C'mon," he simpered, "you gotta take me. You don't know what it's like on the lonesome. It's hard. It's..."

The dark figure slid from the shadows, transforming into a large, thickset man with wide, flaring nostrils and smoldering eyes. Muscular, brown features were framed by an explosion of fiery-orange hair barely contained beneath a blue-knit watch cap. The stink of sour cinnamon grew stronger.

"Don't tell me your problems!" he thundered, jabbing a blunt finger into Clarence's narrow chest. "Big Simon doesn't give a shit! I got Suzies above me who take their percentage! I only make a small cut off this! You want to play! You got to pay! You want in, you hoist more!" The finger gave another painful nudge.

Clarence collapsed against the hallway's textured surface. Granulated spackling misted down, dusting his hair and shoulders with flakes of white ash. "But CitySec's clamped down on the grocers and stores," he whimpered, clutching the spot where Big Simon's finger had dug deep between his ribs. The area throbbed and was tender to the touch. He knew there would be a bruise. "I can't do double passes anymore."

From outside came the sounds of blaring horns and tires squealing on pavement. An expectant sigh moaned through the doorway, echoing up the hall. The screeches dissolved into a series of abrupt thuds, tinkling glass, and hollow, crunching Duralite. Stunned silence followed. Then voices shouted—some in anger, others wild with pain—while footsteps clattered hastily down the sidewalk.

"Nobody else will touch the stuff." Clarence reached towards a dark-blue sleeve. "You're the only ones I can sell to. You gotta take what I bring."

There was a blur of movement and Clarence found himself lifted from the floor. A forearm slammed him hard against the wall, pressing like a moly-bar across his throat. Blood thundered in his ears, and he gurgled, unable to breath. His vision kibbled and from the darkness a crimson dot blinked on and off, pacing the wild racing of his heart. Flecks of spittle dampened the side of his face as Big Simon hissed into his ear. Waves of hot, sour, cinnamon bathed his face.

"You listen to me probie and you listen good. Nobody tells Big Simon what to do. Nobody!" The arm gave a hard shove, then let go. Clutching his throat, Clarence slid gasping to the floor.

As Big Simon moved back, other figures stepped from the shadows to form a ragged semi-circle of dark-blue silhouettes. "We're the Wiggers and you're a roach." The harsh silken voice echoed along the empty hall. "Be careful or you'll get your ass squashed."

Sullenly, Clarence clambered to his feet. Slumping against the wall, he gently massaged his throat. "But you'll take them?" he rasped, pointing a trembling finger at the debit cards in Big Simon's hand.

The blue-capped head nodded slowly. "This time. But like I say, next time there better be twice this or your skinny ass can keep right on going. Now here—"

A fistful of red Omni cards clattered to the floor.

Dropping to his knees, Clarence swiftly gathered the cards, his scrambling hands scooping dust and carpet fragments along with them. One rested near a blue-suede toe. He reached for it, but at the last second drew back, uncertain. With a jeering laugh, Big Simon kicked the card across the floor. Clarence snatched it from the dust and stuffed it into his pants pocket.

With his back flat against the wall, he rose warily to his feet. Alert to signs of sudden movement, he slid past the semicircle of silent shadows. Once clear, he turned and darted down the hallway and into the sunlit lobby.

The booming echo of Simon's voice froze him at the lobby door. "Remember what I said probie. Don't be coming back unless you got something better."

"I won't," Clarence yelled over his shoulder. "And thanks guys." Waving a tentative hand, he slipped onto the street.

The traffic sounds resumed their normal hum.

"You get them?" a voice murmured from the darkness.

"Yeah." Terrance rattled the plastic debit cards. "Man," he grinned, "it's a twitch playing Big Simon."

"The Wiggers find we're horning on their territory, it won't be pretty," the voice warned. "Especially if this probie talks and finds out he hasn't been dealing with who he thinks he has."

"Luis, you worry too much. Nothing's going to happen until we're ready." Terrance gazed down the passage. Framed in the doorway, Clarence stumbled through the buzzing traffic, clothes flapping, his baggy, blue denims tripping him at nearly every step.

"Look at that." Terrance shook his head. "Now there's a sorry son-of-a-bitch if I ever saw one." He snickered and clapped Luis' shoulder. "If that's a wannabe Wigger, we ain't gonna have no trouble taking the real material."

A Path Less Traveled

Late-autumn leaves spiraled among the building fronts. Buoyed by vagrant winds, they brushed lightly against second story windows before settling back to the ground.

Pedestrians charged along the sidewalk. Grinding the leaves underfoot, they blindly disregarded the bumpers of speeding trams, and the brazen advances of shivering prostitutes clad in revealing, center-split long coats.

A trio of pigeons with puffed chests and bobbing heads, nimbly dodged the flashing feet and continued their patrol of the sidewalk's sunlit areas.

It was late-October. The days of Indian summer were long past. Izzy stomped up the street hating it all.

He had left home insisting he wouldn't be back. Shaking the Want Ads under everyone's nose, he declared the city held more chances for better higher paying jobs than Greenbow could ever hope.

"I'll make it there," he proclaimed.

"Izzy," his friends laughed, "you'll be back before winter."

"No," Izzy clenched his coat collar tight around his ears, "I won't."

He kicked an empty Styrofoam cup, watching it bounce along the curb and into the gutter. *It's a hell of a thing*, Izzy thought, *when you can't even afford to leave town.*

....

He spent the afternoon huddled alongside a sluice pipe at the river's edge. The pipe acted as a windbreak, creating a sheltered pocket where the cool nipping breeze did not reach. Basking in the sun's warm rays, he listened to the murmur of rolling water and considered his options. He had to admit there were none.

The situation was new to him. He'd always been secure in a place to live, reasonably steady work, and enough money to get by. But now, emancipated from even the slightest obligations, Izzy found himself consumed with the terror-tinged thrill of boundless freedom and unwanted isolation. He had no idea where to go or what to do. His only thoughts were to crawl into a corner and hide. Maybe some generous soul would notice and take pity.

Vagrant clouds drifted leisurely across the sky. One gauzy mass obscured the sun, casting a shadow over his nook. It lingered a moment, allowing the true coolness of the day to chill his skin, then slipped aside.

Shifting slightly, Izzy tucked his arms close and flattened his shoulders against the concrete retaining wall. Light-dappled water trickled from the sluice pipe. With drooping eyes, he tracked its course down the rocky bank and into the river. The sun's penetrating heat, the velvet stillness of the air, the constant drone of traffic, and the murmur of water, conspired to drain away his stress. Nodding off, Izzy could almost imagine he was back home.

The house hunched beneath a mound of forest-green kudzu. Patches of weathered clapboard peeped through the green canopy. He could see where white paint had peeled away, exposing the gray pine board underneath.

"They should do something about that before it's too late." He examined the thick vines that twined around the porch pillars and hooked over the gutters. The plants seemed intent on engulfing the entire structure and pulling it into the ground. "Hell," he murmured, "it was too late when we were kids."

Pushing through the mildewed picket gate, Izzy shuffled up the flagstone walk, careful to match his stride to the circular patches of clear stone. He smiled, recalling when the open surfaces were nearly square. There had been ten of them then, tromping, shuffling, wearing it back. Now, without the foot traffic, the grass and weeds were reclaiming lost ground.

"I wonder," he mumbled, "if they'll grow over after I'm gone."

Idly, he kicked a piece of sod from the rock surface, exposing a narrow joint between stones. Izzy considered the straight edge a moment, then vigorously scuffed back the remaining growth until the slab's entire surface was clear. A wry smile twisted his lips as he surveyed the rest of the walk. The cleared stone appeared distinctly out of place. *Only one out of twenty.* His eyes squinted. *But at least one.*

With each step, he breathed deeply of the humid afternoon air, savoring its fertile musk. Unlike other times, today he wasn't eager to reach his destination. It would mark the end of the only life he'd ever known.

Clumping up the swaybacked front steps, he stopped to nudge the porch swing. The support chains gave short, rusty barks as it rocked back and forth. Fingering the scar on his chin, Izzy recalled how at age seven he, Eddie, and Claire had played the rough and tumble game of Three Musketeers. Swooping in great arcs, they pushed and shoved until only a single Musketeer remained on the swing—exclaiming victory over his, or her, fallen comrades.

It had been that way all through their lives—the three of them, fighting, squalling, and caring. They were closer than family, more than friends. It would be hard saying good-bye. Not like with his sister, Mavis or his bar-buddy, Tommy Ray. They wanted him to stay, not because they cared, but because they were afraid that he might do well.

Hinges squealed as Izzy slipped through the screen door and into the hallway. He smiled inwardly. It was impossible to sneak into or out of the house. Boards creaked with each step as Izzy moved across the worn, uneven floor. The house smelled deliciously of okra, ham hock, and red beans. He inhaled deeply and smacked his lips. Claire knew it was his favorite dinner.

"Uncle Izzy! Uncle Izzy!" A tiny, dark-haired figure scampered across the room and leapt into his arms.

Izzy stumbled back with the impact. "Hey Bud, it's good to see you too," he laughed and crushed Eddie Ray Jr. to his chest.

The boy squealed with delight. "Dinner's not ready yet and we got a surprise for you."

"Hey!" Eddie Sr. boomed, stepping from the bathroom. "You ain't supposed to tell him that." Rising to the balls of his feet, he zipped his pants fly and grinned. "C'mere you!" Bulling forward, he dragged Izzy into a monstrous bear hug.

"Claire!" he yelled over his shoulder. "Izzy's here!" There was a clatter of pans and Claire slipped into the room.

Her face was lit with a smile and Izzy wondered if he'd ever seen her so lovely. Slim, with hazel eyes, her auburn hair pulled back under a scarf, compared to Eddie's swarthy hirsute she was a goddess—serene, delicate, ephemeral.

Wiping her hands on her apron, Claire stepped close. Soft tremors shook her shoulders as she burrowed her nose into the hollow beneath Izzy's jaw. As he pulled her tight, warm splashes trickled down his neck and dampened his collar. She sniffed once before breaking the embrace and turning quickly away.

"Take a load off." Eddie gestured at a patched lounger. Once a shaggy, overstuffed monstrosity, now its seat and arms were worn smooth; the crosshatch of underlying weave exposed like a piebald scalp.

Izzy shook his head and stepped to the couch. "Nah-h that's your chair. This here is fine with me." As he stretched out, Eddie Jr. scuttled over to nestle between his feet and effectively lock him in place. Dabbing at her eyes with the apron hem, Claire settled onto the cushion next to him.

"Get ya anything?" Eddie made as if to hoist himself from his seat. "Got a couple three beers I've been saving."

"Maybe later." Izzy shrugged himself into a comfortable position. "Right now, it's good just to sit."

"I wish you weren't going," blurted Claire. "It's better you should stay here among friends than head out there among strangers."

Izzy patted her clenched hands. "Not to worry." He gazed deep into her eyes. If it hadn't been for Eddie… "I can take care of myself."

"What'll you do when you get there?" Eddie leaned forward and rested his elbows on his knees. Sunshine splashed through the window, blurring the dense hair of his forearms into hazy gauntlets.

"Damned if I know." Izzy stared at his work boots. Three months ago, he'd bought them with the last of his discretionary cash. Constant sun, heat, humidity, and walking had worn their shiny finish to a dull luster. "All I know is there's nothing for me here in the way of work and I want to do something. There's gotta be a better life than scrounging."

"Know anybody out there?" Eddie scratched his armpits then sniffed his fingertips. Apparently pleased with the odor, he smiled and sat back.

Izzy shrugged and shook his head. "Not a soul."

"How you gonna live?" Claire slid closer until their knees touched. Her hands remained a white-knuckled lump in her lap.

Rolling onto one cheek, Izzy patted his back pocket. "I got a little saved up. It'll carry me a while. Hopefully long enough to land a job. I read in the papers where they got a Job Service there that helps you find work and pays you a little something while you're looking. They even find you a place to stay." He squeezed Eddie Jr. between his feet. The boy giggled and tried to strangle Izzy's toes. "That should help stretch things."

"I see the local mill's hiring again," Eddie added hopefully. "Maybe you can get on there?"

Izzy snorted in disgust. "They're not really hiring, and you know it. They're just a hope factory. They wring it out of their workers and ship it off to the big city swells. You've seen how they do things—on for three months, off for two. Just long enough to keep a body hanging on, but never enough for unemployment or bennies."

Eddie grimaced and scratched his chin. Black stubble rasped loudly with each scrape of his fingernails. "Well at least it's a sure thing compared to the city."

"Maybe," Izzy conceded. "But there's no way to get ahead or break even. Hell, even your business is just squeaking by." He slapped his thigh. "Nope.

My minds made up. I'm city bound and when I get there, I'm gonna give it my best shot."

Sizzling and popping sounds hissed from the kitchen. Claire jumped to her feet and rushed from the room. With the interruption Eddie and Izzy sat grinning in awkward silence. The conversation had reached a smiling point, with no one sure of what, if anything, to say.

"Just a little boil-over," Claire announced returning to her seat. "Nothing serious. Dinner in fifteen minutes. Oh, by the way, since Jr. here already spilled the beans..." Claire snaked an arm behind the couch back and retrieved a package. "We got something for you." She handed Izzy a thick rectangular box wrapped in wrinkled news sheet.

"I helped wrap it." The boy puffed his chest and slid over to his mother's side.

"Did you now?" Izzy smiled and tore the wrapping loose. Lifting the lid, a flash of brilliant orange dazzled his eyes. He pulled the garment from the box and carefully examined it in the light. The blanket-lined long coat was heavy and pieced together, he knew, from several of the family's denim castaways.

"The inside's my blanket from when I was a baby," Eddie Jr. offered. "Ma was looking for something warm and I told her she could use it 'cause I didn't need it no more."

"Is that right?" Izzy winked. The boy grinned and nodded his head furiously.

Beaming, Eddie Sr. jerked his chin at the coat. "Claire here spent the better part of last month sewing it together. She used me as a pattern to get it right. Go ahead," he urged. "We're about the same size. Try it on and see if it don't fit."

"Ok." Izzy's throat caught with a sudden ache, and he swallowed hard, just managing to hold back the tears. "Let's see." Forcing a smile, he stood up and pulled the jacket on.

The coat draped securely over his shoulders and its unbuttoned lapels formed a broad orange "V" that ran from collar to abdomen. With his arms hanging loose by his sides, the sleeve cuffs stopped at his knuckles. When he folded his arms, they rode up to his wrists. He gestured spastically several times to check for tightness and was pleased with the unrestricted movement. As he strode around the room, the coat brushed his legs at mid-calf and its hem swished favorably with each step.

Placing his thumbs behind the lapels, he nudged Eddie Jr. and winked good-naturedly at Claire. "I imagine I'm quite a sight. Like to blister the eyes of anyone that looks my way."

Eddie Sr. snorted and clumped him on the back. "It's sure to catch the eyes of them city women. 'Specially with the direction that V's pointing." He kept his face straight for a moment then burst out laughing.

Grinning hugely, Izzy stood still while Claire fussed about him, tugging here, and straightening there, fitting the jacket to his frame. "Them's so you don't lose it." She sniffed, patting the lapels straight. "It gets cold up north and I thought you'd need something warm to wear."

....

Izzy awoke with a shivering start. Blinking sluggishly, he tried to yawn, but discovered his face was stiff with cold. The sky had shifted to a dark navy blue, and he glanced around wondering how long he'd slept.

The late afternoon sun was an angry, orange ball dipping into a banded horizon of magenta, fiery red, and deep aquamarine. The air carried the oily smell of exhaust and held a sharp piercing quality that bit even through his coat.

"Best be moving." Hauling himself to his feet, Izzy tucked his hands into the felt-lined pockets and hunched his way up the bank.

Genetic Drift

White noise crackled through the room. It was followed immediately by Nurse Leeland's disembodied voice. "Dr. Jerome will see you now."

At the announcement, April gathered her purse and elbowed Tom to alertness. "Come-on, we're up." With a grunt, he struggled to his feet and followed her past the sterile receptionist cubicle and Ann Leeland's neutral stare.

A soft, three-tone melody heralded their entrance into a spacious, naturally lit room overlooking the mid-town plaza. They paused before a large window. Framed in rose-tinted glass, CynCity heaved and clawed through roiling clouds of amber smog while Sarong Bay glimmered mother-of-pearl along the horizon.

They turned slowly, soaking up the office's ambiance.

Prints from famous artists, Gorman, Russell, Wu-Tei, Arthur, Ling, even Van Gogh, jostled for space on textured, off-white walls. In the corner, beside a closed door, a Mongolian Sentactic sculpture thrust its broad knobby petals into the room. To their right, positioned against a backdrop of wall-mounted plaques, a rugged, youthful-looking man reclined behind a mahogany and stainless-steel desk. Rubbing his eyes, he spoke calmly into a vid-com unit.

"The tests are conclusive Mr. Connors. Your wife has developed an acute case of hypothyroidism; that's what's causing her obesity and loss of vigor. Since her charts indicate a hereditary predisposition there's nothing I can recommend. You must provide the money for the treatment… There's no need to shout Mr. Connors… No, but if you hadn't waited so long the cost wouldn't be so high… I understand… Yes. Excuse me one moment."

Rising slightly, he gestured at two chairs positioned before his desk. "Please be seated. They're very comfortable, the newest design in orthopedic office furniture from Beijing. I'll be right with you."

Sandals rasping gently over rich, burgundy carpet, Tom and April crossed the room and quietly slipped into the chairs. Up close, the man appeared older—an aging athlete with a well-tuned physique. His white jacket and loose Everclean shirt highlighted an angular face etched by sun and time. Blond hair, dusted sliver at the temples, was brushed straight back to frame clear, blue eyes that sparkled with humor.

Tom swallowed hard. He looks ten maybe fifteen years older than me.

It's the jacket, decided April. *It's definitely the jacket*. She fought back the urge to lick her lips.

"... There were no mistakes Mr. Connors. Inter-laboratory comparisons are all positive. G&G and E&G reports indicate... Yes. Yes of course." Alan Jerome nodded and rolled his eyes. "... I understand, but FHIC guidelines are clear on this matter... That's very generous of you, but I couldn't accept it... I don't care who else has and please don't name names... I didn't make the rules and cannot authorize exceptions... That of course is your option... I'm sorry Mr. Connors, but I really must go." Snapping the link, he turned to his visitors and gave them a slight what-can-I-do shrug.

"Now then," he glanced at the view panel on his desk, "Mr. Wyman and Miss Langston is it. I'm Alan Jerome. What can I do for you?"

"May I use your bathroom Dr. Jerome?" blurted April. "I've just got to go."

"Certainly. That door to your left. And please," there was a flash of dazzling, white teeth, "call me Alan."

"Thanks much." April hurried across the room.

"The light comes on automatically when you enter," he called after her.

The door slammed and the two men sat in silence. Tom stirred uneasily, hands fluttering a moment before settling into his lap. Legs crossed, he cleared his throat and addressed the counselor's left eyebrow. "The sign on your waiting room door says M.D. Are you really a doctor?"

"Oh yes, that and more." Alan jerked a thumb over his shoulder at the collection of plaques. "I'm a graduate of the Federal Physicians College, an FHIC associate, freshman member of the World Genetics Counsel, Northwest Sperm Depository affiliate." He waved nonchalantly. "I lose track. I get them. They go on the wall."

Leaning forward, Tom ran his hand along the desk's finished edge. It was an expensive conference model with built-in wafer technology. Very classy. Very efficient. "Looks like you do pretty well for yourself. All the doctors I know struggle to get by."

Alan Jerome boomed with a hearty laugh that crinkled the corners of his eyes. "I am now, but you should have been there when I entered practice as an independent health care provider. Two years of seven-day weeks. Twelve to fourteen hours a day. No vacation. I was barely able to pay the bills. And dealing with insurance companies," he shook his head. "What a nightmare."

"So, when Federal restructuring occurred, I shifted my emphases to genetic insurance counseling. People needed someone to interpret the new laws and requirements. "Besides," he grinned and clasped his hands behind his head. "The field promised to be quite lucrative."

"I'll bet." Christ, Tom thought, I don't believe it. This guy's gotta be over 50.

"I paid off all my debts the first year. Six months later I started a fertility referral service. After that ...well, I own a home in an exclusive subdivision near Fallstaff and Breck, out near the foothills. I take vacations five times a year and drive a cherry-red Nica Tempest." The dazzling, white smile returned. "I guess you could say I'm doing pretty well."

Tom bobbed his head. He was still nodding when April eased herself into the vacant chair and whispered in his ear. "The bathroom's tiled in a Mondrian style. It's gorgeous. There's even a bidet." She turned to Alan Jerome. "Your office is simply wonderful."

"Thank you," he laughed lightly. "I think so too. And now that we're all here," Alan set his desk console to Consultation and activated the office stenographer routine, "let's begin shall we."

"For your legal protection and mine, regulations require I notify you that this conversation is being recorded." April beamed as he rolled his chair sideways, centering himself at the desk. "Please insert your IDs into the receptacles before you."

Fumbling his ID card from his pocket, Tom mimicked April who had already slipped her card into a recessed slot along the desk's edge.

A monocular eyepiece emerged from the desktop. "Mr. Wyman if you would look into the scanner, right eye first... Thank you. Now left... Very good. Miss Langston, if you would please."

As the eyepiece retracted, Alan Jerome stared intently at the console screen. "Web traffic is heavy this morning, so it'll take a moment. While we're waiting, you are here for...?"

April swelled visibly and enfolded Tom's hand with her own. "We're here for a conception verification."

"Received authorization last month," Tom added.

Alan wriggled his eyebrows. "Fast workers." His gaze lingered a moment on April's neckline.

April flushed and Tom grinned broadly.

The desk chirped as the personal memory cards popped from their slots. "Retinal verification positive. Please remove your ID's." Alan stroked several options on his console. "Now, let's download your GenMed files and see what we've got."

As the view panel screen filled with columns of information, Tom and April scooted their chairs closer for a better view.

D. K. Phinster, M.D., P.C.P.		**F.H.I.C. Lic. # A-3556-L**	
HEALTH CARE PROFILE File #: 371.97k		HEALTH CARE PROFILE File #: 233.45d	
Name: Thomas Simon Wyman		Name: April Marie Langston	
Height: 1.705 Meters Weight: 80.45 Kg. DoB: 7-15-2016 Age: 25 Status: Single w/ Marriage Option Occupation: Jr. Accnt, ICT Inc.		Height: 1.902 Meters Weight: 59.53 Kg. DoB: 3-21-2017 Age: 24 Status: Single w/ Marriage Option Occupation: Manager, SecCom Corp.	
Residence: 155-456-90 Southbridge Subdivision Quad. 4, #A-205. Net#: 1357@free.com Cell#: 500-9999-1121-1 FID#: 222-91-3445-A FHIC Policy #: 001-22534-12		Residence: 155-456-90 Southbridge Subdividsion Quad. 4, #A-205 Net#:2122@free.com Cell#: 500-2343-1121-4 FID#: 637-24-9918-K FHIC Policy #: 279-88761-35	
Hanifan Test Series		Hanifan Test Series	
MP	ESD	MP	ESD
G&G: 1/6000	+/- 0.045	G&G: 1/8330	+/- 0.033
H&G: 1/800	+/- 0.23	H&G: 1/1800	+/- 0.09
E&G: 1/1900	+/- 0.002	E&G: 1/2500	+/- 0.001
P&G: 1/5.3	+/- 0.009	P&G: 1/9.7	+/- 0.05
Insurance Rating GIQ: 29.97		Insurance Rating GIQ: 13.38	

"Hey," Alan chuckled, "we're neighbors. I live in Southbridge too. Quad 3. Wonderful place, isn't it? The patrols and laser fencing really provide a sense of security, don't they?"

"They sure do," April agreed. Tom grunted and continued searching the display.

Alan examined the files a moment longer then turned to the couple. "Well, it all looks good. You're well under 35 Miss Langston, healthy and prime for childbearing. Nice looking too if I might add." His eyes twinkled and April felt a current of heat thrill through her body.

"Mr. Wyman." Alan Jerome's tone was gruff, his expression stern and man-to-man.

Tom squirmed at the sound of his name. "Yes."

"Your GIQ rating appears a bit high, but I'm sure everything's fine."

"Dr. Jerome?" Alan cocked an eyebrow and touched a finger to his ear. "Excuse me," April giggled, "Alan. I've never seen an in-depth health care profile before. I just pay the premiums. This first segment is self-explanatory. It's a rehash of the information we verified on our arrival. But what does the rest mean?"

"Which part is that?" Alan Jerome glanced at the screen.

"The Hanifan Test Series."

"It's statistical analysis results," Tom interrupted. "See." He pointed at the view panel. "The MP column lists median probabilities and the ESD column lists error ranges within a Standard Deviation." He waved at the screen. "It's all right there."

April turned slowly in her chair until she was staring at Tom's ear. "Tom dear," she hissed, "advanced stats were required for my communications degree. I know what MP and ESD represent, what I don't understand are what the other acronyms signify!"

"People… People…" Alan Jerome raised his hands. "We're connected. I feel your tension. This is an important life decision, naturally you're anxious. But please, there's no need to bark at one another."

Tom inspected his fingernails, suddenly contrite. "Sorry. It's just this is all so… so…"

"Mr. Wyman," soothed Alan, "you'd be surprised how few citizens, let alone health care professionals, understand the intricacies of an HCP."

April pursed her lips and counted to ten. "Dr. Jerome, she said tightly, "if you would please continue."

Nodding slightly, Alan Jerome assumed his best lecturer's voice. "As you can see the Health Care Profile contains basic Web information, personal statistics, as well as a Hanifan Test Series summary. The full HTS consists of four reports which address every chromosome in your genome." He pointed at the screen.

"The G&G or Geno-genetic Report directly correlates an individual's gene map with known diseases and syndromes.

The H&G or Here-genetic Report uses linkage analysis to correlate genotype with hereditary abnormalities.

The E&G or Enviro-genetic Report correlates genotype with the disease-related impact of an individual's physical environment and personal lifestyle.

The P&G or Psycho-genetic Report correlates genotype with an individual's psychological profile."

"Interesting." April tugged reflectively at her right ear.

Tom groaned and wiped a sleeve across his forehead. The office temperature seemed to be set ungodly high. "Can't we get on with this? It's such a waste of ti— Ow!" He bent, rubbing his shin where April had kicked him.

Alan examined his thumbs, waiting for the couple to quit glaring at one another, before continuing. "Each report lists a series of variables which are used to determine an individual's genetic cofactor for a specific disease. While the FHIC identifies specific hereditary and environment-based disorders as uninsurable, there are other situations where genetic cofactors play a clear role in a person's insurability.

For example, let's take an E&G situation with a known G&G correlation. Say you've a genetic susceptibility for hypertension, you smoke, are overweight, eat fatty foods, and don't exercise. In this scenario your genetic cofactor for hypertension may range between 80 and 100, a significant disease potential that's uninsurable under any policy."

"But," he raised a finger, "if you don't smoke or associate with people who do, ("Remember secondhand smoke?" Tom and April nodded.), eat right, and exercise regularly, then your cofactor may fall around 10 or 20 – a low disease potential that is insurable."

Leaning forward, he propped his elbows on the table and steepled his fingertips. "For each individual there are practically hundreds of thousands of genetic cofactors. They are plotted onto a Genetic Insurability Scale of 1 – 100, then distilled into a single rating value called the Genetic Insurability Quotient. The Federal Health and Insurance Commission uses this rating to qualify individuals with health coverage and determine their premium.

GIQ's between 0 and 30 are insurable under standard Federal and private full-coverage healthcare plans. Ratings over 30 but less than 70 are considered risks, insurable only with extended policies listing specific gene-related exclusions. And persons with ratings over 70 are considered genetically uninsurable; they can be covered for physical injury, but nothing else." Folding his hands behind his head, Alan Jerome leaned back and stared benignly across the desk.

April shook her head as if clearing a fog. "That's it?"

"That's it," he grinned. "Of course, certain directives alter specific cases, but most people find this explanation the easiest to follow."

"It seems rather severe," she snorted.

"Not at all. To maintain quality of life, we must strictly enforce medical equality. No one can hide from their genes. Advance HTS screening relieves the public from bearing the financial burden of another's genetic disabilities." Alan's smile widened into a sharp toothed grin. "Shall we continue with the verification."

Bending close to the console, he pulled up another screen.

Prenatal Diagnosis Committee: Chapter 712		Lot# 235.78A
Paternity Test (Wyman & Langston)		Date: 09-19-2041
Chromosome Selections	Paternal VNTR	Maternal VNTR
Xm234.8 Zx176.1a Wy891.4 Aa553.6b	50 72 149.97 180.01	50.1 72 150 179.993
PoP: 99.97%	ESD: ± 0.03	Paternity: (verified)

"H-m-m, the probability of paternity with four Variable Number Tandem Repeat's is usually higher, but unless you wish to contest the 0.03%," he winked roguishly, "it's your child."

April averted her eyes and blushed into her collar.

"No," Tom huffed, sitting straighter in his chair, "there's no doubt it's mine."

"Humm." Alan scratched idly at his nose. "I don't see the fetus's sex listed. You must have declined for some reason."

"We wanted to be surprised!" April blurted.

"Of course." He winked and April blushed again.

Turning back to the console, Alan tapped the display with his finger. "I see your PDC has prescribed a standard ob-gyn pregnancy management schedule. Maternal venipuncture every six weeks with interphase cytogenetic testing of differentiated fetal blood samples. And real-time ultrasound every trimester to verify fetus gestational development." He shrugged casually. "It's a bit more rigorous than most, but since this is your first, I guess they're just playing it safe."

Stroking his lip, he leaned closer to the view panel. "Your file indicates an initial maternal venipuncture yesterday morning and since full in-utero G&G work-ups can take 10 hours, the results should be ready."

The screen blinked as data scrolled across the display. With each line, Alan's smile stiffened into an expressionless groove. Reaching forward he tilted the panel from the couple's view.

Perspiration moistened Tom's forehead and beaded his upper lip. "Something wrong?" The question came out squeaky and uneven.

Alan squeezed his chin between thumb and forefinger as he examined the data. "There's an aberration within the fetus' G&G analysis. Interphase testing indicates a discrepancy in specific loci of chromosomal region Xq27.3."

Tom's lips quivered. "W-what's that mean?"

Alan swiveled about, staring thoughtfully at the ceiling. He laid his palms flat on the desktop before turning his attention to Tom. "To be blunt Mr. Wyman, it means your fetus has Fragile X Syndrome."

Tom blanched and his hands clutched the chair arms. He remained mute while April burst with a flurry of questions—"What is it? Is it serious? Why weren't we informed earlier?"—all within a single breath.

Alan Jerome grimaced. "Please calm down Miss Langston. I'll try to answer your questions. Fragile X Syndrome occurs when foliate-sensitive breakage sites appear on the X chromosome. This genetic condition causes a range of developmental problems, including learning disabilities and cognitive impairment, which manifest in greater or lesser severity as a child ages. Fragile X is hereditary; it can be passed silently down through generations in a family—from father to daughter but not son, and from mother to son and daughter—before a child is born with the syndrome. Since conception authorizations use preexisting analysis results, we can only assume a false-negative discrepancy in one of your HTS scans."

Breathing smoothly, he surveyed the couple, noting the effect of his words. April sat bolt upright, her eyes wide and her lips slightly parted. Tom buried his face in shaking hands. Tears welled from between his fingers and plopped noisily to the carpet.

"In this situation," Alan Jerome continued, "regulations require reanalysis of parental G&G and H&G reports and necessitate an official query. I reiterate, this conversation is being recorded, so please be truthful."

He fixed his clear, penetrating gaze upon April. "Miss Langston, to your knowledge, has there ever been an incidence of Fragile X Syndrome or unexplained intellectual disability in your family history?"

Glassy eyes blinked once, twice. "W-what?" April stammered. "Oh. Never. Never." She began nervously preening herself.

Alan Jerome turned to Tom. "Mr. Wyman, to your knowledge, has there ever been an incidence of Fragile X Syndrome or unexplained intellectual disability in your family history?"

Tom stared at his reflection in the desk's steel supports. A long, narrow face peered back. Sounds receded to a white hum. The question barely registered.

Forehead knotted with concern; April tugged lightly at his sleeve. "Tom," she prodded, "answer the man."

Tom Wyman looked up, his eyes red and brimming with tears. When he spoke, it was with a raw, weak voice. "The doctors gene mapped me at birth," he whimpered. "They insisted I was clear."

"Tom?" April hooked nervous fingers through her hair, pulling it out straight from the sides of her head.

"Please answer the question Mr. Wyman?" Alan Jerome's eyes bored steadily. "Would you like me to repeat it?"

"No. No need." Tom took a deep breath and swallowed hard. "Yes, an older brother. He was institutionalized at 5 and died seven years before I was born. But," he looked up bewildered, "that was well over thirty years ago. Surely it can't…"

"Thank you." The console beeped and Alan turned to the panel. He spoke from the corner of his mouth as information scrolled down the screen. "I initiated reanalysis before invoking the official query. A questionable procedure", he shrugged, "but it saves time."

"The results confirm your statements. Miss Langston, you're clear. Mr. Wyman, reanalysis has uncovered a maternal recessive linkage for Fragile X. This will affect your GIQ rating I'm afraid." He punched several touch keys and read some more. "But it shouldn't be too serious."

Tears boiled down April's face. "Tom!" she howled, beating her fists against the chair arms. "Why didn't you tell me!"

Sobbing, he knelt beside her. "They said I was clean." He reached out and she slapped him away. "I never questioned their analysis. Never dared reanalysis." He leaned closer, letting her fists drum weakly against his chest and shoulders. "Please", he moaned, "I didn't know. I… I…"

"Now we'll never have a child," she wailed and collapsed weeping into his arms.

Holding her tight, Tom rocked slowly side-to-side. "I'm sorry," he sobbed. "I'm so sorry."

Alan Jerome watched from across his desk. *Such a nice couple,* he thought. *The guy's a bit of a geek, though. It's too bad really, but rules are rules.* "I'm sure your PCP instructed you concerning this eventuality. The Federal Health Care law states:

"Abortion is mandatory when the occurrence of significant fetal genetic abnormalities indicate high probabilities of physical and/or psychological disabilities."

You are, of course, entitled to a second opinion, but I assure you recent developments make DNA analysis 100% accurate. That, by the way Mr. Wyman, is why your recessive trait was missed. Standard testing procedures at the time of your birth had a margin of error of plus or minus 3%."

Tom and April remained silent. Their world had suddenly shifted from pleasantly defined security to random, threatening shadows. Clutching tighter, they sought stability in each other's arms.

"Do you," Alan Jerome began, his eyes flickering between the two, "desire re-evaluation?"

Mutely, they shook their heads.

"In that case…" He stared at the screen, subvocalizing his commands. "I've scheduled an abortion procedure with your PDC tomorrow at 10 AM. The sooner this is taken care of the better. You can try again next month if you like. You'll need re-authorization of course, and since your chances for a viable fetus, even with Mr. Wyman's GIQ reassessment, are fairly high, I suspect your next attempt will be successful."

A desperate smile broke across April's puffy, tear stained face. "Do… do you really think so?" she sniffed.

"Certainly," Alan reassured. "If it doesn't, you can always enter into a conception contract with a suitable donor or even employ in-vitro fertilization. Both avenues tend to cost," he rubbed thumb and forefinger together, "but either way, well at least the in-vitro way, you're guaranteed clean genome. And with your GIQ Miss Langston you're nearly 100% assured of a healthy fetus."

Tom rose unsteadily, wiping tears from his eyes. "I see our time's nearly up." Sniffing, he squared his shoulders and helped April to her feet. "We thank you. Next time…"

Alan made a chin-chucking motion with his fist. "That's the knock but remember what I said about in-vitro."

"We'll remember," piped April, "but we want to keep it natural if possible."

"All is," Alan said, sliding from behind his desk. With quiet ceremony, he gathered the couple and ushered them from his office. "Come again for verification or should you require a referral."

Passing the receptionist desk, Tom's subdued "Good-bye" and April's half-hearted wave drew a curious look from Ann Leeland. Heads ducking in embarrassment, they hustled for the outer door, stopping briefly to hug each other before pressing through into the empty hall.

A sleepy smile slid across Alan Jerome's face as he leaned against the doorframe. "Mrs. Leeland please forward a recording of this meeting to FHIC underwriters. Include an analysis of Mr. Wyman's G&G and H&G reports and recommend his GIQ be reindexed to 32.07 with exclusion FX-532."

"Yes sir." She frowned, stroking her badge. "Mr. Jerome, you're aware this new classification will restrict his procreation coverage. Future conception authorizations will be difficult if not impossible to obtain. They'll be forced to explore alternate avenues of fertilization."

"So, they will." Alan's mouth quirked slightly, and he glanced at his watch. "Hey! I've a 12:15 lunch engagement at Ricos. If I leave now, I'll just make it. Hold down the fort while I'm gone."

"Yes sir." Ann Leeland sat rigidly in her chair as he rushed through the waiting room and clattered down the hall. Sighing heavily, she turned to the console and steeled herself to work.

It Happened on Bleaker Street

The word was out. Be off the street by 9:00 PM. Draw the shades. Turn up the sounds and by no means look out your window. This was an official event to be witnessed only by the participants and several well-positioned, objective observers. Nobody else. Citizen's Watch and CitySec contacts agreed to intervene only if the situation escalated beyond counsel pact limits.

Towering rows of tenement housing created a narrow, open-ended coliseum. Streetlights flooded the arena with a pale orange brilliance. Traffic lines and parking squares glowed in the light, dividing the playing field into a yellow and white gridwork. At mid-block, an abandoned two-seater huddled near an alley entrance. Stripped and mute, its dark windows reflected the approaching contestants.

They swaggered slowly from opposite ends of the corridor—two ragged lines, one electric red, the other faded blue. At mid-point, they fanned out across the street, facing each other in mute, vibrant rows. The evening throbbed with an undercurrent of white noise. The low humming of streetlights blended with the far-off rumble of traffic, amplifying the tension between the groups.

Then, a blatant hand gesture from the blue. Voices stirred to murmurs. A hawked rumble of spit arced from the red. Voices rose to shouts. Team lines pulsed, thinning and thickening, erupting with frenzied motion as the grandstanding began.

There were daring displays of bravado. Individuals faked charges at opponent ranks. Less foolhardy members shook weapons, pounded their chests, and shouted insults from the safety of their respective lines. Taunts and curses hurled back and forth in contests of ego frustration.

Who would break first?

A glistening scimitar of light and a young man staggered backwards. With first blood drawn the forces surged together.

Screams of rage and pain. Blades flashed. Clubs rose and fell. Bodies folded, staggered to their feet, and collapsed again. A fist rose from amid the repeated crunching blows with a small round object clenched in its fingers. An arcing, metal rod sparked blue-white, and the object tumbled into the gutter, rolling beneath the silent mini-tram.

With a muffled, Whumph, the tram leapt several feet in the air then crashed to the ground. Scorching waves of heat singed hair, skin, and nearby clothing. A body slumped against the curb burst into flame.

The vehicle became a fiery beast lunging skyward. Beveled windows framed wild, flickering eyes. A grill-rimmed maw gave voice to violent, bellowing rage. Twisting and roaring, the beast exhausted itself with the effort of taking its first step. With a frustrated growl, the flames withdrew into its sullen, glowing heart. The grill teeth sagged molten white. The face and body softened and collapsed in on themselves. The dull, red eyes drooped closed. Thick, ropy streams of metal and plastic meandered along the pavement as the chassis wilted into an amorphous green puddle.

The contestants paused, startled by the explosion. Hesitation quickly gave way to action as the teams regrouped and continued the battle more fiercely than before. Wet cracking thuds and sharp metallic rings rebounded from the building walls as the antagonists came together again and again.

With a final flurry of blows the groups split. Howls accompanied the sound of running feet. Faded blue torsos tumbled down the street. A mob of jeering red-clad victors yapped at their heels.

Bodies sprawled on the pavement. Most lay still, bent in awkward positions. A few moaned and twisted feebly in the center of dark spreading stains. From their box seats, the watchers consulted wrist dials and nodded—six minutes and only one penalty. Satisfied, they slipped away to deliver their reports.

....

"All right!" Backs were slapped. "Yeah!" Shoulders were pounded. First one, two, then the entire group of scarlet heroes skipped back to the scene, crowing their exploits.

"Didja see me man? Didja see when I nailed that mother right between the eyes?"

"How 'bout when I sliced that sumbitch. Ow-wow. Didja see that?"

"Naw, I was too busy dusting four of them back."

A shock of wiry orange hair scanned the crowd. "We lose anybody?"

"Don't think so. There's a couple been dinged up some, but they can still walk. The Wiggers took it hard, man. I count six, maybe seven down."

"Good enough."

A thin young man glanced uneasily at the faces milling around. "Hey, anybody seen Fuerto?"

"Nada." Terrance brushed dirt from his shirt cuffs. "Haven't seen him since the start."

"No! No!" Luis muttered and darted off into the darkness.

"What's with him?" Dinky-D jerked his chin at Luis' fading back.

"He's worried about his brother." Terrance casually dug coagulated blood from beneath his fingernails. "The little prick probably got clipped and went crying back to the crib."

Dinky wiped his hands on his shirt, streaking dark, red lines across the chest. "Man, he babies that little shit."

Terrance nodded and continued walking in silence.

Rico trotted up and danced tight, manic laps around the moving pair. "Man did we take 'em or what?"

"You bet." Terrance forced a grin. "All the way downtown! Ain't that right!" he shouted, circling a fist over his head. "Ain't that right!"

"Yeah!" The group cheered, waving their fists in the air. "Los Manos Rojas number one!"

"Hey guys," a voice called from the sidewalk shadows. "C'mere. You gotta see this." Laughing, Joy Boy jabbed a thick metal rod into the side of an inert body. There was the snap of electricity and the corpse jerked. "Check it out. The fucker's dead, but he still jumps." Joy Boy jabbed again. The body twitched again. "Outrageous, hey."

"What you got there?" They crowded around. Several hands stretched forward but pulled back before making contact.

"Cool isn't it." Proudly, Joy Boy held up the rod. "It's a prod stick like the security boys carry." He wriggled his eyebrows. "I made it myself."

"Christ!" Terrance grabbed Joy Boy's arm and jerked it down. "Quit flashing that thing around. We were only supposed to have knives and clubs." He glanced uneasily into the surrounding darkness hoping the watchers had left. "It was agreed on in the war counsel."

"But it is a club." Joy Boy blinked innocently. "It just delivers an extra punch is all." At this Rico snickered and Dinky-D slugged his arm. Encouraged, Joy Boy continued.

"Look, anybody I clip with this sucker is fried gone. It carries a jack-pack delivering 30,000 Volts on contact. See." With a twist, he slid a plastic sheath partway from the rod handle exposing a compact mass of micro circuitry. Nestled in its center was a jack-box pirated from a city power transformer.

"Twisting the handle base turns it on and off."

Terrance nodded reluctant approval. "Well, if nothing else, you're good at this shit."

"Damn straight." Joy Boy grinned and slipped the sleeve back into place. "Besides it was their thermo that scragged the tram." He hooked a thumb at the greenish lump. The fire had dwindled to a pulsing, dull yellow glow.

"That's right." Dinky stepped forward. The bio-lume ruby implanted between his eyes flared to brilliance, turning his blood-streaked face into a devil mask. "Those bastards tried to fry us first."

Mouth hanging open, Rico glanced about the suddenly quiet crowd. "Hey! I thought that wasn't in."

"It wasn't," Terrance responded dryly.

"So, what happens now?" Dinky picked a flake of dried blood from his chin. He examined it a moment before rolling it into a ball between his fingers and flicking it aside. "I mean why did we bother with a war counsel if it didn't matter?"

"Cause now their ass is gone." Terrance slammed a fist into his palm. The wet smack echoed back from the building walls. "We didn't break the war pact, see. When word gets around, they got their asses kicked even though they rooked, their reputation is trashed. Ain't nobody gonna deal with 'em, especially the Suzies. In fact, I bet an alliance of say, us, the Peters, maybe even the Chaques, goes visiting some night and by morning they're all gone. No more Wiggers."

"Am I right?" He leered at the circle of tense faces. "Am I right?" Heads bobbed vigorous assent.

"Alright." He paced the company of eager red figures. "Everybody stays mum about Joy Boy's ah-h-h… club." Snorts and chuckles rose from the gathering.

"Joy Boy," Terrance laid a thick, meaty hand on the lanky youth's shoulder, "Tag any Wiggers that are still moving. Make sure there're no survivors."

He glanced at the bodies scattered along the street. "Hell, there's not that many. Nail them all again, just to be safe. And make sure it looks like you're hitting them."

"You got it," Joy Boy cackled and scampered off.

"Can I give it a try," Rico begged, running after him.

"Me too," added Dinky-D trotting along behind. "I wanna try it too."

"Juno!" Terrance called to a tall, gangly youth with spiked, raven hair. "Gather up the others and shag 'em home." He cupped an ear to a barely audible, though steadily growing siren wail. "And be quick about it! We got to bug in a big way."

....

"Mi hermano!" Luis splashed through a crimson pool and fell to his knees beside a thin, crumpled figure. He carefully gathered the limp body in his arms and drew its dark curly head to his chest. As he lifted, blood surged over his hands and across his lap. The fresh tributaries wound their way to the pavement, adding their coppery volume to the already spreading lake.

"Ah Jeeze..." He nearly let go when red bubbles frothed from the deep gash across Fuerto's throat. Luis' gaze flicked from the gaping second mouth to strangling eyes that pleaded for help he couldn't provide.

"Nothing I can do bro," Luis sobbed, hugging him close. "Nothing I can do."

A trembling hand clasped Luis' wrist. Fuerto tried to speak, but only managed a soft gurgling. Redness gushed from his mouth as his fingers tightened, relaxed, then tightened with a final spasm. His eyes emptied and Luis groaned as the hand fell away.

Terrance approached slowly, stopping just outside the circle of blood. Hunkering down, he slowly rubbed his face. "Shit," he muttered. His pant legs pinched the skin along the backs of his knees where dried blood had stiffened the fabric. Ignoring the discomfort, he continued to squat.

"Hey Loue," he began softly. "Looks like we did it. Won from Bleaker all the way to LoDo. That's a lot of distribution."

Luis nodded but said nothing. Blood saturated his clothes. His hands and cheeks were sticky with gore. Pink tears trickled down his chin and plopped onto Fuerto's calm, upturned face. Dead eyes glowed orange in the streetlights.

"The Wiggers are finished." Terrance clenched his fist. "We got 'em by the balls for breaking the war pact. The Suzies will work with us now. We're a power." These last words were forced through clenched teeth. In a scene of red on black on red, Luis clasped Fuerto's body to his breast. Moaning softly, he rocked gently back and forth. The ichor under his knees squelched with each shifting movement.

Terrance perked his ears as siren wails pressed closer. "C'mon Loue," he urged, "we gotta bug. CitySec's coming. The thermo drew 'em in."

"We're done," Rico panted jogging up to the scene. He stopped suddenly, almost falling on his face. "Jesus what happened?"

"Junior got himself cut." Terrance dragged a finger across his throat and shook his head. "He's VSF, man. Very severely fucked."

Dinky-D approached warily. "The others have hit it. We're the last." Nodding at the news, Terrance continued to stare at the bloody pair of rocking marionettes.

Joy Boy sauntered through the blood pool, his sneakers making sharp sticky sounds with each step. "Hey, I just tried the burned guy. He didn't move a bit. Fire must've cooked his nerves. What do you think Loue?" Resting the club on his shoulder, he waited patiently for an answer.

"Junior's dead!" Terrance snarled. "C'mon Loue." He extended a hand. "Leave him! We'll get the bastards who did this next time."

"Get your ass in gear!" screamed Dinky-D.

Luis hunched lower and remained kneeling. "Goddamit!" Slipping forward, Dinky brandished his vibro-knife before Luis' face. "You'll move or so help me I'll carve you like your brother!" Grabbing him by the collar, Dinky dragged Luis to his feet and shoved him unprotestingly along the street.

Terrance watched them stumbled down the block, then turned to Joy Boy. "You know what to do."

Nodding, Joy Boy jabbed his staff into Fuerto's body. Once. Twice. Three times.

"That's enough. Let's go." Skirting the thickening mire, he motioned Joy Boy to follow.

Joy Boy cocked his head and chuckled. "He-e-e-e. Maybe once more."

Terrance snagged his arm, careful to avoid the club. "I said that's enough. Let's hit it." Together they followed the others.

A block away Luis leaned against a building corner, watching as the pair turned and drummed up the street. "Mi hermano," he whispered, beating the wall with his fist until blood welled from chewed knuckles and tatters of flesh clung to the rough brick surface. He was still pounding when thick, ebony hands grabbed his wrists and gently led him away.

Dado

Slowly, ecstatically, Dado caressed a long gray hair that protruded from one nostril. He let it glide between his fingertips, slipping nearly to the end before giving it a slight tweak. His right eye twitched with each satisfactory spike of pain. *Still alive*, he mused. *Some day's it's hard to tell.*

He gave the hair another tug and winced. *The pain helps.*

A chill breeze blew in from the bay, bringing a dull ache that throbbed from his feet to his teeth. *God!* He flipped the hem of his patch coat over his exposed ankles. *Used to be I could run buck naked all day in this. Now all I'm good for is to sit here and shiver*.

Wedging his cane against the concrete floor, Dado gave a gentle shove. Rocking was better than sitting still. He thumped the arm of his battered, tube frame rocker. Yep, he felt warmer already.

"You know, there's comfort to be had in knowing you're going to die." He spoke aloud, not so much to hear himself, but to fill the silence.

Nearby, a brown-armed boy sawed at the porch steps with a jagged piece of metal. "What's the big deal?" he called over his shoulder. "Everybody dies. Especially gerries like you."

"No, he's not!" A fury of loose-fitting sack cloth and unruly, golden hair erupted from the arching wall-hole of their current squat. Though several years younger and pounds lighter, Carrissa fearlessly charged her brother.

"Yeah, he is, snoopster," the boy chuckled, throwing her off. "One of these days he's gonna roll over and rot."

"No, he's not! No, he's not!" Fists flailing, she charged again. This time the boy slammed her in the stomach and knocked her down.

"That'll teach ya to mess with me," he sneered as she dragged herself away.

Whimpering, the young girl pulled herself up the rocker leg and clutched Dado's arm. *Sibling rivalry*, he sighed, laying a protective hand on her head.

It never goes away. *Though I must admit the lad deserves a good booting.* "Jojo there was no call for that."

The boy hunched back to work, steadfastly ignoring the old man. "It's true and you know it." He heaved a loosened chunk of concrete into the alley. "You're gonna die just like you said."

"But Grandpa," Carrissa cried, "I don't want you to go. If you die, whose gonna teach me numbers and stuff."

"Like you're ever gonna need 'em," Jojo scoffed.

She clutched Dado's arm to her thin chest and gazed up at him through hazel pools that filled quickly with tears.

Hugging her close, he buried his face in her hair. It held the light, musky smell Dado always associated with youth. *Babies have it,* he sighed, *most children too. We seem to lose it about the same time we lose our innocence, then gain it back when we realize our mortality.* Wetness trickled down his cheeks and he fought to keep his voice steady.

"We all got to go sometime 'rissa. Most people don't know when that is. But me, I know I got another year, year and a half, tops. And to tell you the truth old Dado is ready." *Though if I were completely honest,* he thought, *I'd admit to being terrified. But that's the way of it isn't it. Fear and anticipation, regret and contentment all rolled together.*

He brushed a curl from her forehead and watched it twist from his fingers back to its original position. "So, you see, I'm not going anywhere, leastwise not right away. You'll have to put up with me for a while yet." He made a face and ruffled her hair. Carrissa smiled faintly. "Now don't you worry anymore about it."

His fingertips lingered over 'rissa's hair, gently stroking the silky locks as he passed a tired gaze across the rubble that was their back yard. Tumbled concrete slabs and twisted rebar avalanched from the lot next door. Like a stroke victim whose left shoulder sagged, the adjacent apartment complex slumped into their area. It's other half, still upright and solid, sheltered their few neighbors.

Settling deeper into the rocker, Dado slid a hand along its seat edge, absently caressing the rough plastic weave. Ten years ago, his daughter Charline had discovered it on a rummage run. Its frame bent and broken, its webbing rotted, she'd wired the chair back together and refitted the seat and back with woven straps of opti-fiber. Over the years it had become his favorite settle. *It might be lawn furniture, but I'll miss it,* he decided.

Moist breezes brought the ripe scent of seaweed and city spoilage to his quivering nostrils. In this area the smell of incoming tides drove most people away, but Dado liked it. He'd lived by the beach all his life and wouldn't consider living anywhere else, no matter how pungent the odor or how high the water.

Fish-ribbed clouds scuttled by high overhead. An amber, mid-morning sun rippled through the open spaces between the ridges. *Mackerel skies*, Dado's lips twitched silently with the words, *but no mare's tails. It'll be cloudy for the next day or so, maybe a little rain. Looks like things are shaping up for another slushy winter instead of honest-to-goodness snow.*

Though temperatures had been summer-like for the past few weeks, there were signs that winter crouched in the shadows, biding its time, ready to pounce. Mounds of gray-brown ice huddled in the deep, dark recesses of alleyways. Dado chuckled. *I don't know but there's probably ice left over in some godforsaken alley from when I was a kid.*

"But why?" Carrissa sniffed and tugged his sleeve.

"Hum?" Her question jolted Dado from his reverie, and it took him a moment to remember where he was. "What's that?"

"Why're you ready to go?" She tucked a curl of hair behind her ear.

"Cause it's time and I've seen too much." He stared into the distance, watching as a glistering swarm of brilliantly, colored VTOLs lifted from an up-city Heliport. Green, red, amber, and blue, they flashed and flickered in the afternoon sun. The low thrum of their engines pulsed through the air.

Bottle flies, Dado snorted. *They look like bottle flies buzzing around a bloated fish.* Darting and weaving among the towers, the aircraft circled several times before disappearing over the horizon.

"You kids don't know what things were like when I was your age."

Jojo rolled his eyes and groaned. "If you're gonna bore us again, I'm gonna go do something else." He stood and began walking away.

"You'll sit your ass right down there and listen young man." Dado pointed an imperative finger at the stoop. "'rissa you too."

"Ah-h-h," Jojo muttered and plopped back down. Carrissa settled herself next to the wall, careful to keep out of her brother's striking range.

A sharp yowling lifted from behind a nearby mound of rubble. Hungry eyes pinpointed the sound. Jojo and Carrissa automatically checked their hunting belts, then slid from the concrete porch slab and began creeping across the open space in a slow, sure-footed crouch.

Rising carefully to his feet, Dado shook his cane at the stooped backs. "And just where in hell do you think you're going?" he growled.

"You heard it," Jojo whispered sidling to the right. Carrissa nodded and fanned left.

"Get back here and sit down!" he bellowed. "Food can wait."

"What's more important than eating?" Carrissa looked questioningly at her grandfather. Dado always said hunting is what kept their clan going. Without the meat she and Jojo brought in, they would starve.

"You're getting some kind an of education, even if it kills me. The years may have forced me to give up teaching, but I'll be damned if I'll let my offspring live in ignorance. Besides," he scanned the distance, "it's too far away. Chances are it'd be gone by the time you got there."

With Carrissa trailing uncertainly behind, Jojo stomped back to the porch, disgruntled at being kept from his quarry. "If you're gonna drum us, why can't it be about stuff we can use? Why bother with this old crap?"

A breeze ruffled the fringe of white hair that circled Dado's head. His dome, deeply tanned from years of exposure, nestled in the center of white hair like a nut-brown egg. "There's a need for both," he said quietly, motioning them closer. "You got to know why things are to have any chance of changing what is. Otherwise, you'll just end up with the same thing."

Settling himself, he planted the cane between his feet and gripped its pommel. "Now I'm reminded of a writer by the name of Heinlein."

"Whose he?" Carrissa interrupted.

"Probably some dead gerrie," Jojo snorted derisively. "Dead, gone, and useless."

Dado fixed a baleful eye on the boy. *Such arrogance. It took me years to understand things I didn't want to know. Should I really expect any less from them.* "Yes, he is dead. He used to write about the potential futures of humanity. That's us." He circled his thumb. "Unfortunately, the things he predicted didn't exactly come true."

Jojo rolled his eyes back and did his best to seem disinterested.

"Pay attention!" The barked command was accompanied by Dado's cane slamming against the porch, inches from the boy's leg. With a high-pitched yelp, Jojo scooted back several feet. Dado shook the cane tip at his wide, startled eyes. "This is for your own good."

Taking a deep breath, he continued. "Anyway, this Heinlein fella once asked: "*Can any species survive without a willingness to fight?*" Over the years I thought about this and decided not if it's going to succeed it can't."

He waved his cane at their surroundings. "Take a good look around. What do you see?"

"Nuthin," Jojo muttered.

"I see some grass and flowers." Carrissa plucked a pale green blade and popped it into her mouth.

Jojo leaned far over and punched her arm. "Rag doll."

"Ow!" she cried, clutching her shoulder. "Don't hit me! And I am not a rag doll!"

"Whyn't you make me stop rag doll." He punched her again, this time in the thigh. Carrissa howled louder.

"Leave her be," Dado said wearily.

Feinting with several jabs, Jojo smirked and sat back.

"Your sister caught the gist. See that plant there." Dado pointed at a small, red-leafed scrub growing out of the foundation next to their ankles. "That plant twists its roots deep into a crack in the foundation. There's nothing there for it to eat except rock, yet it grows and reaches for the sun."

"It's just a weed." Ripping the plant from its purchase, Jojo rolled it into a ball and tossed it into the yard.

Dado started to reply when the air filled with a chorus of shouts and pelting feet. Like geckos in the hot sun, Jojo and Carrissa silently flattened themselves against the wall. Their bodies became a single ear focused on every noise. They flexed their toes, ready to bolt at the slightest threat.

Dado's hand slipped beneath his breast lapel and remained there until the sounds faded away.

Cautiously, first Carrissa then Jojo disengaged from the wall. They inched quietly across the concrete, eyes flickering warily from side-to-side. Settling back to their former positions, they looked up, clear-eyed and unperturbed, waiting for their grandfather to continue.

Nodding to himself, Dado took his hand from the pistol strapped beneath his armpit. "Now where was I," he mumbled so low his lips barely moved. "Ah yes. Life lives wherever and however it can. Any niche, any opening offers an avenue for survival and hope."

Carrissa stared upwards, mouth hanging open. "Told ja dummy," Jojo hissed, twirling a finger around his ear. "Grampa geeze has gone wacko."

"However," Dado raised a finger to the sky, "in decay lie the seeds of rebirth. Life feeds off itself, consuming the bodies of its forebears; that's those who came before," he explained.

Jojo turned on his best humor-him grin, while tuning out the lecture. Carrissa continued to gape uncomprehendingly as Dado charged himself up with his oration.

"Take this city for instance. When I was your age, its streets were clean, and all the buildings towered to the sky. There were few gangs and no pariah packs. People traveled without weapons and the police protected all of us."

"What a load," Jojo snorted, flipping a rock into the air. "Everybody knows CitySec don't care what happens—'specially down here."

Dado ignored the interruption. They'd had this argument before and every time he was left trying to defend the integrity of his memories against the child's pragmatic experience of the present. Besides, he had to admit that for all practical purposes Jojo was right. City Security only protected those who worked or could pay.

"Yeah well." Frowning, Dado sank lower into his chair. "Nowadays, everything's scuffed and worn. Afraid, we hide from ourselves and each other."

"I'm not afraid." Jojo thrust out his lower lip.

"Me neither," Carrissa piped, tugging her hunting belt to a more comfortable position.

Dado rolled his eyes. "I know you're not. I was just trying to explain—"

Curling his lip, Jojo hawked and spat on the ground. "So, what's this got to do with anything except you trying to scare us?"

"Be patient." Dado made a quieting motion with his hand. "I'll get to that. And I'm not saying you're afraid. Either of you."

"Yeah Jo." Carrissa jutted her chin. "Now shut up so's I can hear."

"Do you rag doll?" He sneered and punched her in the shoulder.

"Ow!" she yelped. "Quit hitting me." She rubbed the spot. Black-and-blue swellings were spreading over the faded yellow remnants of Jojo's older assaults.

"Like I said before, whyn't ya stop me." He bunched his fists and weaved from side-to-side.

"I told you to leave her be," Dado warned, his voice low. "That's twice. Don't let there be a third."

Jojo stared blankly at the old man, then deliberately leaned over and punched Carrissa again.

With a whir, the walking stick whipped through the air. There was a sharp crack and Jojo howled, clutching his knee.

"Thanks Grandpa." Carrissa scooted closer to his chair, putting distance between herself and her brother.

"Don't thank me. One of these days you'll have to fight back, or he'll keep whomping you."

"Rag doll fight back? No way." Jumping suddenly to his feet, Jojo loomed over Carrissa and brandished his fists. She cringed against the wall as he snickered and sat back down.

Dado watched carefully as Carrissa's face turned ugly and her hazel eyes gleamed with hate. *Won't be long before the boy gets one hell of a surprise*, he chuckled to himself. *Hope I'm here to see it.*

He cleared his throat and stamped his cane several times. Jojo and Carrissa glared at one another before slowly returning their attention. "We saw things coming a long way off, but we just didn't want to admit it." He stopped and swallowed. "People were angry and afraid. They wanted change, and they wanted it now. A faction in the government decided to use this discontent to push their own agenda. They called it, The People's Contract, and while they touted it as necessary, it went too far."

Tears plopped onto his chest as he tapped his staff on the concrete. "It changed everything. Folks didn't realize what advantages and services they had until they were stripped away."

He winced, remembering the turmoil of those days; the health and welfare riots; the random bombings and assaults; the long queues of job seekers and families receiving food doles. No bridge overhang was empty of tenants, no alley safe from muggers. New and tougher laws were passed to quell the general unrest. Prisons were filled before their construction was completed, forcing the courts to release all but the most persistent and vicious of criminals. In the end, things blew up in everyone's face.

"In the rush to give power back to the people, we forgot who those pushing change through the government considered people." He stopped to catch his breath. His heart was hammering with the still repressed rage of what could have been—what should have been.

"Now," he clucked bitterly, "there's no free rides. Hell, no paying rides either. Nobody can afford them."

Carrissa yawned and her chin bumped her chest. She started, blinked back sleep, and glanced sheepishly at her grandfather. Dado continued, oblivious, caught in the web of his memories.

"Under restructuring everyone was in the same boat, government, business', citizens. God, we fought like animals over the bones of an ancient giant. Yammering, slavering, trying to take what our neighbors had, we panicked and kept panicking until everyone was panicked out."

His cane swung between his fingers in leisurely, measured arcs. "It took that kind of exhaustion to settle things towards equilibrium. In the end, those who had started with the most continued to prosper. As for everyone else, many managed to scrape by, some found themselves all but destitute, and others just plain destitute. In case you're wondering, that's us." Carrissa nodded silently and Jojo flashed a profane, three-finger sign.

"And this," Dado raised his arms, "is what we have today. Your legacy is a society turned inward. You know," he mused, "I used to write a bit. I'd make up stories about future events only to discover what I'd created eclipsed by reality."

"Why we gotta listen to this!" Jojo kicked the wall. "What's it got to do with anything." He jumped into the yard and snagged a lump of concrete from the ground. With a sidearm flip, he zipped it at a piece of rebar jutting from a broken pillar. The lump rebounded with a sharp clang.

"It's fine when you teach us stuff we can use like dogging, shooting, where to find food, and what scritches to look out for. But when you feed us this, you're just another complaining geeze. Honk. Honk. Honk."

"Sides," Jojo scrubbed a grimy hand against his sack shirt, "most of the time we can't understand you." He nudged Carrissa with his toe. "Ain't that right rag doll?" Reluctantly, Carrissa nodded her head in agreement.

Dado stared sadly at his feet, his toes wriggling softly in the homemade sandals. "Maybe your right. Maybe it's no use talking about the past. You just get caught up in it and can't change." He gazed at Carrissa's upturned face.

"Maybe it's best to let life find its own way instead of trying to reinforce old patterns. Left alone, who knows what you'll come up with. Maybe more of the same. Then again, maybe not. Maybe something better."

Dado shifted uncomfortably in his chair. "Well," he bellowed and jerked his cane upward, "what are you two still doing here listening to a blathering old fool like me." The cane quivered as he held it at arm length. "Get out there and hustle up some dinner or else it's stale biscuits for everybody."

Grinning, the children gathered their hunting implements and charged off. "Remember what I taught you," he yelled at their retreating backs. "Keep to the shadows and watch out for tweakers and pariahs." Only Carrissa turned to wave.

Dado watched until they disappeared around the corner. Head hanging, he pulled himself to his feet and shuffled through the breach into their squat.

Never Enough. Just Enough.

His breath puffed in faint white clouds from between his quivering lips. His ears burned and his nose wouldn't stop dripping. The wind had long since stamped his features into a permanent grimace of pain and frustration.

Izzy hunched his shoulders against the chill temperature and stumped blindly along the side street. Tugging his collar high above his ears, he attempted to shield his face from the worst of the cold. He glanced once at his reflection in a storefront window, then refused to look again. The haggard features smudged with grime and coarse black stubble were unrecognizable.

A gust of icy air stung his eyes and he hunched lower into the collar. "Forty days." His thoughts tumbled back to the morning. "Just forty days."

....

Izzy wound his way through a maze of partitions, following the obscure directions provided by the front desk. Panic struck only once when he thought himself lost amid the empty, gray corridors, but a quick glance at a perimeter directory indicated his appointment was only three turns away. With a ragged sigh, he continued forward.

Paperwork rattling in hand, he shuffled through a cubicle entrance. A sign mounted to one side of the entry read: **Doyen Processing**. Inside, an officious taper in a severe, black jumpsuit stood behind a narrow counter that evenly divided the cramped floor space.

"I'm Mr. Dwight," the man's voice rang high and nasal. Head held erect by a stiff white collar, he sighted down a waxen nose, scrutinizing Izzy with a slow, disdainful gaze. His hands, protruding from bright white wrist cuffs, lay flat and still on the countertop. Sniffing lightly, he flipped several fingers. "Please be seated."

"Brought my paperwork." Izzy held up the fistful of static sheets while installing himself in the only available chair—a molded plastic model designed for discomfort. "Everything's in order and up to date."

"I'm sure it is." Tweaking his cuffs, the man glanced at a view panel concealed behind the counter. "Mr. Izzard Kaplinski is it?" Izzy nodded. Mr. Dwight retrieved a stylus from the countertop and began twirling it in his fingers. "Mr. Kaplinski, do you know what day this is?"

"Yes sir." Izzy swallowed hard. "It's October 30th."

"October 30th." Tapping the stylus against his lips, Mr. Dwight began circling the cubicle. Izzy craned his neck trying to keep him in sight as he passed behind the chair.

The man didn't walk, he glided with slow, precise movements. His body seemed unreal. Only his head and hands appeared human. The rest was something poured into a human-shaped mold of amorphous obsidian. In the pale, overhead light, the torso and limbs disappeared—their dark edges fuzzing. Like a blind spot, Izzy's mind erased the body, drawing the head and hands together into a caricature that floated through the air. Izzy blinked and rubbed his eyes trying to shake the image.

"Mr. Kaplinski, it's been exactly 40 days since you entered our job seekers program." Stopping at the counter's far corner, Mr. Dwight set the stylus down and frowned. "That means your allotment is up. And since we've been unable to place a person with your, um-m-m… skill set, I'm afraid we can no longer offer our services."

Mouth hanging open, Izzy stared across the cubicle. The words took a moment to sink in, but when they did his jaw snapped shut and he began to protest. "B-b-but," he stammered, "there's gotta be something? An extension maybe? Look," he held out his paperwork, "I've been busting my ass hunting for work. I've filled out hundreds of applications, maybe thousands. I've shown up for every one of your employment seminars and worked the database levels you assigned me till I can't see straight."

Mr. Dwight's nose wrinkled in distaste. "Mr. Kaplinski, please. Profanity is not allowed in this office."

"There's gotta be something," Izzy pleaded, his arms spread wide in supplication. "I'll take anything. Do anything."

"The Civilian Job Search Department doesn't work that way," snapped Mr. Dwight. "We follow strict ethical codes. Personnel are placed according to their optimum employment level. Anything less disadvantages the employee. Anything more inconveniences the employer."

"What about retraining. I can learn new skills."

The sneer that writhed across Mr. Dwight's face silenced Izzy's appeal. "The CJSD does not retrain. That task falls to the employer."

Sliding behind the counter, he primly clasped his hands on the countertop. "For the record, I am pleased you're exhibiting initiative by applying in person. We encourage such efforts. There have been many cases where applicants succeeded in acquiring positions through such determination. Even," his eyes closed halfway, and a smile nudged his lips, "after our services were retracted."

"Yeah?" Izzy growled, crumbling the paperwork in his fist. "Name one."

Mr. Dwight's face went blank. He didn't like being questioned, especially by... by this. His lips pursed. *Imagine such impertinence, that they should forget who and where they are.* "Many," he replied coldly.

"It's tough out there." Izzy threw the static sheets to the floor. "And I never talked to nobody that got a job without working through you guys. The only ones I've heard that have, were luck-outs or outright buy-ins."

Mr. Dwight sniffed and turned aside. "You've had 40 days of our services as required by law. There's nothing more we can do. Once you've found a job, you'll be eligible for our services again."

"But it isn't fair!" Izzy stood up and slammed a fist onto the countertop. Face blanching, Mr. Dwight jumped aside and pressed a stud under the shelf. Two black-clad security guards crowded into the cubicle. Thick, square blocks of neckless meat, they filled the cubicle's half-open space and effectively blocked Izzy into a corner.

Carefully, lest it should touch his clothes, Mr. Dwight two-fingered Izzy's paperwork from the floor and dropped it into a dispose-all recycler. "Please," his voice slid around the words as if they might soil his tongue, "escort this... gentleman...away."

With his wrists and upper arms bound by vice-like hands, Izzy was directed, sometimes with his toes barely touching the floor, to the exit. He offered no resistance as he was ushered through the dole crowd and encouraged out the front door with the stinging slap of a wide, meaty hand.

Tired and angry Izzy worked his way through the late morning crowds. Pedestrians edged aside as he stomped along the sidewalk. When foot traffic was this light, everyone kept their distance. Izzy tucked his hands into his pockets and trudged along, keeping a third eye out for street Johnnies and itinerants.

A ragged blue-clad figure dodged among the pedestrians. Izzy danced aside as it came near. He'd been in-city long enough to know you had to watch your pockets. Once, shortly after moving, he fell prey to the bump and snatch. Two rangy youths jostled him in passing. Boys or girls he couldn't tell, their baggy, blue clothes concealed all signs. Half a second later, he felt an emptiness in his back, right pocket. When he looked up the couple had disappeared into the crowd along with his wallet. In one shot he'd lost most of his carefully hoarded scratch and it had been hell replacing his IDs.

At an intersection Izzy glanced up to check the traffic. In the distance, a tower lifted its ragged peak skyward. A fringe of naked girders was visible as fuzz sprouting along the building's top edge. Part of an uptown rejuvenation project, it marked the border between MidDo and LoDo.

"Reminds me of that Dwight character," Izzy muttered. "Stick thin with a fringe. A real prick. Someone should shove that pen of his up his ass."

A small, tense group of people surrounded him as he waited at the curb. The stoplights flickered and a cluster of trams whizzed by. A narrow gap opened in the traffic flow. As one, the tiny knot of pedestrians bolted across the street and onto the opposite sidewalk. Behind them, a green-suited figure dashed onto the crosswalk, attempting to follow in their wake.

Brakes squealed. There was a soft, mushy thud and an outrageously colored pinwheel of green, white, and red, spun through the air. Still glowering at a mental image of Mr. Dwight's sneering face, Izzy continued down the street oblivious to the shouts and blaring horns.

He turned at a wrought iron gateway and climbed the canted, flagstone steps of a reconditioned brownstone. Once elegant with polished, marble lintels and scrubbed brick, the building frontage was now soot-tarnished and mottled with long white streaks of pigeon dung.

Lobby doors squealed as Izzy shoved through the entrance. Inside, he vigorously rubbed his face and yawned. *Sleep. I need some sleep, then some serious thinking. Maybe I'll pound the pavement some more.*

As an afterthought, he paused before the elevator and gave the up button a half-hearted punch. Nothing. No lights blinked. No machinery hummed. The damn thing hadn't worked in all the time he'd lived there. "Figures." His narrow shoulders sagged. "Why should Otis start working now?"

Izzy stared at his twisted reflection in the elevator's polished doors. Eyes bruised and pouchy, deep lines etching his slack face, he felt older than his 36 years. With a deep sigh, he pressed his forehead against the cold, metal frame. *It's a wonder I keep trying.*

Giving the doors a kick, Izzy turned and wearily dragged himself up the three flights of stairs to his furnished cubby.

His footsteps echoed hollowly as he trudged down the hall. Slapping a palm against the seal lock, he automatically stepped forward and nearly collided with the cubby door. Nothing had happened. Brow furrowing, he tried again. Still nothing. Frantically, he beat his palm against the lock pad.

"Won't work," a gruff voice sounded behind him. "It's been secured against entry." Izzy jumped as the super sidled up next to him. Short and overweight, with a slight hitch to one leg that gave him wobbling motion when he walked, it was amazing how stealthy the man could be. "Saw ya come in and thought I'd head you off before ya broke something."

"What right did you..." Izzy began furiously.

"Sorry." The super shrugged. His shirt collar rasped against the thick tufts of hair sprouting along his neck. "Word came over the com-net that you was axed from the CJSD program. That means your last dole was garnished for rent and I can tell you right now, it didn't cover the week."

"But my stuff's in there." Izzy's gaze chased about the empty corridor, vainly seeking the points where his voice echoed along its length. He really didn't have much to begin with, but having it taken away hurt.

"Sorry. I'd help you out if I could, but I can't. It's my job." He shrugged again.

Izzy's hands fluttered from his sides, to pockets, then gripped his ears. "Where does that leave me?" he muttered.

"Where else." The super hiked a splayed thumb over his shoulder.

Sounds grew faint and the corridor lights dimmed. Izzy sensed more than felt a swirling movement pulling at him, dragging him down. "At least let me grab my coat. This," he plucked his shirt, "won't keep me very warm tonight."

The super eyed him squarely and nodded. "Alright. You ain't been badger like most of the doles. I'll let you in, but," he held up a finger, "only the coat, unnerstand. The rest gotta stay."

Nodding abjectly, Izzy stood aside as the super waddled forward and laid a thick palm against the lock pad. As the door hissed into its wall recess, Izzy darted inside.

Before the super shooed him out, he managed to grab his coat and the Omni card he'd stashed for emergencies—twenty-five credits worth. It managed a light meal with fifteen left over. He felt the card as a hard, flat plate in his pocket. An inane line from a poster he had as a kid, strayed through his mind. "Never enough, just enough."

"Yeah right." Izzy wiped a drip from his nose and shuffled faster down the sidewalk. The evening air was sharp and penetrating. "Just enough to starve to death."

Garbage Run

Riding low, its belly filled with city spoilage, the Eden's Run drove outward from Sarong Bay, heading for the drop-off that is the Great Banks. Swells rolled and tilted its deck as the lumbering scow plunged through a roiling, leaden sea. Crew members swayed along the open catwalks ringing its hold, their knees bending and releasing with the unconscious habit of experienced sailors.

Festive holiday tunes blared from bull horns affixed to the pilot house. The melodies drifted through the salty air, fading, and rising with the rushing wind and waves. Inside the helm's cramped confines, it tinkled as light background to the engine's dull throb.

With pursed lips, Captain Majors watched the crew negotiate the narrow walkways with heavy rebreather tanks strapped to their backs. From her position, they looked like ants shouldering logs. The corners of her mouth twitched slightly as the jingle of sleigh bells rang clearly from outside the command bubble.

"Christmas ants on an apple core," she chuckled. "Now all we need is snow."

A sneeze sounded beside her, and she threw a quick glance over her shoulder. A tall, young man stood before the pilot board. His rough, sinewy hands dancing over the controls. Captain Majors looked him over with a practiced sweep of her eyes. Outfitted in standard-issue pea jacket and dungarees, he looked much like any other seaman, except for his earlobes. Long, dangling lobes pierced with platinum spikes peeped from under his black, woolen watch cap.

It's always their ears, she reflected. Give me a man with big earlobes and I'll show you a man with a big dick. Captain Majors chuckled silently to herself. Those were my younger days when I chased em up and down the piers. Let some go. Caught a lot more. She caressed the firm bulge hanging over her belt. That was what… three kids and a figure ago? Ah-h-h well. Rolling her shoulders, she turned back to observing the crew.

Eddie Barkles sniffed and wiped a rough, blue sleeve along his runny nose. He always caught one winter cold, usually from suddenly shifting temperatures. *And here*, he thought, fingering his tender nostrils, *I figured this season might be different*. He shrugged inwardly. *It's just as well. Keeps me from smelling the cargo and most of the captain's 10 Cr per gallon perfume.*

"Weather's been ungodly warm for this time of year wouldn't you say Captain?"

"Aye. It has." Captain Majors remained anchored to the deck plates. Legs spraddled, hands clasped behind her back, she stared impassively out to sea. Her cheeks, chafed raw by salty breezes, billowed slightly with each breath. "Keep a steady hand Mr. Barkles, we're nearly there."

Leaning forward, Eddie studied the ship's few working instruments. They had lost a quarter knot in speed and readings from the DM sapper scan indicated a 20% rise in particulate density. Frowning, he tapped several of the displays. "These old boats", he grumbled with disgust, "don't have any of the new telemetry modules. Instead, we rely on outdated retrofits. Uh-h-h Captain..."

"I see it Mr. Barkles." Wriggling her stocky frame several steps across the cramped cabin, she peered at the pilot board. NODE and RDG redline vectors had inched upwards from when they left dock. No surprise, but higher than expected.

Eddie coughed softly as a few tendrils of Jasmine musk pushed past his clogged sinus'. He wiped his nose and cocked a questioning eye. "Think there's any danger?"

Captain Majors tucked a shock of frosted, red hair beneath her braided watch cap, and peered out the cabin's gym-glass bubble. "Let's hope not," came her barely audible reply.

The skies were clear with a faint haze softening the horizon. A late afternoon sun reflected rainbows of red, blue, green, and purple along the rolling ocean surface. The Eden's Run pressed through an apparent archipelago of tiny, brightly colored islands—floating conglomerations of garbage that scattered like spinning tops in her wake.

Scratching an itchy left butt cheek, Captain Majors eyed the flotsam carefully. Bigger than jimmies, these aggregates indicated premature cohesion. It was a bad sign to be sure, but not a major concern. So long as the particulate counts didn't rise above 50 PPT and the ship's speed wasn't impaired by more than a third, they'd be fine.

She canted her head towards the navigator and murmured in a calm voice, "How's she riding Mr. Barkles?"

"Drafting at 120," came the immediate reply. "Topping at 133. Speed three quarters and holding."

"Very good. Keep her steady." Captain Majors smiled to herself. The man may be homely as a wart on a dobber's behind, even with his lobes, but he's a fine pilot.

Small clouds of gray-white gulls squawked and dipped through the air. As they drew close to the ship, a salvo of short pops from the foredeck sent them into a twisting flurry of shrieks and frantically beating wings. At the next volley a white form tumbled into the sea.

Nice shot. Captain Majors nodded, admiring the marksmanship. *On the wing off a rolling deck. Not easy. Not easy at all.* And some of them were hitting every time. Working the garbage concession was boring and the crew needed their little diversions. She peered at a small, patched hole in the far upper right corner of the cabin's bubble. *Just so long as they remembered the rule of aiming away from the ship.*

"Whatcha think Captain. What with this heat maybe something's stirring, hey?" Eddie swallowed hard and wiped his nose again. A quick glance at his jacket sleeve told him he'd been doing it all together too much. It was crusted from wrist to elbow with partially dried streaks of yellow mucus.

"Not to worry Mr. Barkles. I've been on this run for ten years now and have seen it before. It's only El Nina kicking up her skirts. Happens regularly." Grinning, she gripped Eddie's shoulder with a confident hand. "But just in case," her thick penciled eyebrows rose slightly, "we'll report our observations to CityCom when we dock."

Coughing nervously, Eddie ventured a wane smile and nodded. "That's the lad." With a hearty slap on his shoulder, Captain Majors turned away. "Is our speed still steady?"

"Yes Captain. Holding at three quarters."

"Very good, but just to be safe have the deck hands check for clumping along the hull."

Swiftly, Eddie issued the commands over the comlink and watched with satisfaction as crew members bustled along the rails, peering down the scow's sides.

Head bent to one side; he tapped an earphone. "The crew reports all O.K. Captain. No appreciable build up."

"Very good." Captain Majors scratched vigorously at an ear. "Set watches for every half hour. Once we've cleared the site, have a pike detail scrape the sides, especially the stern and rudder sections. Don't want any surprises, do we Mr. Barkles?"

"No, we don't," Eddie agreed, vigorously nodding his head.

"Open the channel to the engine room. Low volume. We can already feel them, but I want to hear how hard the engines are laboring. Can't trust the instruments in this soup. Best to go by the senses."

"Aye Captain."

They continued in silence, with only Eddie's occasional cough disrupting the rhythmic hum whispering from the speaker grill. The engine's steady throb pulsed through the diamond plating beneath their feet, resonating their skulls with its calming vibrations.

The oscillations deepened slightly, and Captain Majors flicked an unobtrusive glance at the instruments. No red-lining and no drop in speed. Suspension count was up slightly from before, but so far all within tolerance. With a satisfied grunt, she returned to her vigil.

Presents! Her lips hardened. I've got to remember to get presents tonight. God, the kids will go ballistic if there's not a head-high pile under the tree. And Alex, damned if I know what he wants. "Something from you," was all he'd say. Which means something nice. Which means I haven't a clue. Augh! The man is impossible.

"You single slobs have it made," Captain Majors shouted over the engine thrum.

"What's that?" Eddie cocked an ear. His hands danced along the pilot board, adjusting screw torque and rudder angle. He had to constantly compensate for drag to maintain speed in this density.

"I said you single slobs have it made," she yelled again. "You don't have to spend nearly every penny on presents."

"Not so's you'd know it," Eddie responded sourly. "Christ, what with friends and immediate family, this holiday takes a mighty big bite." He snorted loudly. "My season bonus is already gone and I'm already eating into next year."

"Robbing Peter to pay Paul." She nodded and heaved a sigh. "It seems we save all year just to spend it now."

"True," Eddie agreed, digging a pinky furiously in his ear. "Very true." He leaned forward and checked the LDR telemetry. "CoSat says we're in position."

Captain Majors dabbed a finger at the corner of one eye and stepped closer to the observation bubble. "Very good Mr. Barkles. Notify the deck crew to stand by."

Bull horns positioned at strategic intervals along the gangways crackled to life. Crewmen with prod poles hastened along catwalks suspended around the great, mounded hold as "All Stations!" blared through the air.

"Crew in position awaiting your command."

"Very Good." Captain Majors sniffed once and clasped her hands behind her back. "Let's begin shall we. The sooner we finish, the sooner we're home."

"Aye. Aye. Captain." Grinning, Eddie touched his throat mike and gave the orders.

With a heavy grinding the foresprit of the ship split wide. Chains clanked and capstans whined as the mountain of refuse, impelled by conveyer paddles, tumbled from the bow. It spread across the waters in an arcing fan of slowly sinking detritus. Only a rainbow slick of oil and grease marked its passing.

The crew dug frantically with their poles, prying soggy remains from niches along the inner hull. When the final chunks splashed into the ocean, they waved their arms signaling all clear.

"All clear?" came the call from the pilot house.

"All clear!" came the response from the crew chief.

The bow portal slammed shut with a low, booming gong, like the closing of massive temple doors. Captain Majors knuckled a kohl-rimmed eye. The digit came away smudged with azure and black liner. Uttering a noncommittal grunt, she wiped it off on her coat lapel. "Let's take her home Mr. Barkles."

"Aye, aye, Captain." Eddie made several rapid adjustments to the pilot board settings, correcting speed and rudder angle to compensate for their alteration in draft.

Waves drumming against her empty hull, the Eden's Run pivoted in a great circle and headed for home. Drawing shallow in the rolling swells, the ship's tri-bladed screws lifted clear of the surface. Freed from the thick soupy sea, they screamed to high speed before plunging with a torque-twisting groan back into the gray foam.

Eddie inched a silver flask from his breast pocket and winked slyly. "What do you say to a Christmas nip Captain."

"Don't mind if I do." Unscrewing the cap, Captain Majors took a long swallow, then passed the bottle back. She smiled, admiring the glimmer of Eddie's ear spikes as he tossed off his own portion.

Burping slightly, she patted her chest. Alex might smell the liquor on her breath, but so what. Out of sight. Out of mind. What her husband didn't know wouldn't kill him.

Luck Out

With a soft grunt Alice dragged her swollen belly across her thighs. "Just where the hell do you think you're going?" she barked from the couch.

"I'm going out," Luis muttered, jerking a heavy, brown coat over his shoulders. "Gonna look for work." He buttoned the collar tight around his neck, then tugged the sleeves down until only his gloved fingers showed. Turning side-to-side, he examined himself in the catchpenny mirror mounted beside the entryway. A fresh crack ran its length, twisting his reflection into off-centered halves. Satisfied no colors were visible, he reached for the door.

"Liar!" Alice snatched an e-copy of FanTeen from the couch arm and flung it across the room. It grazed Luis' head and crashed against the doorjamb.

"Bitch!" He grabbed his ear. "I'll knock you out! I swear I'll knock you out!"

"Bite me!" she snarled, struggling to her knees. "Don't lie to me. You're going to dangle with the Rojas."

Eyes glittering, hand cupping his stinging ear, he raised a shaking fist. "I said I was going to look for work and that's what I'm going to do."

Alice screwed up her face. "I'm getting out!" Her voice mimicked his of a month earlier. "Don't need the crib no more."

Nostrils flaring, Luis took two steps and stopped. "Wait right there, woman!" His voice trembled with a brittle edge. "You just wait right there! I said I was out and I am. Fuerto getting cut took care of that."

"Yeah?" Glaring across the room, she settled back onto her ankles. "Well then Mr. Ex, tell me where you're going to look for work?"

Luis hunched his shoulders and traced a rough semicircle on the rug with his toe. "I'm heading off to Central. See if they have anything."

Gathering her maternity tunic close, Alice examined his face. "Everybody knows Central's locked tight," she said gravely. "And Job Service won't touch a piker. You've got to know somebody to get in and mister… you don't."

"I know, but maybe I'll luck out." Luis shoved his hands deep into the coat pockets. "I got to try somewhere," he mumbled. "There's nothing around here."

Alice heaved to her feet and waddled across the worn carpet. "You'll need more than luck." She kissed him softly and licked the scant hairs on his upper lip.

Carefully he wrapped his arms around her waist. "God, it's like hugging a balloon." She gave him a mock slap and kissed him again.

"We've blood between us." He ran his fingers gently through her long, auburn hair. "That means something to me." Alice smiled, lower lip catching between her teeth. Pulling her arms from around his neck, Luis kissed her palms. "Be sure to lock up after I go." Twisting several thumb locks, he drew the dead bolt and opened the door. "I don't want to be worrying 'bout you while I'm gone."

....

"Ah, Christ," Manny tapped the screen with a gnawed fingernail. "Look at that will ya. Can you believe it's already coming?" He slumped back, disgusted. "And T-tide just done."

Scraping a chair across the room, Rod leaned over Manny's shoulder and squinted at the view panel's display. Each sweeping LDR pass refreshed the composite image into a long irregular bank that inched across the screen. His eyes grew wide. "Jesus it's big. Last time I saw anything like it was the 59 – 65 swell. What a mess that was." He wiped hairy knuckles across his mouth. "How far out?"

Manny tapped several keys and a column of data appeared in the display's corner. "Telemetry has it at thirty miles."

Carefully, Rod searched the screen for telltale afterimages. "What's the range?" he asked, absently stroking a stubbly cheek.

"Christ!" Manny sputtered. "You can read as good as me. It's right there." He stabbed a finger at the screen. "CoSat says a 95 to 15 core with a contemporary crust."

"Yeah. Yeah." Rod reached across the board and snagged a battered coffee mug from the upper console shelf. "Looks like we're in for it."

Nose wrinkling at the smell of sour perspiration, Manny began furiously fanning the air. "Jesus!" he gagged. "You ever hear of a bath? They don't kill ya know!"

With studied indifference, Rod leaned back and took a long, slurping pull at the mug. As he tipped it up, an ancient chip molded into the chubby red ceramic figure atop its handle issued a mournful *Ho-Ho-Ho*. Smacking his lips, he set the mug aside and belched. "Speak for yourself. I mean…", Rod waved his fingers before his nose, "come on."

"Watch it," Manny hissed. "Don't you even try mixing it up." He looped a wiry, black dreadlock behind his ear.

They sat several moments in stony silence then broke into loud raucous bellows. Manny's fierce glower twisted into a wide grin. Snickering, he slapped Rod's shoulder. "So," he said, suddenly serious. "What do we do?"

Rod frowned and ran a hand lingeringly across his bald dome. Thoughtfully pursing his lips, he reached for the Com mike. "We call the coordinator. It's her job."

……..

The control room door creaked open, and a slim, brown woman stepped into the room. She wore a tailored neon jumpsuit that suffused the air with a brilliant orange glow. "Hey guys." She waved a tentative hand. "What's up?"

"The fan Julie girl. The fan." Manny gestured at the panel. "It's jingle bell time."

"You can't be serious?" She stood inside the doorway, arms akimbo. "That's over a month away."

"Not this time sister," Rod drawled. "Telemetry clocked it at 10 MPD. It'll be here in three days."

"What!" she exploded, throwing her hands in the air. "That's too soon. We're not even close to being ready."

"We've got to be," he stated flatly.

"We can't," Juliana groaned. "We don't have the personnel to handle it. Seasonal support won't be on for another five weeks."

Rod shook his head. "Ain't that just like a dame. A problem comes up sudden like and it just can't be handled."

Turning, Juliana raised a warning finger. "I'm tired of your shit," her voice grated low and glacial. "Watch your mouth or I'll have you up on harassment charges."

"O-o-o." Rod fluttered his fingers and rocked back. "I'm scared." Then with a derisive snort, "Don't get your pretty little head in an uproar."

Fists bunching, she circled the room. "That's it fat boy. Forget the rules. I'm taking you down myself."

Tugging at his waist band, Rod bent forward. "Oh yeah. You and whose army?"

Chest-to-chest, arms stiff at their sides, they stood in an upside-down V. A limber sapling propped against up a rugged boulder. Mouths twitching, eyes narrowing to slits, they mimicked changes in each other's expression.

"Hey! Hey! Hey!" Manny shouted from the sideline. "Would you two cut the crap. We got enough problems."

Slowly they relaxed and Rod dipped his head. "Sorry," he sighed, squeezing the bridge of his nose. "This situation has me on edge."

"Sure," Juliana nodded, backing away. Her gaze never left his face. "Sure."

"Come on. I'll show you what's what." Rod gestured to a console chair. "You're the best coordinator we got. And sister have we got trouble."

Taking seats, Rod and Manny briefed her on the incoming tide. Fingers drumming the cabinet surface, Juliana slouched in her chair as they related the latest CoSat scans and F-RAM simulations. Occasionally she roused enough to ask a question, but mostly remained slumped, eyes half closed, absorbing the information.

When they finished, she took a long shuddering breath. A worried look flickered between the two men. "It came on awful fast. Wasn't there any warning? Didn't the scow lines report any buildup?"

"Yeah, for the last two weeks scow captains have been reporting unusually high particulate levels of 50 PPT and greater." Manny spit into the trash can beside him. "It seems the screwups at CityCom have been ignoring the reports. The tide ain't supposed to happen now, so it ain't."

Juliana shook her head and cursed. "The stupid sons of… If we'd known when this first started…" She pounded her fist on the table. "Ah-h-h forget it. It's no use pointing fingers now."

She rubbed her face and stared vacantly at the far wall. "It's big. We'll need to coordinate with borough and coastal sectors."

Mouth setting in a grim line, she slapped the chair arm. "Manny, you were right about the fan. Get down to personnel and see if they've anyone in the pool. Tell them we need backs, any backs, and we need them now."

"You got it." He hustled from the room.

Scooting her chair to a vacant terminal, she began furiously tapping keys. "Rod, let's review equipment status."

……..

The personnel office was a labyrinth of partitioned cubicles, guarded by a single secretary draped in loose-fitting, gold lame and white chiffon. With the stern expression of a sentry on picket duty, she denied access to all but a chosen few.

Bursting through the door, Manny rushed her desk. "Marline you gotta help us! Who you got to spare?"

Eyelashes clumped with mascara, fluttered beneath a towering, red bouffant. Slowly, they rose to meet Manny's desperate gaze. With deliberate care, the secretary extracted a nail file and began shaping her nails. At each stroke, gauntlets of red plastic wrist-to-elbow bracelets rattled and clacked.

"Sorry," she drawled around a massive wad of gum. "All assignments have been made for the next five weeks. If you wanted extra personnel, you should have put in for them six weeks ago when requisitions were processed."

Manny danced and hopped as if the floor had suddenly grown too hot. "Look, something big has come up and we found out about it just now! We need help!"

Marline yawned and blew dust from her nails. A disgusted look flashed across her face as she examined her splayed fingertips. "I said all personnel have been assigned for this period."

"Don't you have anybody?" he whined.

Quirking the corner of her mouth, she released a staccato burst of snaps and pops. "That," the tower of hair bobbed slightly, "is the only meat around here."

Behind the partially open door, a young man leaned against a narrow, chest-high counter patiently completing each line of an electronic job application. At the sound of the secretary's voice, he darted a glance over his shoulder and hunched closer to the form.

Manny scrutinized the prospect with the obvious distaste of someone discovering a noxious mass on the bottom of his shoe. Black hair slicked with Espuma. Dark almond eyes set deep in olive skin. Tight fitting chinos. Red shirt, open to mid-chest despite the brisk winter weather. Worn, ill-fitting, pseudo-leather shoes. Thin arms. Narrow chest. He hardly looked rugged enough. An iridescent triangle of crimson dots flashed briefly from his bare, left hand.

"Ah-h-h Christ," Manny moaned, "A banger. Come on Marline," he pleaded, turning back to the desk. "You're killing me here. You sure there's no one else?"

She jerked her chin at the young man. "That's it. You take him. We'll put him on temp."

Disgusted, Manny wrinkled his nose and yelled across the narrow space. "Hey kid!" The young man apprehensively tapped his chest with a static wand. "What, you blind? See anyone else around here? Yeah, I'm talking to you. You here for work or just taking up space?"

"The names Luis. Luis Adena. And yeah," he stared warily across the room, "I'm looking for work."

"It's not slick and you'll have to wear different threads." Manny pointed at his clothes. "They won't be as styling as what you got on and I guarantee nobody will be impressed by 'em."

Luis fingered his shirt uncertainly then lifted his chin. "No matter. I'll take it."

Head shaking, Manny started for the door. "Alright. Leave the scrawl with Marline here and grab your stuff." With a flurry of furious scribbles, Luis finished the application and handed it to the receptionist. Gathering his coat, he rushed to the door, dropping a glove in the process.

"Hey kid," Marline's voice grated behind him, "you lost something." Turning, he followed the insistent directing of a red-tipped finger. Smiling thanks, he ran back to retrieve the glove.

Manny rolled his eyes. *A pisher. A damned pisher.* "Come on kid, hurry it up," he groused. "We ain't got all day."

....

The door rebounded with a hollow clang as Manny slammed into the control room. "Here's all I could get. Calls himself Louie Adena." He fell into the nearest chair and spat. "Louie here's a gangbanger."

"The name's Luis," the young man corrected, scanning the room. Three-dimensional coastal relief maps and a Cousteau-series of ocean shelf resonance charts covered the off-white, metallic walls. Comic strips and regulation memos obscured a door-mounted static board. In the corner beside a row of lockers, an empty doughnut box protruded from beneath the trash compactor lid. Six chairs surrounded a central table whose coffee-stained surface hinted at hours of downtime. A pile of static newssheets and E-magazines were stacked neatly on one side.

Juliana sat up straight in her chair. "That true about the gang?"

"Was." Luis' eyes traced an optical cable snaking across the floor to where it disappeared beneath the built-in command console. "I been out for a while."

"Out or just slacking," Juliana pressed. "We can't have an affiliation presence here."

"Out!" came his sharp reply.

"Why?"

"Man," he snarled. "This is bull shit!"

"I asked why?" Juliana's gaze was hard, insistent.

Luis gaped at her. "What... I... Because my woman's carrying my kid! Alright! My crib told me to ditch her, but I couldn't."

"And?" She slowly traced a dried coffee ring with a fingertip.

"And nothing. My life is none of your business." Folding his arms, he sat down and glared sullenly at his shoes.

Rod stepped forward, his bulk blocking the overhead fluorescent lights. "Kid we don't mean to pry, but you want to work here, you come clean with us all the way to your asshole. Now answer the lady's question."

Luis fingered a small tear in the chair's upholstery. His stomach gurgled from the smell of rancid coffee and hot electronics. Taking a deep breath, he spoke to Juliana's left shoulder. "My brother was killed in a one-on-one. He looked up to me, depended on me, and it got him dead. Now I got a kid on the way, and I want to be around to make sure he don't end up dead too. Ok!"

Juliana caressed a tattooed tear on her cheek. "Yeah," she whispered. Then louder. "Yeah, you'll do."

"What!" Manny slapped his forehead in disbelief. "You believe that! Why he's just a little…"

"What's that on your lip?" Rod broke in, squinting at Luis' faint mustache. "Looks like a stain of some kind. There're towels in the bathroom. Better go wash it off. A-ha-ha!" he laughed explosively.

Chest puffing, Luis rose to his feet. "It's my 'stache," he growled, neck craned back to see Rod's face. "And where I'm from nobody makes fun of another man's 'stache."

"Oh, so you're a man are ya." Rod grinned. "How old?"

"I'm seventeen!" Luis snarled.

"Seventeen." Rod turned slightly, taking in the others. "The kid's seventeen." Juliana stared back blank faced, Manny with a look of disgust.

"Well kid here's the scoop." Rod brushed unseen dust from his overall sleeves. "Right now, you ain't where you're from, you're here. And we don't have time to babysit you."

"What he means to say," Juliana hurried to explain, "is when you're on the job, you leave your problems and attitudes home. Joking is fine. It eases the tension, but…"

"I don't take orders from no woman," Luis interrupted.

Rod chuckled and winked at Manny. "And she thought I was bad."

"You listen to me," Juliana snapped, "and listen good! This job can be dangerous and until you know the ropes, you jump when one of us says jump. That means any of us."

"We've been working together over five years now," Manny added, gnawing at an errant piece of thumb nail. "A working team. She's site coordinator. Rod's job foreman. Me, I'm senior assistant; the next in line, get it. And you," he arched an eyebrow contemptuously, "are temp help. Follow orders or you're history." Leaning sideways, Manny spit the pieces of nail into a nearby waste can. "Understand?"

Luis bit the inside of his cheeks. Keep it steady. Keep it smooth. Can't afford to lose this job. Not now. Not with Alice pregnant. He shrugged violently and nodded.

"G-o-o-o-d," Juliana eased to her feet, "we're communicating. Now let's get down to it. I'll be brief. This is for your benefit Luis, so listen up. You familiar with the holiday tides?"

"What ya take me for?" He sniffed and adjusted his cuffs. "Course I am. When they come in the sewers back up into the streets. Man does that stuff stink."

"So, you live along the bay side or close to it." She nodded as if adding one more fact to a growing list of facts. "Well then you're probably familiar with what we do. The tides last from one to two months at a time and our job is to clean the beaches while they're here and after they've gone."

"A-h-h crap," Luis groaned. "You're slimers."

She folded her arms, expression blank. "That's right. You got a problem with that?"

Sullenly, he shook his head. "I didn't think so." Juliana crossed the room. "You know what tide is coming up?"

"Yeah, the T-tide just finished so the C-tide should be here in another two, maybe three months."

She leaned across the console. "Normally that's true, but this year there's been an early turnover in the ocean's thermal layers. The tide's arriving in three days. And it's big. Real big."

Luis cast his eyes around the room. "If that's so where are all the other workers? You got them stashed in there?" He pointed at the row of lockers lining one wall.

"Now listen to that Manny," Rod smirked. "You're all the time saying how kids today are stupid. It just ain't so."

He turned back and stared Luis straight in the eyes. "We usually bring on a seasonal crew of three of four, but this year we were caught off guard and they are not available. Your it."

Eyes starting, Luis fought to still a rising wave of panic. This situation wasn't at all what he expected when he left the cubby. He started to speak when Juliana slapped a colored topo map hanging beside his head.

"The Bay area is divided into 50 coastal-watch sectors of 10 miles each. Ours runs from Verrazano to Mammaron Point." She indicated a section of yellow-inked coastline. "With your help we should just about be able to handle it."

"Yeah, if we break our backs and don't sleep," Manny grumbled.

Ignoring the comment, Juliana gestured at the console. "Can you handle a ComNet system? It's an older model," she twitched a shoulder, "but it's all we have."

Luis ran his fingers along a row of winking icons. "Yeah, this ain't so different from Joy Boy's. I guess I can work it." He sounded doubtful.

"Good. We've all got to handle CoSat uplinks, report relays, and emergency communications." Juliana ticked them off on one hand. "But don't worry. It's just basic protocol. Nothing difficult. You'll pick up what you don't know in an hour."

"Now let me show you what we're up against." Sitting down, she began downloading orbital images of the coastline to the screen. "The tides begin just past were the city barges dump their loads." An arrow slid across the display indicating an LD position 50 miles from shore. "That's where we start tracking. As swells hit the dump area, they amass a core of high-density solids. This conglomeration incorporates decades of accumulated refuse; that's why core sizes are given in years. Are you getting all this?"

Wrapping his arms tightly about his chest, Luis nodded.

"I can slow down if it's too much, too fast."

"No," he shook his head, "I got it."

"All right." With a deep breath, Juliana turned back to the screen. "We use multi-phase, chromatographic scans to determine the age range of substrata associated with each tide and the relative contents we're dealing with. We have to be careful." She glanced quickly at Luis. "There have been instances where waste dumping included hazardous materials."

As her fingers danced across the touch panel, the display filled with multi-colored images of lens-shaped, cross-sections. A Key appeared along the right margin, assigning specific values to each section. "We use LDR soundings to determine the tide's relative suspension mass, age density divisions, and dispersal range."

Juliana indicated the central sections of yellow, red, green, and blue. "This year we have not only a 95 – 15 core of over one million displacement tons, but a substantial accretion of this season's incidentals as well."

She traced the violet fringe with her finger. "If we're lucky the initial influx will hit in three days with the primary core peaking just before Christmas. Chromatic banding suggests normal levels of toxins, so danger from that direction should be minimal."

Scratching the scruffy gray fringe over his ears, Rod peered anxiously at the screen. “Any sign of fragments?”

Juliana’s eyes hardened. “Nothing reported. Scans are set for 700 kilo’s and up.”

“We should be checking for smaller,” he insisted.

“700 is as small as orbital LDR telemetry can isolate. It’ll have to do.” She smiled. “I’ll just keep a sharp lookout when we’re on site.”

“Oh, that’s right,” Rod huffed. “You’ll be safe in the AT post while we’re outside slogging through the crud.”

Juliana winked. “I’ll be watching extra careful.”

“Yeah.” He shuddered. “But you’ve never seen damage a swell this size can do. I have.”

She patted his shoulder. “Trust me.”

“What are core fragments?” Luis inquired.

“Those,” Manny crooned, “are the things nightmares are made of.”

“But what are they?” he persisted.

“It’s like this kid.” Rod loosened his collar and propped a foot against the console edge. “As the lady said, this stuff has a heavy central core. Now this core starts off as a semi-solid. Not rock-hard mind you, but thick like a lump of clay. Usually, the waves mash it into a slurry, and we just rake up the slop when it hits the beach. But every once in a great while, a solid chunk slips through. That’s when you got to watch out. Waves carry it in and wham, it takes out everything in front of it.”

He paused and rubbed his face. “Thirty years back I saw one come in. And yeah!” he snarled at Luis’ smirk. “I’m that old! I was a kid like you, fresh on the Fraiser Hook watch. The Yule Tide, that’s what we called it then, rolled in and a fragment the size of a Maglev engine slipped past the LDR. When it slammed into the sea wall, we lost 5 men. Some were crushed outright. Others got dragged off by the undertow.”

Luis stood silently, solemn faced, then whistled. “Only thirty years? I’d have thought forty, maybe fifty.” Juliana giggled and Manny cracked a wide grin. Rod looked hurt for a moment before breaking into loud guffaws.

Placing a hand over her mouth, Juliana strangled an errant chuckle. “Core fragments reaching shore, let alone striking anything, are freak occurrences. They’re nothing to worry about.” To Luis there was something in her offhand dismissal that seemed menacing. He glanced quickly at the door.

“Christ!” Manny exploded. “Enough with the history lesson. Louie here ain’t scared are ya?” Luis slowly shook his head. “Na. Didn’t think so. He’s a kid. Immortal as they come. The world’s his oyster. Come on, let’s get this over with." He reached into a metal locker and dragged out a shiny, one-piece, orange jumpsuit. The stench of mildew and plastic rolled from the open compartment. "Stand up kid."

With a few rough tugs Manny spreadeagled the suit and held it to Luis' shoulders. "We wear one-piece P-suites of treated vinyl and Kevlar. They got coated Dura-grip gloves, neoprene work boots, a hood that seals around your neck, and an optional filter mask. I suggest you use the mask. It can get pretty rank sometimes. And," he patted the suit's hood, "there's even a built-in Com-link that helps us talk over the noise and keep track of each other." He returned the suit to the locker. "Know how to use a pistol?"

"Hey!" Rod broke in. "The kid ain't ready for that."

"If he's gonna be out there with us, he better be." The console beeped and Manny reached over to make a quick adjustment. He snorted at the change in readings and turned back. "Well?" He stared at Luis.

"Yeah, I can handle a gun." Luis narrowed his eyes. "Why?"

"Look who I'm talking to. The kids a banger. Sure, he can handle one." Manny's eyebrows crawled up his forehead, nearly disappearing into his thick curly hair. "It's like this. Sometimes the beach rats don't run away and ya gotta be ready for them."

Luis searched the grim features of the other two. Their stolid expressions made them seem cold and remote. "Won't the suit protect me?" he asked, pointing at the locker. "It's Kevlar and I never heard of a rat could chew through that."

"Kid," Rod took a deep breath and let it out slowly. "Beach rats usually scavenge in packs and don't always have tails. Sometimes they're human and you know how they can be in groups."

He paused to study his feet. When he looked up his eyes were steady and humorless. "Normally this is no problem and we've the manpower to set up defensive perimeters, but since we're short staffed we gotta be prepared to fend for ourselves."

"Not that anything is likely to happen," Juliana added quickly. "There'll be extra CitySec patrols, and the scoops usually scare most of them away. It's just that every so often, one or two will get bold and then…" Shrugging, she stared hard at Luis. "You do what's gotta be done. You clear with that?"

Luis blinked and nodded slowly. The knots in his stomach kept him from speaking.

"All right then," Rod boomed, at ease now that the painful topic was broached. "During the crunch, we work fourteen hours on and ten off.

Holidays and religions take a back seat. Even a purist like Manny here has to fire up a menorah on his own time."

"Hey! Hey!" Manny shook his fist. "Watch the disrespect. If it wasn't for one of my people being nailed to a cross, you'd still be swilling beer with snakes."

Rod ignored the insults and continued. "There's a lot of grunt work, but some technical stuff too. That's why familiarity with basic ComNet protocols is helpful. We work every day until cleanup is done. If you work out, we'll see about setting you up seasonal. Do you want the job?"

"Wait a minute!" Manny shrilled. "He already said he wanted the job. He can't back out now."

Rod rounded quickly. "You said it earlier," he pounded his fist on the console. "We need someone out there we can depend on. If the kid is half-assed about it and quits partway through, I don't want him backing me. We've told him the score and you see that it made him a little green. I'd rather face the wall alone, than with someone who didn't want to be there."

Turning, he spoke directly to Luis. "Look kid, no grief, and no shit. We really need the help, but if you're in any way uncertain, we don't want you. There're other backs out there, but you're here now. What do you say?"

Luis nervously plucked his nose. It was true. He felt like bolting. This type of work and responsibility were beyond his experience. Not that he had a choice. With his voluntary secession from the crib, it wasn't safe to pull jobs on the street. Besides, legitimate offers hadn't been exactly pouring in and the part time jobs he was used to were low pay and less reliable. This was full-time seasonal, and with the city for god's sake. Besides no one, except Alice and Fuerto had ever said they needed him. Well, that's not true. At the Rojas' initiation they'd asked the same thing as the fat man here, but then it was different. Then, it was join or die. These guys were asking him, in or out. Luis gave them the same answer he'd given the Rojas. "You can count on me."

"Great." Rod crushed his hand. "Be here at 5:00 AM sharp. Starting tomorrow you'll receive crash training on aeration and filtration equipment, and decontamination procedures. By the time the tide hits, you'll be checked out on everything including the Port-a-John. Oh, and there's a ton of records to fill out." He winked. "We'll supply the wands."

Fresh Meat

Shoulders hunched, collar turned high, his fists jammed deep into the coat pockets, Izzy stiff-legged along the sidewalk. His eyelids were heavy with exhaustion, but he forced himself to move quickly.

"You th-think it's c-c-cold n-n-now," his teeth chattered with spasms of uncontrollable shivering, "just w-w-wait until it gets r-really dark."

Izzy hugged himself tightly and twisted his entire body from side-to-side. His feet performed a tiny jig as he searched his surroundings. "Better quick f-f-find some p-place to h-hole up for the night or I'll f-f-freeze."

Across the street, a light flickered from within the dim recesses of an alley. Blinking sluggishly, Izzy jerked a hand from his pocket and rubbed his eyes. Was it really a light, or just the temperature playing tricks with his vision?

There. It happened again—a brief flash of yellow-orange, different somehow from the bronze light of the humming streetlamps. A reflection? Izzy scanned the block for sources.

No trams. No window lights. No one with a pocket flash. There was nothing.

Sidling across the street, he peered into the alley. A brightness guttered and wavered in the depths. *Definitely not artificial. Looks like... couldn't be. Fire? Here?* Mind racing, he glanced up and down the block. *Why not here? It's a cold night. There are others got to keep warm.*

He slipped into the alley mouth, carefully feeling each step before committing his weight. Glass and gravel crunched underfoot as he inched warily through the darkness. His toe nudged a soft object that squealed and hustled away. Izzy clamped his teeth against a scream. *Rats! I should have expected them.*

Grimacing, he pressed ahead.

Ten steps ahead the alley jogged right. The corner walls flickered orange and red with the light he had spotted from the street. From this distance, he could hear soft hissing and crackling. It was a fire for sure. He'd spent too many nights as a boy crouched around a campfire not to know the sound.

He began creeping forward when a taloned shadow reached for him across the fire-lit wall. Breath exploded from his lungs and his heart threatened to burst from its cage. The shadow retreated and Izzy collapsed against the brick face.

"Jesus!" He clutched his chest. It took a moment for his heart to slow and his breathing to even. Patting down his neck hair, he peered around the corner.

An old man crouched beside a half-drum filled with dancing, orange flames. Gnarled hands rubbed and chafed together, wringing warmth from the sputtering embers. At the sound of Izzy's approach, he snatched up a club that lay beside him.

"Come outta them shadows and show yourself." The voice was firm, but the weapon trembled in the old man's hand.

As Izzy stepped forward, the man let out a slow hissing breath. "Heard you coming but wasn't sure who you were." He squinted and leaned closer. "From the looks of it, you're too fresh to be any danger."

He waved Izzy in and gestured to a spot across the fire. "You might as well come sit and enjoy what heat there is. It's getting mighty cold, but don't you be trying nothing." He shook the club meaningfully.

Turning back to the drum, the old man tossed a small, black object into the blaze. Immediately a column of oily, gray smoke coiled into the air. "There's no food, but there rarely is these days. Some boiled water over there." He jerked his chin at a steaming soup can. "It's all I can offer." Almost as an afterthought he added, "The name's Midge."

"Izzy. I'm Izzy." Hurrying to the drum, Izzy opened his coat and leaned over the flames. Plastic and rubber smoke burned his eyes and throat, but he was too cold to care. He huddled over the fire until his shivering stopped.

Izzy closed his coat, groaning with delight as the warmth baked into his chest. It felt just like the flannel pads his mother applied to his chest when he was little and had a cold. Heated in the oven, they felt so wonderful he would beg her to heat them up again and again.

With a contented sigh, Izzy sat back and relaxed.

Staring across the makeshift brazier, he examined the old man. Fire glow illuminated a lean, grizzled face with sunken cheeks that couldn't have hidden more than three or four teeth. The scraggly, white hair and beard—yellowish grey in the firelight—were singed from hovering too close to the flames. Tattered clothing sagged on his bony frame and, like his hair, bore the scorch marks of excessive heat. While Izzy watched, a purple tongue nipped from between cracked lips with a faint rasping sound.

The old man said nothing and barely moved. His gaze intent on the dancing flames, he seemed a flickering holo-sculpture of shadow and light. Izzy wanted to reach across and touch him, just to make sure he was real.

Crack! Pop! Bright, smoldering globules leapt from the fire onto Izzy's pant leg. Frantically, he swatted them off.

Cursing softly, he checked for damage. The skin exposed through the still smoking holes in his pant leg was sore, but otherwise intact. His hand hadn't been so lucky. A blister was forming on his palm where a mass of molten plastic had stuck.

"It happens," Midge croaked, pointing at Izzy's hand. "You get used to it. Just hold it to the flames," he instructed. "Fire draws fire. It'll smart at first, but only for a bit. Then you won't feel it so much."

Izzy tentatively extended his arm with the palm open to the flames. The blistered area screamed as if freshly burned. Yanking it back, he glared at the old man.

"Ya gotta keep it there till it quits hurting or it won't work. Come on, try it again," Midge urged. "It won't kill ya and I'm serious. It'll work."

Slowly, with many withdrawals, he pressed his hand forward. The pain grew until nearly unbearable then began to subside. Izzy unclenched his eyes in disbelief as it diminished to a barely discernible soreness. Pulling his hand away, he ran a fingernail across the spot. The blister had collapsed to a hardened mass. He looked at the old man, amazed.

"Told ya." Midge's lips split into a wide grin. Izzy counted quickly—yep only four. "You're a newbie ain't ya?" The old man shifted his squat. "Fresh on the street?"

Izzy nodded slowly, uncertain as to the wisdom of admitting such a thing.

"Choice or shove?" Midge asked, raking grimy fingers through his beard.

"Couldn't get a job and my forty days expired," Izzy explained. "Dole didn't cover rent, so they tossed me out a couple weeks back with what I have on." He plucked his coat lapel.

Head bobbing, Midge poked a broken curtain rod into the fire. The flames subsided, then burst into new life. "That's a tough break."

"Damned bureaucracy!" Izzy spit the words.

The old man rocked back and forth, cackling silently. "Not to worry son. Out here bureaucracy is in short supply. But then again so is everything else."

"Yeah. Yeah." Izzy rubbed his face. "Good thing I saw your fire. By the way, thanks for letting me hang. I was freezing."

Midge snorted. "That's a mixed blessing. We can have a fire tonight cause it's too cold for the pariahs."

"Pariahs?" Izzy didn't like the sound. "I haven't been in-city long. What are they?"

"Local gangs and what not. They like to tease folks like us." Midge stared deep into the flames. "Sometimes to death."

"Don't worry too much about them," a harsh voice broke in. "Better to watch your back from those you know." Izzy started as a tall, gangly shadow moved into the firelight.

He was a long, lean man, with a sharp prominent nose and glittering, black eyes. A sparse, wiry bristle covered the chin, but became patchy the higher it climbed his hollow cheeks. Limp, greasy, brown hair brushed his shoulders and the ragged duster he wore was spattered with dark, oily stains.

Midge nearly fell over himself scrambling to Izzy's side. Indifferent, the stranger folded himself into the vacated spot. "Who's the newbie?" His eyes bored hard at Izzy, examining him with meticulous care.

Voice trembling, Midge cocked his head to one side. "This is ah-h-h Iz... Iz... Izzy." Izzy leaned away as the old man huddled closer.

A lanky arm reached around the drum and took Izzy's hand. The grip was like a vise. "Sonny's the name. Sonny Calb. That's a nice coat you've got there." He chucked a scabrous finger at the orange lapels of Izzy's jacket. "Bright too."

"Thanks. Some friends give it to me when I left home. I was lucky to get away with it when I got evicted a while back."

"Yeah, I heard that." Sonny scratched his chin. "Followed you in here." He examined his fingernails then stared straight into Izzy's eyes. "Been listening."

He gestured at the can of water and silently Midge nodded his head. Reaching over, Sonny took a swig from the steaming can, belched, and set it down.

"Boots look good too," he commented.

Izzy shrugged. This cataloging of his clothing was making him uneasy. "I've had 'em for a year or so. They're pretty well beat up."

"Bettern' mine." Sonny shook his shoes until their soles flapped. "Hey Midge!" he barked. "How 'bout a taste?" The old man jumped at the harsh request. "C'mon," he demanded. "I know you. You ain't never without a taste."

Reluctantly, Midge pulled an amber, plastic bulb from his coat pocket. His hands shook so severely he nearly dropped it in the fire as he passed it over.

"Careful," Sonny warned catching the bulb. "Don't want to burn it up." Biting the nipple, he gave the bulb a healthy squeeze. His cheeks puffed as they filled with liquor. Rinsing it around his mouth, he swallowed and smacked his lips. "Have a taste," he passed the bulb to Izzy, "on Old Midge here."

Keeping his eyes fixed on Sonny, Izzy took a small dram. It burned down his throat and he gasped, accidentally breathing a little into his lungs. Eyes tearing, he bent forward exploding with deep, ragged coughs. Midge retrieved the bulb while thumping Izzy's back.

Sonny laughed and slapped his leg. "Wrong pipe. That'll do it every time." He whooped and carried on as if it were the funniest thing he'd seen in quite some time.

The laughter bit off in mid-guffaw and he turned angry eyes on Midge. "Hear about Daffy Jack? Got himself necklaced the other day."

"Necklaced?" Izzy rasped. The coughing had subsided to sporadic events, and he could talk again. "What's that?"

"It's a pariah fave," answered Sonny. "They drop a gas-soaked tire around your neck and light it. Whumph!" His arms leapt skyward, making Izzy jump. "Human torch," he laughed, eyes twinkling in the firelight.

"But Daffy?" Midge sadly shook his head. "Can't be. He was so fast."

"Not this time." Sonny sucked his teeth. "Got snagged in the round room over by 45th and Tule."

"The idiot." Midge was still shaking his head in disbelief. "There's no way out there."

"Yeah well…" There was silence as Sonny leaned back and crossed his legs. Midge seemed to shudder and collapse into himself. Izzy glanced back and forth between the two.

"Who say?" The old man finally managed.

"Got the glib from Scramblin Jane. Said she was nearby when it happened. Claimed she heard and saw everything."

"Know who done it?"

"She wasn't sure. The Black Peters probably. That's their yard-up anyways."

Sonny stretched and yawned hugely. Reaching into his pocket he extracted a short-bladed knife. It glinted as he twisted it back and forth. "Ya know," he spoke slowly to the polished metal. "I don't feel like a tussle tonight. No, what I feel like is a bit of old-fashioned tonsil hockey." He stopped the movement and leered at Midge. "What ya say pops?"

Whimpering, Midge tried to slip behind Izzy's back. "Hey! What's going on?" Sonny drew himself to his feet. Izzy bristled and stood up. "What do you think you're doing?"

Sonny edged around the fire drum, its light playing their huge shadows against the alley walls. "Don't worry new boy," he gently licked his lips. "I'm saving you for later. Right now, I got older pussy in mind."

"Like hell," Izzy growled and lunged for the knife. Too late he realized it was a mistake. Sonny's free fist lashed out, catching him on the jaw, just below his left ear. As he spun sideways, a foot struck him in the stomach driving the air from his lungs. Izzy fell backwards. His head connected with a ripe thud against the wall. There was a bright flash of light and n… rs… smahing… into nels.

Sonny's hatchet-face swam in and out of focus. At times Izzy could count the bristles on his chin, see the caked, green plaque between his teeth. "Too bad," Sonny snickered. "I like my meat lively. Now…," his voice faded away.

The last thing Izzy saw before the tunnel closed was Sonny standing before Midge, holding the knife to the old man's throat. "Open up and take it pops, or you'll be missing the rest of your teeth."

Light pinched out. Images surged in and out of darkness, swelling and contracting as they danced across his mind. Claire handed him a jacket with orange lapels. "So, you don't lose it," she laughed, patting them straight. He saw the blur of a hundred thousand smug, patronizing faces; their voices lifted in a roar. "Sorry, we can't use you." Midge cringed in an alley corner; his eyes wide with terror. Leering beside a flaming cauldron, Sonny waved a huge dagger. Mr. Dwight's puckered face turned and spoke. "Forty days Mr. Kaplinski."

"Forty days," Izzy murmured.

There was a point when disembodied hands rolled him from side-to-side. Probing, searching, he was powerless as they ripped and clawed at his body. The jostling was followed by an insistent tugging on his legs. He came apart and floated away.

……..

Pale, morning sunlight stung his eyes. Stiff, barely able to move, Izzy tried to examine his surroundings, but at every movement of his head the world blurred, and the acrid taste of bile scorched his throat. "Take it slow," he moaned. "Slow."

His head throbbed and it was with great effort he managed to sit up. Alley walls spun and warped. The ground heaved. Izzy squeezed his eyes shut, clenched his jaw, and fought a growing urge to vomit. When the world quit lurching, he opened his eyes.

The fire drum was smudged with cold soot. Inside lay a few twisted, black lumps of unburned plastic. Both Midge and Sonny were gone. He wasn't surprised. Sonny's long-coat lay in a heap beside the drum. *Now why would he leave his coat*, Izzy wondered.

Lifting his arms sent pain lancing across his shoulders and down to his fingertips. Carefully, he explored the back of his head and encountered a large pulpy area with a slightly raised ridge in its center. Fingers trembling, he could just sense the puckered edges of a short, deep gash. His fingertips came away sticky red.

Dropping his arms, Izzy closed his eyes and drew a slow, shuddering breath. *I'll live*, he thought. Almost immediately other discomforts began insinuating themselves. His buttocks were numb, and he was shivering violently. *I'm cold.* He made to pull his jacket close and became aware for the first time his coat was gone. His feet ached. Looking down, Izzy saw his shoes were missing. Midge or Sonny, he couldn't be sure which, had robbed him.

The sons-a-bitches, I... "Oh shit!"

Izzy frantically searched his pockets. They were empty. He went limp against the wall, stunned at discovering his last few credits missing. Now, even the remote possibility of calling home for help was gone.

Numbness crept into his mind, and he gazed along the alley toward the street exit. The pavement was cold and littered with jagged fragments of plastic, glass, and metal. It would be stupid to run that gauntlet barefooted, he decided. Pulling Sonny's discarded duster close, he tore strips from its lining and quickly bound his feet.

Dragging the duster's remains about his shoulders, Izzy teetered to his knees. He swayed there, bent nearly double, one arm braced against the wall. "Can't stay here," he groaned. "Got to get out." Gathering his strength, he pushed himself erect and tottered down the alley.

Shakedown Cruise

Swaggering through the door, his cocky gait and arrogant attitude were all Alice needed. Rolling from the couch, she fell squealing into his arms. "You got one! You got one!"

"Yeah!" Luis threw his coat into a corner and strutted around the room. "I'll be busting ass through the holidays at City pay." He paused before the wall mirror to preen his hair.

"Whatcha get?" She bounced back to the sofa, sloshing and swaying like a water-filled beach ball on cushioned sand.

He became absorbed with positioning an errant lock that draped along his forehead. "I… um-m-m… I," Luis stammered, glancing quickly at Alice's twisted reflection. "I'll be cleaning beaches for City Sanitation." He winced.

"So, you're a slimer," she stated pragmatically. "That means seasonal pay and no bennies."

Plopping beside her, Luis leaned back and stared at the ceiling. "It also means no presents and you'll be on your own over Christmas and New Year. Probably even Valentine's Day."

Alice sighed and tucked her feet beneath her. "No matter." She smiled and poked him in the ribs. "It's still terrific. Besides, it's not like we had plans or anything. And L.A. Jr. here isn't due till March."

"You're right. You're right." He reached over and patted her knee. "We got anything to eat? All they had down there was stale doughnuts and bad coffee."

Immediately after dinner Alice began planning, making expense lists, organizing their household budget, even designing a slush fund for when the seasonal work ended. Luis wasn't surprised. In school she was good at math and there wasn't a crib gathering she took charge of that wasn't hot with schmooze and booze. After everything was set, she'd cram it full of extras bought with left over money. And there was always money left over. Alice was good. *Man did she piss off the sisters.* He chuckled. *They didn't kick up when she dropped out. But I do it, and my neck gets sore from watching my back.*

Grabbing an E-pad, Alice began eagerly jotting notes. "We'll get a carry-cot and a few toys."

She chewed her thumb reflectively. "We'll need clothes. Baby for the next two years. I'll pick up a few things for me. And you, you can't be wearing your old colors all the time. Not if you want to get a steady job."

Or live, he thought, morosely pacing the apartment. Six steps to the kitchen area where a fold-up table and chairs stood open. Mismatched plates smeared with the congealed remnants of dinner sat on a narrow cupboard ready for washing during the next tap period. One step to the nearly empty box fridge. Six back to the living room where Alice sat on the threadbare two-seater. Five to the worn mattress lying against the wall, and two more to the stained closet where their privy nestled behind a hastily tacked up sheet. Luis turned slowly. Cramped now, when the baby arrived it would be worse.

"Rollos has things cheap," Alice muttered, scratching frantically on the pad. "I got a cousin works there can get us discounts."

"We need a new micro-oven. The old one just barely boils enough water for us to drink and I'm tired of lukewarm food." She tapped her front teeth with the static wand. "Maybe get the Tri-D fixed. You're always saying how sick you are of 2-D."

Luis sprawled onto the sofa. His eyes lingered over a crack on the far wall then strayed to patches of peeling, off-white paint, chipped molding, and soot-streaked windows. "How 'bout us getting a new place?" He idly plucked stuffing from a hole in the sofa's arm.

"What? You gone dim. How we gonna pay for new rooms?

And stop digging at that!" She slapped his hand. "We can't afford a new one."

"I just thought we could," his hand strayed back to the hole, "you know, get better digs. It'd be little less hassle, maybe."

Alice shifted to a more comfortable position. "Luis, you know this job won't last more than three months, maybe four, tops. We barely make rent as it is, and you want to drop what we have on a new place." Gathering her hair, she flipped it over her shoulder. "And what about your kid? Hm-m-m? You answer me that. He's gonna need all kinds of stuff besides clothes and food. And I'll tell you right now, Gerti won't midwife for nothing."

Luis groaned and bent forward clutching his head. He hated it when she used her reasoning tone. "They said they'd see about putting me on permanent seasonal."

"O-h-h like that means anything," Alice snorted. "Look if we stay here that buys us some time. We'll be able to stretch our money, see. Till you get something permanent."

"Yeah, you're right," he sighed, slipping deep into the couch. "I just thought we could, you know, get outta this hole."

"I know. I know." She lightly caressed his arm. "But we can't swing it just yet. If they offer you steady seasonal, then we'll talk about moving."

That night Luis fell asleep to Alice's scribbling and planning.

....

The next three days at the garage were a frantic hustle of activity—equipment checkout, status updates, situation briefings, operations handling, strategic planning. Luis found the general mayhem of organization and coordination exhilarating, a lot like war counsel with the Roja's. The job was brutal, its excitement a rush, but as the tide core drew nearer, Manny and Rod's banter grew increasingly vicious. Every barb appeared aimed at him, their put-downs, their jokes. Luis' periodic blow ups only made things worse.

"Christ, kid!" Manny stormed. "Wouldja listen to me! Suction on!" He grabbed a red lever and shoved it forward. "Suction off!" He yanked the lever back to its original position. "It's that simple. So, what's your problem?"

"I got all that!" Luis shouted, pounding his fist against the scoop's side. "But what I don't got are the variable power settings and how they're changed according to flow." Breathing heavily, he thrust his chin at Manny. "And it's pretty damn obvious you haven't a clue either."

"Hey Manny?" Rod hollered from the adjoining command room. "You gonna let some kid tell you don't know your stuff? He's a slick one. Bet he's after your job. He sure seems to know more than you."

Scowling, Manny bugged his eyes at Luis. "You listen to me you little prick. If you think you're gonna queer it for me with the boss, you got another thing coming. Why I oughta…"

"You ought to go inventory the filter sections in the back."

Manny froze with his lip curled in mid-syllable as Juliana strolled into the garage. Tucking a clipboard under her arm, she approached the two. "Hit it. I'll take over from here."

She turned to Luis as Manny slouched away mumbling under his breath about smart-ass punks. "Don't let him get to you. He's an ass from way back."

"I heard that!" Manny hollered from the gate room.

"I'm sure you did," Juliana retorted.

She winked at Luis, then raised a sympathetic eyebrow. "So, how's it going?"

"I'll tell you how it's going," Rod bellowed from his console seat. "The kids a bellyacher. If he thinks this is tough, just wait till we're out in the field."

"Shut your mouth," Juliana tossed over her shoulder. "And get back to work. I'll handle this."

Luis squeezed the scoop's guide bar and shook the machine. "What gives?" he strained through clenched teeth. "What gives? I mean, they got nothing better to do than dump on me all day?"

"They're a pain that's for sure." She smiled. "But it's not a shot at you. That's how they treat everyone, even me. Get used to it." Her smile faded. "Lord knows I've had to. That Manny sure can be a prick. And Rod… Oh man, some days I'd like to tear him a new one."

Juliana sighed and crossed her arms. "But they're good at what they do. No matter how abrasive they may seem, the fact that they continue to give you grief means they accept you. Just give them back as good as you get."

"It's not like I've been complaining," Luis added defensively. "They just can't answer my questions."

"Not can't. Won't. I've been watching. They're seeing what you can do on your own. How you react under pressure. If you can think." She tapped her forehead meaningfully.

Luis snorted and shuffled his feet. "That's bull shit."

Juliana laughed lightly. "Maybe. But how else they going to get to know you. Besides, Rod's right. This is nothing compared to moving mountains of sludge. Here it's fun and games. Enjoy it while it lasts."

"Yeah right," Luis muttered. He glanced at her face and pointed at the tattooed tear. "Been meaning to ask, not that I'm prying or nothing," he added sarcastically, "but your man doing time?"

"Was." Juliana tugged at a suddenly too-tight jump suit collar. "He's gone now, maybe ten years back. Got blasted away in a two-by." She cleared her throat and forced her lips into a thin smile. "But enough of that. It's history. Are you Ok?"

"Yeah." Luis nodded, averting his gaze to the far wall. "I'll be fine."

"Good." Turning abruptly, she yelled, "Manny get back in here!"

"Now what?" he growled, sauntering belligerently from the back room. "First you got me learning the kid to handle equipment then I'm booted to inventory. What's next?"

Juliana jerked a thumb over her shoulder. "You're back on checkout. Get to it."

"All right. Come on kid," Manny grumbled, flicking his hand at the scoop. "So, you think you know it all huh? Well, it's time I showed you how to vary power settings according to intake flow. There's a pattern to this so pay attention."

....

Each night Luis slogged home, bone weary, mind racing with facts and instructions. He slipped along streets slicked with refuse ground by seven million tramping feet. Pushing, shoving, cursing their way to unknown destinations, hordes of shoppers, clerks, and business officials jammed the sidewalks. With an alacrity born of experience, Luis wove his way through thickets of sharp elbows and shin-cracking heels. A particularly buxom woman spiked his instep as she jostled by. Luis howled and nearly fell, but with a desperate lunge kept his feet. Falling in rush hour shopping crowds was potentially hazardous. Unnoticing, uncaring, the crowd trampled anything in its path.

Blaring horns and flashing signals blurred with holiday decorations and festive banter to create a shifting kaleidoscope of colored sound. Rushing streams of wheeled and tracked transports hurled sheets of liquid filth onto sidewalks and cringing pedestrians. Holo-Santas hawked toys and merchandise from nearly every window. Flickering, silver bells pealed Christmas tunes through the hazy brown air. Snowmen and elves capered among light rimmed doorways, cajoling passersby with their cuteness. Gyrating, scantily clad Santets enticed would-be shoppers with their shivering wares. Beefeaters strutted before dun-colored office towers, rousting bell-ringing charity solicitors from lobbies, doorways, and building facades.

Nativity scenes sprouted in every available open space as bands of itinerant carpenter families invaded the city. In one life-size, outdoor display, Luis noticed the baby Jesus had been evicted from the manger, his resting place taken by a snoring, ragtag dinge. Mary, weeping saintly tears, cradled an empty wine bottle in her steepled arms.

Building surfaces not decorated with Christmas ornaments or advertising, were blasted with graffiti—some artful, most not. Overlapping symbols defined borders of the latest surf-and-turf gangs. Doors, walls, and windows emblazoned with curlicues and diagonal slashes indicated premises protected for a fee.

In the clear portion of a Deli window, a lone paper turkey caught Luis' attention, some shop manager's half-hearted attempt at capitalizing on T-Day past. *What was it*? His mother had told him once, before she left. He beetled his brow. *What was it? Thanks for giving the bird day. Something like that. It wasn't important*. Shuffling past, he tried to side-step the larger masses of garbage.

Chill winds howled along the skyscraper canyons. A pasteboard reindeer, dislodged from its moorings, tumbled through gutters filled with icy sludge. Cyclones of loose newspaper and gift wrap twisted in the frosty air. Pulling his coat tighter, Luis followed the press of people into the dim calm of an underground subway.

Clicking through the turnstile sniffers, he paused to wipe cold mist from his eyes. Even here the trappings of X-Mass dominated. Dirt and smoke varnished pillars spaced throughout the hall were wrapped halfway in spirals of red and green ribbon. Near the ticket office a bedraggled 20-foot Santa rattled *Ho-Ho-Ho* as he endlessly placed a star on top of a blue-flocked, plastic Spruce. The ceiling bobbed with a host of neon pink angels and scratchy muzak blared an out-of-tune rap version of Silver Bells. He grimaced. *You'd think they could at least play something newer instead of this oldies crap.*

Crowds milled about the embarkation platform. Luis checked the overhead digital and sighed. Cross-town Maglev's were always behind schedule, especially with the dwindling number of shopping days.

The press of bodies increased as the digital display clicked fifteen, twenty, then twenty-five. From just behind his ear, a Midtown businessman grumbled about the damned inconvenience, the damned lowlifes, and the damned holidays. For the next ten minutes, Luis suffered a hushed diatribe damning every possible person, place, and thing in the city.

His legs, as well as his ears, had begun cramping from being too long in one position when, with a rush of air and grating squeals, the tram pulled into the station annex. Luis shoved aboard a car packed with damp, steaming passengers and wedged his way to the far end. He grabbed a loop just as the car jerked forward. Huddled in his thoughts, he was watching the tunnel lights flash by when a gloved hand grabbed his arm and roughly spun him around.

"Well, hey. Here's the little prick." Two bodies splashed with red and black backed him against the emergency door. "Where you been man?"

"Rico! Dinky-D!" Luis' voice quavered. "How's it going man?"

"Where you been keeping yourself?" Dinky-D pushed his narrow, rat-like profile forward. The sharp tang of Ocher stung Luis' nostrils. He tensed, suddenly alert. They were wired, dangerously wired.

"Yeah!" Rico spat. "We not good enough for you anymore."

"Oh, haven't you heard?" Dinky smiled brightly. "Luis here's working for the city. He's a big man. Ain't that right?" He tousled Luis' hair.

"Yeah." Rico nodded thoughtfully. "Seems I did hear something 'bout that. Scraping up people's shit if I recall." They broke into laughter. Reaching forward, he jerked Luis' coat lapel popping the collar open. "Forget where you come from? Who your friends are?"

"No," Luis answered, mindful to keep his hands exposed and open, "but I told you guys I was out."

"No." Dinky-D shook his head. The red, bio-lume crystal embedded between his eyes blinked and shimmered. "Just lost is all." He casually pulled a vibro-blade from his back pocket. "I'm sure you'll come around."

"Leave him be!" A large man stood up three seats away, his head nearly bumping the overhead support bar. Rheumy eyes stared from a weathered, brown face framed in an impressive polar guard white beard. Dressed in a mangy, red suit edged with yellowed pseudo-fur, to Luis the man looked to be a seasonal bell ringer for one of the LoDo shelters.

Dinky-D turned, a crooked smile illuminating his face. Knife snaking back and forth, he advanced on the old man. "A mistake," he said simply. "You made a mistake."

Rico licked his lips in anticipation. "Cut the geeze. Cut him." His hands twitched and his feet did an eager little jig.

Passengers crowded to the car's opposite end, studiously ignoring the progress of events. Luis watched in horrified silence as the elderly man waited blank-faced and let Dinky-D close in. With no effort, no appearance of desperation or fear, he suddenly stepped forward, slid past the menacing blade, and twisted it from Dinky's hand.

Bones gated and snapped. Dinky screamed, clutched his arm, then collapsed to his knees. Rico remained frozen in a half crouch, his eyes wide, jaw slack, and arms extended from his sides. As the train hissed to a stop the old man turned and said in a quiet voice. "I suggest you and your friend get off. Now!"

Rico dragged a groaning Dinky-D to his feet and staggered from the subtram. "We'll get you geeze!" he screamed from the debarkation platform. "Just wait! We'll get—" The door shushed closed on his threats.

"I won't hold my breath," the old man muttered and resumed his seat.

With a blare of horns, the Maglev pulled away. Through clear plexiglass windows, Luis watched Rico drop Dinky-D and, with fists waving, chase the train several yards.

As they slid into the tunnel, he approached the old man. "You'd better watch your back pops. They'll do it." He stared at the flickering tunnel lights. "I'd look into finding another way home if I were you."

"I appreciate your concern son, but I've dealt with their likes before. Anyway," he chuckled at the empty space around them, "it sure cleared out this car." The old man extended a broad, vein-knotted hand. "The name's Nik. You are…?"

"Luis." The old man's grip was crushing and as they shook, Luis noticed a series of barely visible lines stretching along the back of his thick, corrugated wrist.

"Please," Nik gestured at the bench. "Have a seat."

"Thanks." Flexing life back into his fingers, Luis slouched onto the seat. "I wasn't really in any danger, you know. They were just reminding me about my responsibilities."

"Right." Nik nodded slowly. "Reminding." He fixed brown, rheumy eyes on Luis and asked, "You trying to get out or stay out?"

"What?" The sudden directness of the question caught Luis off guard.

"I got ears kid," Nik answered flatly. "They may be old, but they still work. I heard everything they was saying. So, which is it?"

What is this, Luis thought. *Suddenly everyone wants to know my affiliation*. "Trying to stay out," he mumbled, staring at an overhead panel advertisement. Angled from the tram ceiling for easy viewing, the panel showed a bare-breasted couple striding along scrubbed avenues and manicured lawns, extolling the virtues of the new Lustron fortress communities.

"That's tough." Nik's deep brooding voice drew him back. "I know." He raised his sleeve exposing a dark, inky band that circled his forearm just above the wrist. The five lines Luis had noticed earlier radiated from a weeping eye centered on the band.

"The Vigils. We owned the toughest hood around. Nobody messed with us. Nothing happened on our turf that we didn't know about or have a piece of. We fought the world for what we had and what we wanted. And when it took from us, we paid it back."

Nik tugged his sleeve back into place. "I was 18, an old man when the wall come down. Four cribs got together and made for us with Zips, thermos, and Long Toms. Wham! Bam! My hood was gone—the houses burned; the streets trashed. We fought 'till there was nothing left. My Mama got herself shot in the back running from the front porch. Never did find my girl. She got burned up I guess." He sighed heavily. "That's when I decided to bug."

Luis listened as the old man's eyes looked deep inside. "The homies hassled my ass, as you say, reminding me of my responsibilities. When an old friend of Mamma's helped get me a job, it got worse. Like your good buddy there, they tried knives; I got a couple of nice scars to show for it. When they laid guns to my head, I said enough and moved out. Got an apartment on Third.

Been there ever since. It's one of them subsidy types the government was pushing at the time."

"With all that behind, you shoulda known it was stupid to butt in," Luis scolded. "Not that I don't appreciate it," he added. "You saved me from a major thumping. This time anyway."

The white beard twisted with a wry smile and nodded somberly. "When this area started organizing, I wasn't too worried. I know what they look for in a party fool. When they bothered me, I fought back. Now I'm pretty much left alone. I stay around, I butt in," he winked at Luis, "because I'm used to it and got nowhere else to go. But if I had me a kid, you can bet your sweet ass I wouldn't want to bring him up around here. Get me into one of those protected areas. Give him a better chance to survive."

"You mean somewhere like that." Luis jerked his chin at the Lustron advertisement. It had recycled to the beginning, panning across planned environmental space to focus on the couple.

"No," Nik chuckled. "Those places are too spindlebutt for me. Besides," he rubbed his thumb and forefinger together. "You got to be bringing home plenty of scratch. No, I was thinking more like Swell Hill or Beau'Mich Alley. You know, up-city past the river, where it don't stink so bad."

A speaker crackled to life announcing their arrival at the next annex. "My stop." Luis rose and stretched out his hand. Nik took it and squeezed. "Been good talkin."

"You mean, listening to an old fart chew your ears off."

Luis grinned. "Yeah, that."

"Remember," Nik speared him with a gnarled finger. "To get out, you got to stay out. There's no halfway."

Page 58, Lower Left Column

CynCity Globe Friday, November 29, 2041

GANG MEMBERS KILL ELDERLY TENANT

CynCity – World Press Associates

Marta Mohler enjoyed her whiskey and enjoyed her friends. Together they did her in.

Four weeks ago, Mohler, aged 63, became one of hundreds known to have been killed for the one thing of value they possessed: an apartment.

With the devastating economic changes wrought by Federal and State restructuring nearly 40 years ago, many elderly citizens, already burdened by raging inflation and inadequate pensions, found themselves impoverished. Their only benefactions lie in subsidized housing and the temporary grandfather status afforded them under the then, new Universal Health Care law. As of last year, the government yanked that UHC cushion away.

This social redress, combined with already tenuous economic situations, pushed many of CynCity's elderly to destitution. Their plight quickly became intolerable to regional representatives who demanded something be done.

Seven months ago, the Federal Health and Welfare Bureau under the superintendency of Rep. Argent Bielman, P-Jersey announced that persons over 60 years of age could claim and sell their government-subsidized apartments.

With the pressure for city housing growing, suites of three or four rooms situated in older semi-protected neighborhoods were suddenly worth 500,000 credits or more. Even smaller studio apartments could be sold for 200,000 thousand credits.

This lure of money has proved especially strong for the lonely who believe wealth will draw friends, for the poor who dream of cashing in and spending the rest of their lives in comfort, and for those fearful of infirmity who barter their lodgings for now costly, long-term medical care.

Such greed and raw capitalism can be vicious, particularly for elderly citizens, like Mohler, who live alone.

As with many of the known victims, Mohler probably never realized with whom and with what she had become involved. Living in a single bedroom apartment, she spent much of her time drinking with friends, said Captain Victor Raboy of City Security's Homicide Division.

"Among her acquaintances were two young men, members of an East Quadrant street gang called Zwart Piet (Black Peter)," he said. "They knew she was living alone and wanted to appropriate her apartment. So, during a drinking party they tricked her into signing a trust agreement; on her death ownership of the apartment would transfer to them. Afterwards, under the pretext of buying more liquor, they took her to nearby Sarong Bay and injected her with a lethal dose of Indigo-B." (See editor's note.)

After burying her on the beach escarpment, they sold the apartment. (Investigators believe they killed an elderly couple in a similar setup.) The pair drew the attention of City Security after buying a flashy Aviron sports coupe with the proceeds.

Like many disappearances, Ms. Mohler's case would have remained unsolved, her killers unpunished, were it not for a lucky break. Three weeks ago, City Sanitation engineers uncovered her body while purging beaches of this year's relatively mild Thanksgiving Day tide. Said R. MacNurra, an employee of City Sanitation District 12:

"——, there I was raking when the tines caught on something just beneath the sand. I felt a lurch and up she popped, half out of the hole. Scared the bejesus outta me. Good thing the grinder caught her foot first or it would have been really messy."

At least 100 elderly residents across the city are known to have been murdered for their dwellings in the last six months. Currently, the whereabouts of 4,500 elderly who disappeared after selling their flats are being investigated.

While killers have included friends, neighbors, and family members, authorities fear what appears to be the growing involvement of organized crime in these cases. Residents are warned to be cautious about individuals or organizations offering cash and/or long-term, in-house health care in return for apartment ownership. Seek legal advice before entering into any agreement.

Citizens should know that not all individuals or CFA (Care-for-Apartment, Cash-for-Apartment) organizations are fraudulent. For legal advice or to verify a company's status call the City Better Business hotline at 900-333-3333.

To report questionable solicitations or illegal activities call the City Security Crime Stoppers hotline at 900-666-6666.

Persons living in patrolled communities should call neighborhood security services before contacting City Security.

Editor's Note:
Indigo-B (Purple Fugue) is a narcotic of the Wenthall Color series developed by GenMed Laboratories. This drug and its sister compounds, such as Saffron-Y (Yellow Blaze), and Vermillion-R (Ocher Joker), are popular among local street gangs who often associate a particular drug with their affiliation colors.

Apartment Hunters

Setting the static news sheet aside, Nora leaned back and removed her glasses. Sighing heavily, she slowly massaged her eyes. *I just don't know what this world's coming to. When I was a youngster, my parents used to complain about how bad things were. I'm glad they never lived to see this.*

A melancholy smile creased her face. *Well old girl it's a cinch you won't have to worry about it much longer.*

Nora reached for a glass of distilled water, one of the few luxuries she allowed herself—tap water, while fine for cleaning, tasted nasty. She sipped carefully and let it trickle over her tongue. *Ah-h-h*, she smacked her lips. *That's nice. Clean. No chlorine. Just the right temperature.* She moved to set it aside when a sudden pain in her armpit bent her sideways and sent the liquid slopping across her lap; a needle-sharp reminder that vanished as quickly as it arrived.

Straightening slowly, Nora stared with dismay at the puddle of water sinking slowly into her dress. *Now it's this. What's next? Incontinence?* Tears starting, she grabbed a handful of rough tissues from a box beside her chair and began dabbing at the liquid.

The tissue pile had grown to three crumpled sheets when her apartment com unit trilled the beginning theme from *In Your Face*, a flat-screen sitcom Carl had loved. He'd loved it so much; he programmed the theme onto their call chip. At first Nora hated the noise and regularly beat on the security com whenever it played. Eventually time wore its groove, and the notes became familiar friends delivering fond memories.

Gathering a knit shawl about her shoulders, she levered herself from the overstuffed lounger and inching forward with her cane, toddled to the door. Her glasses, dangling from polycarbon mesh cord, bounced against her thin chest at each shuffling step. Reaching the entryway, she paused to rest. *Can't fly like you used to*, she chided herself. *Time's coming when you'll have to give up answering your own door*.

After several wincing tries, she managed to lift her hand high enough to activate the eye-level surveillance panel built into the corner wall. The display filled with hissing snow and the faint outline of a gray-suited figure. Grumbling about incompetent technicians, Nora pounded the unit until its image snapped into focus. She hooked her spectacles behind her ears and squinted at the screen. In the lobby's outer vestibule, a clean-cut young man waited patiently beside the digital camera.

His plain, nondescript face was framed by slick, helmet-cut, brown hair. A crisp charcoal gray suit, lapelless in the modern sales rep. style, fit snug around his narrow shoulders. As he craned his neck, a strip tie tucked tight beneath his collar glinted metallic red in the cold sunlight shining through the exterior doors.

Though the camera's fisheye lens distorted his features, he looked bland enough. But then, Nora considered, everything looked bland when viewed through a com screen. It was only in real life that objects displayed their true colors.

Pressing lightly against the touch-plate, Nora leaned to the panel grill. "You buzzed me?" she asked, then jerked away as if shocked.

Dishwater gray eyes fixed on her bodiless voice. Thin lips split into even rows of dazzling white teeth that nearly overloaded the camera's glare sensors. "Miss Abernathy, I'm James Wilkes from ApCo." He held a holo ID beside his face. "Our representative spoke with you last week."

"That's Mrs. Abernathy," her voice quavered, "and the vidrep said they'd call back to schedule a visit."

"What's that? You mean…" The young man's expression became perplexed. "Oh dear. I am sorry. Since your name is on my list, I just assumed they'd arranged an interview. I had so many appointments in this neighborhood today, I forgot to call ahead and confirm."

Plainly ruffled, he drew an E-pad from an inside coat pocket and began briskly jotting notes. "Staff incompetence," the young man grumbled loudly. "My fault. My fault. Should always remember to confirm." Tucking the pad away, he flashed an apologetic smile. "I'm sorry Mrs. Abernathy, for any inconvenience. I'll have the office call and schedule a proper interview."

"You'll be returning tomorrow then?" she breathed into the com.

"Oh no," he chuckled. "More like four to six weeks."

"Six weeks!" She stared aghast at her apartment. It seemed larger than a moment before; growing, as if it knew her condition. "Why so long?"

"I'm scheduled to be in this area until Thursday," he replied.

Nora's voice began to rise. "Can't you fit me in before you leave?"

"Sorry, but business is hectic. I'm afraid I'm booked solid. This is the only time slot I have available." Leaning forward, the young man lowered his voice to a conspiratorial whisper. "To tell you the truth, it's nice to have a break. Especially an unexpected one." He straightened and winked into the camera. "Well, I must be going." With a brief wave, he turned to the door.

"Wait!" she squeaked. "Can you do it right now?"

He paused, hand resting on the handle. "Well sure, but I thought you wanted an advance call."

"But six weeks. I can't wait six weeks." Shaking, she pressed the lock release. "Please come up won't you. I'm in apartment 290."

"Of course," he assured.

The inner door buzzed, and James Wilkes pushed through into the main lobby. He took his time, letting his eyes examine the surroundings, taking in the disrepair. It was a standard subsidy retro, well over 60 years old. The Marlite wall panels were chipped and discolored with age. Decades of ground-in dirt nearly obliterated the floor's terrazzo starburst design. Running a finger along the wall raised a rime of dust on his fingertip. Humming softly to himself, he approached the elevator, pressed a small, recessed touch plate, and waited.

....

Hobbling back to her chair, Nora retrieved the news sheet and hastily searched for the article she had just read. She prompted her vid-com and, with trembling fingers, keyed the business hotline.

"Hello. This is Nora Abernathy. I read an article in today's paper. It said to call your number to verify CFA businesses… My name again? Oh, Nora Abernathy. That's A-b-e-r-n-a-t-h-y. I live in the East MidDo Subdivision on 45th and Bleaker. Complex 4, apartment 290. My FID number is 997-472-2291A… The company? Its name is ApCo. Their vidrep called me two days ago… I'm calling because their representative is here… No, he's not in my apartment, but he is on his way up… His name is James Wilkes… No, I didn't get his ID number, but he did show it to me… Yes, of course I'll hold." Leaning close to the receiver grid, Nora glanced nervously towards the door. "Yes, I'm still here… He is… They are… Thank you so much. You've eased my mind considerably."

So. Nora switched off and let out a long slow breath. *They're for real. I'd hate to think that nice looking young man was a phony. He looked a little like Carl. I wonder if he's as big. Snickering, she swatted herself on the butt. Nora you wicked thing. You're too old for that.* Heading for the door, her melancholy smile returned. *No, not too old, she thought sadly. Just too tired and too late.*

....

As the elevator lurched and groaned its way to the second floor, James Wilkes studied his reflection in the car's polished metal walls—rehearsing he called it. With practiced ease his countenance slid smoothly from one expression to another. The good-natured chum; the determined though concerned professional; the sympathetic friend; the astonished stare; the 'appalled by the indignity of it all' grimace. Satisfied with his repertoire, Wilkes began inspecting his appearance. He smoothed his hair, straightened his tie, and managed a final tug at his jacket sleeves as the elevator jerked to a halt. Stepping from the car, he took a moment to get his bearings before turning right down the hall.

Full-spectrum ceiling panels turned the corridor into an endless, brightly lit tunnel. Squinting upwards, Wilkes grinned in satisfaction. *All working. Most good.* Experimentally, he thumped a wall and stamped his foot. In each case he received a gratifyingly dull response. At some point, probably within the last 20 years, the building had been retrofitted with sound-absorbing dura-panel. *Cheap but effective*, he grinned. *Getting better.*

The brightness of the ceiling lights made it difficult to read the faded apartment numbers. Several times he leaned close to determine his progress. Arriving at 290, Wilkes pressed the apartment buzzer, waited several seconds then buzzed again.

The door thudded open against a chain bolt and a sullen eye sunk deep in loose folds of wrinkled skin peered through the narrow crack.

"Hello Mrs. Abernathy. I'm James Wilkes." He produced his business ID. *Take it slow. Gerries often have short term memory lapses.* "We talked a few minutes ago… over the security com."

"Yes, I know," she snapped from behind the shielded door. "I've been checking up on you. The Better Business Counsel says your organization is legitimate."

Wilkes' eyebrows lifted slightly. This one was alert. He'd have to be careful. "It's always best to be safe," he agreed, tucking his ID back into his pocket. "May I come in or would you prefer to conduct our interview with me out here and you in there?" He flashed his most winning smile.

The eye squinted and a corner of the mouth twitched upwards. "Do come in."

Still smiling, he stepped through the foyer and into the living room. The front windows were phase tinted with a peeling UV screen block, and it took his eyes several moments to adjust to the gloom. A floor lamp standing in the room's center cast a feeble light into the surroundings. Grouped in a ragged circle around the lamp, a lopsided Zero-G lounger leaned against an end table, and a cluttered port-a-tray stood beside an ottoman footstool. E-magazines and static news sheets cluttered the floor space immediately surrounding the furnishings. Along one wall an ancient vid-com unit perched next to a low-hanging shelf weighted with knickknacks. Wilkes glanced quickly about the room. That was it. There was nothing else.

Lamp light gave the surroundings a blighted, yellowish complexion. Floral sheathing lined the walls. Worn, all-weather, blue serge carpet padded the floor. Cobwebs dangled from the walls and ceiling. Everywhere a thick coating of dust softened sharp corners and smoothed jagged ridges.

"Don't mind the mess." Teetering across the room, Nora indicated the lounger. "Please have a seat."

"I'll be fine right here." Wilkes shoved aside a pile of news sheets and patted the footstool. He sneezed as a small cloud of dust rose into the air and tickled his nose.

"Bless you Mr. Wilkes," Nora nodded from the kitchen. "I'm having some tea. Would you care for some?"

"Why yes. Yes, I would. Thank you. Do you mind if I look around?" he asked as she puttered about the kitchenette.

Nora maneuvered slowly amid a clatter of cups and pans. "Not at all. There's really very little to see."

"No kidding," he mumbled.

"I'm sorry," she shouted, intent on filling a battered, ceramic kettle. "Did you say something? My hearing's not what it used to be."

"Nothing Mrs. Abernathy. Just taking some mental notes." Quickly Wilkes circled the apartment. Ghosts of red roses followed his muffled footsteps as he toured the carpet's worn paths. There was a living room with and adjoining dining area, a bedroom with a separate bathroom, and a full-size kitchenette. He nodded. *Not one of your larger places, but serviceable, nonetheless. Probably worth 325,000 credits, maybe even go for as high as 480,000.*

Leaning into the bedroom, he noted a single mattress jammed against the far wall. A frayed, green blanket covered its surface. There was no pillow.

An open closet beside the door revealed three dresses and two pants suits. Once fashionable and of good quality, they were faded and threadbare. Several pair of men's overalls hung in the dim recesses of the closet corner. Quickly, he retrieved his pocket memo and checked the file entries. No warnings. He whistled faintly in relief. *Wilkey boy, this looks like easy money.*

Winding back to the living room he noticed that, of all the furnishings, only the knickknack shelf and its contents were clean. *These gerries*, Wilkes eagerly licked his lips, *when they take care of something it's usually valuable.* He examined several diamond-cut pieces without touching them. *Cheap porcelain and zirconium.* He snorted. *Nothing here but trash. Probably hocked most of her good stuff long ago.*

"Those are my precious things." Nora stretched her hand to caress a chipped plaster spaniel. Wilkes jumped. He hadn't heard her approach. "This is my favorite." She drew a small figurine from the shelf. "My son gave it to me when he was seven. He was so proud. He'd saved for months to buy it."

Wilkes looked closely at the glassine oval glimmering in her fingers. Two large, faceted, green eyes stared back at him. "Very nice," he said smoothly. "What is it?"

"Why it's an owl," Nora laughed. "Don't you see. Here's its beak. Here's its eyes—owls always have big eyes you know. And these little things," she pointed at two nubs protruding from the head, "are its ears." Gently she returned it to the shelf. "I was so tickled when he gave it to me. You know I've liked owls since I was a child. They seem so wise. Don't you agree?"

"Of course," Wilkes crooned. *These geezers and their sog-brain reruns. What an owl*?

From the kitchenette a whistle stuttered then rose to a steady shrill. "Tea's ready," Nora chimed.

"Anything I can help with?" Wilkes asked, following her back to the chair. He watched as she filled two cups with steaming liquid and brought them into the living room.

"No." She set the cups down. "You take the port-a-tray. I'll use the end table."

Rubbing his hands together, Wilkes settled onto the footstool and carefully pulled the tray closer. Lifting the cup, he sipped experimentally at the tea. Black and acrid, it filled his mouth with a choking unpleasant aftertaste. Whatever it was, it wasn't tea. Suppressing a grimace, he smacked his lips and smiled. "Tasty. What is it?"

"It's thistle and dandelion," she offered, pleased at his interest. "A strong suffusion cleans the blood and flushes the liver. I gathered it myself."

"Really?" Wilkes managed a wane smile. "Where from?"

"Oh," Nora waved a hand towards the window, "it grows all over. I got this from the parking lot up the street."

Striving to keep panic from showing, Wilkes wondered if he dared to accidentally spill the remainder onto the floor. *No*, he decided. *It might jeopardize my chances.* Jaw firm, he took a large punishing swallow. His stomach lurched and gurgled in protest at the unaccustomed drink. "Lovely. Just what I needed to warm up. It feels like I've been cold all day."

Nora clasped her teacup with both hands, absorbing its warmth into her aching fingers. "Sorry, but I can only afford minimal heat. It seems I've stretched my ends so long they no longer meet."

"Not to worry Mrs. Abernathy," Wilkes cocked a sympathetic eye, "that's something we at ApCo may be able to help with." Gingerly setting the cup aside, he pulled an E-pad from his breast pocket and keyed its document display. "Given my earlier misinformation, I'd like to verify a few items before we proceed. These are the same, or should reflect the same, inquiries our representative pursued over the vidphone. Let's begin, shall we?"

He sat up straight, voice deepening. "Your name is Nora Abigail Abernathy? Uh, I mean Mrs. Nora Abigail Abernathy."

"That's correct?"

"You are widowed?"

"Yes."

"For how long?"

"Twenty years come April. I was married thirty-five years to a wonderful man. Why he used to…"

"I'm sorry Mrs. Abernathy," Wilkes interrupted, "but my time is short, and we must get through this. Please bear with me." He tapped several touch keys. "Your husband's name was Carl Frederick Abernathy?"

"Yes."

"Any children?"

"Two. Emma and Todd."

"Alive?" Wilkes' eyebrows twitched in alarm. He knew about the son, but not the daughter.

"No." Nora stared into her cup. "Emma died in the encephalitis epidemic of '27 and Todd of Viral TB two years later. Oh… oh pardon me." She blotted a tear from her cheek.

"I see. No immediate family then." He jotted several notes. "You currently live alone?" His wand hovered over the pad, awaiting her response.

"Yes," she answered, wiping her nose. "I have since my husband died."

"This apartment is yours? You've filed for and received ownership from the State? There are no liens against it?"

"That's three questions Mr. Wilkes." She waggled a finger. "But the answer to all of them is the same. Yes."

He smiled and nodded. "That confirms the personal items Mrs. Abernathy, now for the residence."

Wilkes cleared his throat. "Are there any problems with plumbing, heating, appliances, or building integrity that need be brought to our attention?"

"Well let me see. I guess the overheads need replacing. They burned out years ago. This lamp and the bathroom light are the only ones that work."

Nora scratched her nose. "The building water tastes bad and is rationed, but that's normal. It runs fine and doesn't back up. The com-links and kitchen implements are old, but they work when I use them." She grinned mischievously. "The walls are still standing."

Head bowed; Wilkes scribbled busily. He nodded and muttered, "Uh-huh," at each statement.

"There is one thing." She gestured towards the door. "You've got to give the security com a good whack now and then to clear the image. Building maintenance hasn't been able to fix it in all the years I've lived here."

"I see." Wilkes jotted a few extra comments. "So, nothing major."

She shook her head slightly and shrugged. "I can't think of anything else. Nothing's really broken if that's what you mean."

"Very good. I guess that about does it." He pressed several icons then held the pad up for her to see. "What I have here Mrs. Abernathy is a standard property release form. It itemizes the services my organization will render on a daily, weekly, monthly, and yearly basis. In return for these services, you agree to the legal transfer of your apartment deed to ApCo upon your death."

Nora extended her hand. "May I read that?"

"Why certainly." Wilkes passed the pad over.

Adjusting her bifocals, Nora brought the pad close to her chest. For several seconds she examined the document, her head jerking with each scan of her eyes.

Wilkes shifted slightly on the ottoman. Beads of sweat dappled his forehead. "It's all there." He reached forward and tapped the display with a manicured fingernail. "Services, treatments, what we'll provide in emergency situations. All you have to do is sign and everything will be taken care of."

Brow wrinkling, she laid the pad in her lap and began rubbing her temples. "Oh, I just don't know Mr. Wilkes."

Wilkes examined his shoes and counted to five. *Restraint. Don't push.* With a warm-hearted expression, he looked up. "What seems to be the trouble Mrs. Abernathy? And please," he added softly, "call me James."

"A moment." Nora dragged a trembling hand across her face and smiled weakly. "If you would be so kind as to pass me my medicine. It's right there beside you." She winced and pointed an unsteady finger.

Wilkes glanced around and snagged a pneumatic hypo from the tray. He read the label and carefully passed it over. "Damitol. That's a pretty powerful painkiller Mrs. Abernathy."

He looked at her strangely as she took the instrument. She appeared to have collapsed in on herself. The bones of her face and hands stood in stark white relief against sunken, shadowy skin.

"You can see it can't you?" Nora whispered. He nodded silently. "I suppose I look ghastly." She caressed the hollows of her cheeks. "It's death Mr. Wilkes, waiting to climb out."

Nora closed her eyes. There was a soft hiss as she pressed the hypo against her neck. Swallowing several times, she set the syringe aside and gulped her now tepid tea. "I have a progressive cancer and can't afford treatment. So, I sit here waiting." She patted the hypo spray. "This gets me through the worst of it. Palliative care is all Health Services will cover."

Retrieving the hypo from the end table, Wilkes began re-reading the information printed on its side. "Your judgment isn't impaired, is it?"

"No, of course not. The drug deadens pain, not the mind. I'm quite lucid."

He hefted the device and looked down its barrel. "I take it Damitol is lethal in large doses."

"Yes, but that avenue has been denied me. This is a TDS, a timed-dosage syringe. There's a built-in governor that regulates its usage frequency. The dosage is preset. I'm allowed one shot every six hours. No more." She chuckled dryly. "Euthanasia is not considered a valid treatment for pain. Even in terminal cases like mine."

"Fascinating." Wilkes turned the syringe over and over in his hands, poking and prodding at the timing device. The governor was completely sealed inside the casing and couldn't be got at without destroying the device. His fingertips dragged along a graded notch on the side of the syringe that looked like a key-lock control for setting the dosage." He shook his head in admiration. "What will they come up with next?" His eyes lingered over the syringe as he set it aside. With a quick, "Now then," he turned back, suddenly all business, "do you have any questions?"

"Yes," Nora's voice cracked. "It says here," her finger tapped the document, "that you provide health care services. Does that extend to APMs?"

"Ah-h-h, I'm afraid the contract references in-house care only, not major medical."

"I see," she nodded. "And is food service daily, monthly, or what?"

"ApCo provides necessities suitable for one-week intervals. Extras are up to you."

"I see." She stared hard at the document, slowly sipping her tea as she read. *What's she doing, reading the whole thing.* Wilkes cleared his throat. "It's a standard form Mrs. Abernathy. Nothing special." Smile strained, he pressed the stylus forward. *Come on granny,* his cheeks flushed. *Just sign it and be done.*

"It says here that up to 75% of apartment expenses are provided. How can you afford to do that?"

Wilkes shrugged. "It's required by federal mandate." He leaned forward, forearms on knees, wand tapping against palm. "We're allowed some flexibility in handling important service issues, such as heating. We feel the best way is to set up a sliding scale based on personal income. Given your status, I expect you'll fall well within the 70 to 75% range."

Heat. Its mere mention made the air seem colder. Nora drew her shawl tight about her shoulders in an attempt ward off a sudden chill. *Well after signing this, I won't have to worry.* With careful strokes, she scrawled her name at the bottom of the E-pad document, then pressed her thumb alongside her signature. Wilkes retrieved the pad and did the same.

"Now one final procedure. I'm sorry, but it's required with legalities of this nature." He jacked a small cube into the pad's side. "We need a retinal scan. Just an extra precaution. It's for your protection. Please look into the circle at the cube's center."

Nora lifted the box to eye level. There was a brief buzz followed by an intense flash of light. Blinking rapidly, she gazed blindly around her surroundings. The circular afterimage of a huge, baleful eye loomed before her, occluding the room. Whichever way she turned her head, the image floated there, watching.

She felt, more than saw James Wilkes retrieved the pad from her hands. "It helps to keep your eye closed until the flash wears off," his voice murmured. "Now it's my turn."

Right eye closed, Wilkes lowered the cube from his face. "Very good." He smiled and tapped commands into the E-pad. "Very, very good." He pressed a recessed button along the pad's side and a plasti-film sheet rolled from its base. "This is your copy." He handed the sheet to Nora. "We keep the electronic version."

"Is that it?" she asked, still dazed. The afterimage had faded to a hazy blur, and Nora found it easier to make out her surroundings.

"That's it." Wilkes smiled benevolently and shook Nora's hand. "All nice and legal tidy. Your in-house services start Thursday evening at approximately 8 o'clock PM."

"Thursday evening? Why so late?" Her eyesight cleared and she could discern the ready-to-be-gone look in James Wilkes' face that her ears told her was there.

"We've many clients to serve and you're the last on the rounds in this section. Two gentlemen from our health services will deliver an initial load of consumables. They'll have a questionnaire for you to fill out concerning your health care needs. Your answers will dictate the specific services required."

Nervously she chewed a finger. "Oh, I don't know. It's so late. I'm usually in bed by 8:30."

"Not to worry Mrs. Abernathy. They'll be in and out before you know it." He winked and tucked the pad inside his jacket. "We'll take good care of you."

Wilkes rose and dusted his pants. Nora pressed her hands against the lounger arms and began struggling to her feet. He lifted a restraining hand. "No need to get up Mrs. Abernathy. I can show myself out."

"A nice medium place," Nora heard him mumble as he strode towards the door. "It'll go fast."

"Have a nice day," he called, closing the door behind.

Nora fell back into the lounger with a heavy, sinking sensation. *It won't be long now*, she thought.

Forty Days

The evening rush hour had thinned to an occasional hissing tram. Pedestrians turned their collars to the cold, damp bay air, and hustled for home along the sidewalks. Rising winds dogged their heels with flurries of paper and cellophane wrappers. Rats, driven before the chilly gusts, burrowed deep into refuse piles, seeking the warmth of shared bodies.

A ragged figure humped across the street and dodged into the side alley. Sliding silently through the shadows, Izzy hunkered in the lee of an apartment dumpster and hugged himself against the warmth-robbing drafts.

“Forty days,” Izzy croaked through chattering teeth. “Forty days.”

He liked to speak the words. They were comfortable, familiar words that made the days less lonely. Crazy, bumble-headed words that parted the gentile, downtown crowds. Skimble-scamble words that held no meaning. Oh, they might have once, but he couldn’t remember. He uttered them now because he liked their sound.

“Forty days,” Izzy mumbled again. “Forty days.”

With practiced care, he hauled a whiskey bulb from his coat pocket. Mashing its nipple between his bluish gums, he tilted the bulb back and sucked. Burning liquid sizzled down his throat. Izzy snorted lightly as the familiar aftertaste rose into his sinus.

“Bad and badder,” he grunted, smacking his lips. After squeezing the final dregs from the plastic bulb, he tossed it aside and idly examined the sky.

A crescent of sun peeped above an apartment roof. It clung precariously for a moment then, as if eager to be on its way, dipped behind the cornice. Izzy grinned at the setting glow of turquoise and mauve. He liked the colors. They reminded him of better times. He watched until they faded and finally disappeared in the luminescence of a rising, full moon.

It’s a Hunter’s moon. The thought sent a chill quivering through his body. There’ll be plenty of light to see by.

Izzy shrugged his coat higher up on his shoulders. The air was cooling fast. It was time to hunt up a hole for the night. He poked his head around the bin and scanned the alley. Nothing moved. Satisfied, he began rising when a vagrant wind brought the patter of harsh voices. "Have us a time…watch the party fool dance…crisp him good…bitchin light show."

His heart jumped as a foot sneaked around the corner of the alley mouth. There was no time. Stifling a groan, Izzy quickly returned to his squat, tucked his hands under his armpits, and buried his face in his knees. Hunkering deep into himself, he tried to become just another shadowy sack of garbage.

Forty days, he thought desperately. *Forty days.*

The pariah pack hesitated at the alley mouth, their dagger-thin shadows stretching towards the dumpster. Kicking trash aside, a disheveled silhouette advanced into the alley.

The wind seemed to pause and even the rats quit rustling as the figure took several shambling steps forward and stopped. A crimson light flickered from its forehead as it scanned the alley for sound and movement.

Unable to still the shaking of his limbs, Izzy hugged himself tighter. He hoped the bin concealed him from direct view. If the pariah didn't come any closer, it would be enough.

With eyelids squeezed shut, Izzy held his breath and waited.

"Nothing here," the figure called over its shoulder. "Let's try the next one."

Izzy remained tucked in a fetal position, silent, afraid to breathe, terrified lest the slightest noise give him away. He knew their tactics. They liked to make you think they'd passed. Then when you thought all was clear and moved or made a sound—Wham! They were all over you. His ribs ached and he still limped from the last time a pack caught him. He was lucky. They had only beaten him.

He lifted a single, fever-bright eye and scanned the dim alley. Nothing moved. Nothing waited. The alley mouth remained clear of charging figures.

The wind breathed again. Several loose news sheets susurrated across the alley floor to nuzzle affectionately against his feet. Unfolding slowly, Izzy gritted his teeth and inched up the wall. His legs had cramped from holding the squat so long, and unbending was painful.

A single terrified bleat rang through the night. Forgetting his pain, Izzy hunched himself into a partial crouch as the yawp was followed by a chorus of excited howls. The pack had found prey.

Still bent, he jerked his coat tight and hobbled off through the darkness in a direction opposite the baying sounds.

"Forty days," he chanted to himself. "Forty days."

The alley pavement was marbled with puddles of shallow, brackish water. At each step, icy liquid oozed through his foot rags, chilling his toes and ankles. Slipping down an adjoining back alley, Izzy shambled through the darkness, searching for the cubbyhole he knew was there.

It was an old heating conduit some blessed soul had blocked off long ago. Cramped, barely large enough for one, he'd stumbled across the recess months earlier while wandering the alleys. Full of cheap wine, he'd collapsed against the panel and felt it give against his back. Luckily, he'd been too drunk to get up and had to stay the night. He examined his find the next morning and fixed its location. Warm and secure, the vestibule was his favorite refuge when darkness caught him in the neighborhood.

Hoarse screams echoed through the alley's warren-like maze and sent quivers through Izzy's insides. The pack was circling, baying at the heels of their quarry.

He listened, waiting until he was sure. Yes, they were coming his way. Coming fast. Numb fingers fumbled their way along the panel's edge, twisting corroded, butterfly fasteners that held the cover in place. He twitched at each screech of rust, expecting to be overtaken before he could hide.

Footsteps tumbled around the far corner. Hands trembling, he yanked and twisted at the remaining clasps. The alley corner flared with ruby light, illuminating a stumbling, scarecrow silhouette—its chest emblazoned with a bright orange 'V'. The figure heaved from the wall and tumbled his way.

Mewling softly, tears pouring down his cheeks, Izzy pried the cover free, slid into the recess, and quickly pulled the lid closed behind.

A body slammed into the panel. Gripping the inside lip, Izzy braced himself against scrabbling hands. Choking, sobbing breaths whistled a moment then lifted into an agonized cry. A series of scrapes and scuffles were followed by uneven footfalls pounding away from his hiding place. The sounds were quickly smothered by a swelling chorus of hoots, hollers, and stamping feet. Izzy leaned an ear to the panel and listened. They were driving him, turning him towards a cul-de-sac a block away.

He let out a shuddering breath and began to relax when a deep voice, eager and full of excitement, called out. "Hey come on. The others are leaving us behind. Hurry up or we'll miss it."

Izzy flinched and gripped the panel lip tighter. "Let 'em go," came a soft, panting voice. "I got another idea. I'm juiced. How 'bout you?"

"What?" The deeper voice sounded incredulous. "You mean here? Right now?"

"You're up to it ain't ya," teased the softer voice. "I mean you wouldn't want it spread around how you can't rise to the occasion."

"Fuck you," came the gruff reply. "I can get it up anytime, anywhere."

"Yeah. Then prove it meat. Lay it out. Let's see what you got."

There were sounds of giggling and rustling cloth. Sweat trickled down Izzy's brow, stinging his eyes as he strained to hear.

"Spread em wider. That's it. Now bend forward. Yeah. Yeah, like that."

"Ah. Uh. Ah. Uh. Ah. Uh." The short, cadent barks filtered through the metal cover.

"Harder!" a hoarse voice demanded. "Do me harder!"

Izzy could feel his penis swelling with each rhythmic slap of flesh against flesh until it strained against his pants and threatened to burst their fragile seams. His eyes grew wide with terror.

Forty days! He pleaded silently. *Forty days*!

With a final "Ng-g-g-g-ah-h-h," the grunts subsided to slow puffing breaths. There was shuffle of feet and the hissing rasp of a zipper. Izzy's penis deflated as if pricked with a pin.

"That's it?" The soft voice was edged with frustration. "That's as long as you're good for?"

"Hey lay off!" The deeper voice became defensive. "You wanted it. I gave it."

"Yeah, but I sure as hell expected more than that." The sharp words cut through the darkness and echoed in the hollow of Izzy's bolt hole. "A dinge coulda done better."

The enclosed air had become hot and thick with the tang of his sweat. Izzy was finding it difficult to breathe. Bright, stabbing aches crept up his arms, threatening his grip on the conduit cover.

"Listen bitch," warned the deep, now angry voice. "Watch your mouth or else."

"Yeah." Izzy could almost see the chin thrust defiantly forward. "Or else what?"

"Or else I'll drive you into the wall."

With a hushed snort, the soft voice quietly muttered to itself, just loud enough to be overheard. "That's about the only kind of driving you can do."

"Whadja say?" There was a short tussle of footsteps. Izzy braced himself. Burning needles lanced down his fingertips as he pulled tighter against the cover's inside lip.

"Ow!" Izzy winced at the sound of pain. "Leggo you're hurting me!"

"Whadja say," repeated the harsh, demanding voice.

"Nothing!" The soft voice whined between gasps. "I didn't say nothing."

"You better not. Now get your shit on and let's go. The others are probably setting up by now." There was a sharp slap. "I said move it."

Stifled sobs, a hasty rustle of cloth, and the pair moved away. Their steps faded until Izzy couldn't hear them, regardless how hard he strained. A breath he didn't know he was holding gushed from his lungs.

Carefully, he cracked the cover. Cold, evening air rushed in to replace the recess' stale, humid atmosphere. He gulped several greedy breaths, coughing as the coolness spiked his lungs. His head floated and the alley walls began spinning in slow, even circles. Bracing against the duct walls, Izzy waited for the world to steady.

Alley noises returned to normal now that the danger had passed. Water dripped softly from gutter pipes and grates. Rats stirred in the shadows, their feet pitter-pattering across the damp concrete as they scurried from one trash pile to the next. Soft breezes sighed against the brick facing. Izzy inhaled deeply, listening to the familiar sounds. From far away, came the agonized screams of a trapped and wounded animal.

Closing his eyes, Izzy leaned his forehead against the panel and sobbed. "Forty days," he whimpered. "Forty days."

First Rights

Blood moon. A Hunter's moon. The pack hesitates, noses lifting to the wind. Pinched faces leer through veils of matted hair as a taloned finger pointed into the alley shadows.

"There's one! Get it!"

Baying and slavering, they begin the chase.

....

Terrance sidled slowly along the sidewalk, lifting his feet high over the cracked sections of frost-heaved concrete. The air was brisk, but not too cold. Still, he strapped his vest tighter around his chest.

Squinting against the harsh morning sunlight, he surveyed the unbroken corridor of blank-faced buildings, automatically scanning for sign.

Jagged rooftops framed a narrow cleft of sky. Pigeon excrement crusted the building lintels and dripped in thin, white icicles from the cornice edges. Doorways stood solidly locked against the outside; the apartment windows shuddered.

A few half-hearted attempts at holiday adornment were scattered among the frontages. Here a lopsided wreath lay mashed against a window. There a handful of Gabriels with horns poised at their lips, guarded a balcony. And over there, strands of metallic blue garland languished from a sill.

Terrance gave the decorations a fleeting examination, then continued along the sidewalk. None looked worth the trouble, besides, right now he was busy looking for someone.

A motram whined down the street and sped through the intersection without slowing for the stop signal. A backwash of dust stung his cheeks. Wincing, he averted his face and continued down the street.

....

Startled. Caught in the open. The figure squeals and jerks its way down the alley. Clothes fluttering, its only hope lies in stiff-legged escape. Lose them among the shadows. Find a bolthole. Wait for them to pass.

....

With a daring two-step shuffle, he sent a spray of fragments tumbling along the cracked and pitted pavement. He idly tracked their skittering path. Across the street three, hunched figures ducked into a building entryway.

Catching the sudden movement, Terrance dropped into a crouch. He relaxed only after the figures disappeared behind slammed doors. In newly won territory, it was best to be cautious. He hadn't made it to nineteen by being careless.

....

Dank, brick walls scrape his hands raw as he darts through side niches and tumbles down slippery passageways. The pounding feet and yammering voices remain close, trailing his every turn.

....

Terrance scrutinized the sprinkling of pedestrians bustling along the sidewalks. Shaking his head in disgust, he tucked his fingers into his pants pockets and slouched along. Few uptowners risked this side of town and those that did usually traveled in heavily armed groups or under the protecting wing of a CitySec patrol. That left locals and dinges, and scragging them, while fun, was jack poor.

Up-city, that's where the action was. That's where the fat and happy citizens ventured unconcerned from their protected warrens. Normally he'd be there doing the old bump-n-rake, but this morning a Suzzie representative had left word at the crib specifically for him. "Grab a bohome and swing by. – W."

Terrance preferred jobbing with his own, but when a Suzerain affiliate requested your presence, it was wise to comply. Besides, he'd done work for them before, and they paid well.

....

Sharp turns. A pyramid of rubbish sprawls beneath a rusted fire escape. Momentarily hidden from sight, he burrows deep into the mound of trash and worms close to its warm center. Limbs stiff with cold, breath ragged, he's certain the thunder of his hammering heart will give him away.

....

An armed cadre of Citizen's Watch recruits strutted four abreast down the opposite sidewalk. From the corner of his eye Terrance examined the black and white striping of their tunics. Telltale bulges at waist and armpit allowed him to appraise their firepower. All four were strapped, but in difficult to reach places. He shook his head. Pretty much useless. A sudden riff could blow them all down.

"Showoffs," Terrance snorted. CW's were only dangerous in groups and then only when they outnumbered their opponents. Terrance turned his head slightly aside, obscuring his profile. He didn't need their hassle today. Another time perhaps, when his crowd was around, but not today.

Ahead, a slagged minitram spilled onto the sidewalk. Fused permanently to the pavement, its greenish flow partially obstructed the block's slit alley.

Terrance glanced around. The bodies were long gone; the bloodstains worn away by the passage of traffic. Except for the tram, you could hardly tell there'd been a one-on-one.

A whiff of decay rolled from the narrow alley mouth. He coughed and put a hand to his nose. CitySan must've missed one. Terrance quickened his pace. Slimers were always careless this time of year. Focusing on the beaches, they left the rest of the city to fester.

....

A rising tide of voices rage outside his hiding place. He remains quiet, but unable to control his chattering teeth. Snuffling and shuffling the sounds move away, fading to silence. He buries his head in his arms and sobs.

....

Terrance skirted the solidified pools of the minitram's melted chassis and shuffled faster across the crinkum-crankum. His toe caught the thick edge of a sidewalk slab and he stumbled hard against a building corner.

"Hey!" a voice called. "Hey T.T.! Where you been man?" Basking in a pale triangle of sunlight, a lanky, emaciated figure hunkered against the alley wall. Soot-covered, greasy brown hair drooped from a skull stretched tight with skin. Sweaty palms convulsively scrubbed themselves against a smudged, red and black t-shirt. "Missed you last night?"

"Joy Boy. Just the man I'm looking for." Slipping close, Terrance extended three fingers in greeting before leaning back against the building. Knees popping, he slid into a squat.

....

With exploding cries of exultation, hands drag him screaming from the trash pile. Swirling moonlit shades of red slash his face. A hundred, a thousand jeering cherubim with glittering eyes and foaming mouths, shove and punch him from all sides. He falls to the ground and scrambles through a forest of legs and kicking feet. He's allowed to escape, and the chase is resumed.

....

Terrance examined Joy Boy's sallow features. A rictus smile. Uneven, yellowish teeth. Sharp, angular cheekbones. His reddish eyes—swollen cysts ready to burst. *The Boy looks bad, but then he always does.* "You clear enough for a proposition?"

Scarlet orbs rolled sideways in stiff, jerking spasms. "Been booted on the Ocher Joker since last gloam," the death head barred a wide, toothy grin, "but sure, the lobes can process."

Twisting his shoulders to a comfortable position, Terrance reached down and picked up a chip of concrete. "Got a line on a job. You in?"

Hard black pupils glittered through puffy slits. "Who with?"

The shard rattled in his loose fist. He squeezed and it bit into his palm. "ApCo. A Suzzie affiliate."

....

Another corner and he falls face first into a puddle. Choking, his mouth fills with the raw metallic taste of slop bin seepage. In the shadows ahead he spies a figure working frantically. The body slips into a wall recess pulling a lid closed behind. Lunging to his feet, he slams against the cover and shreds his fingernails trying to pry it free. The air fills with a reddish glare as the pack closes. With a hoarse cry, he struggles to his feet and stumbles away.

....

"Hm-m-m," Joy Boy nodded and closed his eyes. "Doing what?"

"Won't know for sure till we connect with the man, but I suspect it's a cleaning job." Tossing the fragment, Terrance listened as it clattered down the sidewalk.

....

Legs wobbling, his breath coming in ragged gasps, he totters down the labyrinth of alleyways. He tries to turn and is blocked. He takes another and is confronted by solid cul-de-sac walls. Footsteps fill the dark void behind him. Wild-eyed, he spins about to confront the eager young faces.

....

"I suspect. I suspect. He-e-e-e." Joy Boy's high-pitched whinny breezed through the alley. "Sounds like you don't know a whole hell of a lot."

"I know enough to know you don't mess with the Suzerain. When they ask for you by name, you jump."

"I hear. I hear." The laughter subsided to trembling sniggers. "But why me? Lots of the others would love to get a piece of this."

"Cause you're the creative type, that's why. And if it is cleaning, it's got to look natural." Terrance jabbed a finger into his palm. "ApCo don't like the rough stuff. It's bad for business."

....

Hands pin him to the ground. A large circular object is slipped over his head. Cords bite at his armpits. He's doused with a fluid that burns his eyes and stings his nostrils. Choking, pleading, he cries as the familiar fumes envelop his face.

....

"Oh well. In that case," he rubbed his hands. "I got some ideas that'll work great. No marks. No trace." Wetting a pinky, Joy Boy reamed first one nostril then the other.

"Got the dry crusties," he explained, rolling the phlegm into a tiny gray ball before wiping it on a pant leg. "Anyway, where'd you disappear to last night? You missed the fun."

"I was hanging back with Braille." Terrance wriggled his eyebrows. "You know how she is. Wanted it right then and there, so I had to perform. Left her begging for more. We caught up after the set up, but" he raised a finger, "not before the flash. It sure was something."

....

A quiet, nasty voice gives instructions. Torchlight tales. Spark, initiation, words filtering through his terror. Smelling of gasoline and urine, he whimpers and claws at the tire fastened around his neck.

....

Joy Boy snickered, thinking of the dinge cornered the night before. "He was a funny guy, wasn't he? Screamed like an Uptowner in a grease free, bang brawl."

"The way he hopped and jumped when you let him up, for a moment there I thought he'd get it off."

"Not a chance. We wired it under his arm pits. Besides Dinky doused him good with fluid. Soaked it right into his beard." Joy Boy squeezed a globule of puss from a lesion on his forearm and carefully examined the mass before flicking it against the far wall. "Didja see him flap when we set him off."

....

A wink of light. A muffled Fumph! Head and shoulders burst into a ball of flame. Hair singes. Skin blisters and chars. Bellowing screams are torn from the soul. No longer human, the dancing stickman bounces from wall to wall. The howling beast-face is barely visible, its screeching mouth the only darkness in the blaze.

....

Terrance gave an approving nod. "Like a rat fat candle." Reaching inside his vest, he scratched absently at his ribs. "I noticed no one was touching him when he went. That was your work, right? Most anyone else would use a punk. What did you use? An auto-ignite?"

"No. No," Joy Boy giggled, his eyes gleaming in the sunlight. "Nothing so crude. I used a posi-static accumulator with a remote override. It's great. Let the guy dance a while to build up the charge, then at your leisure..." He made a pressing motion with his thumb. "Pop the static release. A spark and—Wham! Head jubilee." A beatific smile spread across his face.

....

Tendrils of roiling black smoke veil the moon. Flesh sizzles. Rubber sputters. The shambling figure dribbles a trail of liquid fire.

....

"Gave the new guy the remote. He did fine. Waited just long enough." Joy Boy sighed contentedly. "After we got back to the crib, Tiki took him right there on the floor. Brought him all the way in. He'll fill Luis' spot."

"Pretty boy Louie," Terrance snarled. "Now there's a guy that deserves to be singed."

Joy Boy chaffed his arms and shifted into a new position. "Yeah. Too bad about him. Luis was one of the few I could talk with about buzz wiring. You know, we use to spend hours on the Net. Him on the pad, me jacked up and jacked in." Gently, he fingered the cortical implants along the base of his skull. "Word has it he's looking to skip up city."

....

They block the entrance, prodding the lurching effigy with lengths of pipe and wood. Lurid shadows cavort along walls. Party shouts and laughter echo from demon faces. Groveling, crawling, its screeches reduced to moans, the beast circles, falls, and rolls onto its back.

....

"First he ditches the crib and now he wants to bug the quarter." Terrance slammed a fist into the pavement. "We ever catch his ass around here we'll rip him good." He jammed his bleeding knuckles into his mouth.

"Yeah." Joy Boy wistfully brushed his lips and the corners of his mouth quirked upwards. "We'd have too."

....

First rights. Club lifted high, a youth seeking manhood and his place in society approaches the beast. The cudgel slices through smoke and flame to deliver a crushing blow. With a roar, the pack rushes forward. Weapons rise and fall. Boots stomp. Bones crunch and snap. The crowd growls for more. When the beast no longer moves, they back away, surrounding their newly found brother. Amid triumphant slaps and encouraging words, the group turns from the guttering flames and disappears into the night.

....

With an abrupt movement, Terrance lurched to his feet. "Come on." He slapped Joy Boy's thigh. "Suzzies don't like to be kept waiting."

"Yeah. Yeah." Wincing, Joy Boy reached forward. "Gimme a hand." Grasping Terrance's wrist, he hauled himself to a standing position. "Sure, it's got to look natural?" he asked eagerly, skipping down the sidewalk. "You know suicides are nice too."

Yule Tide

White capped waves march across the ocean's steely surface. Tinsel strands shimmer along their crests, while the troughs churn with great sweeping eddies of holly wisps, knotted bows, snarled garland, and wrapping paper. Amid the swirls, clusters of blue and silver wreaths and crimpled wads of festival lights add their colors to the festive swells.

Battered and piebald, Santa surfs a wave. His faded blue eyes twinkle through the opalescent foam. Captain of the Armada, he waves a green mittened hand and dives beneath the froth. Nearby, Rudolph's red nose bobs to the surface, catches a breath of air, then disappears.

Ornaments jounce and spin in a staggering wassail dance. Two steps forward, one step back, a whirl, a jig, a bob. Unflagging and unhurried, the swells shuffle nearer to the shore.

Dawn light flares across the sky, a red eye awakening from a long-troubled sleep. Sea gulls screech and dive to snag flotsam from the sea. The city scintillates along the horizon. Its skyline decked in a festive holiday shroud of municipal lighting. Foam-capped waves raise their salty voices in a tidal roar of homecoming celebration. "Landfall! Landfall! Landfall!" Spume hisses across the beach with the white noise of a crowd gone mad. A faint tinkling of bells whispers over the ocean breeze.

Waves roll in at stately intervals as ocean tides return the barge dumpings of yesteryears. Each surge disgorges its contents onto the sand, cleansing, ridding itself of the excrement of decades.

Refuse clots the shores, befouling structures erected along its edge. High tide injects a roiling mass into the sewer conduits. The outflow stalls and backs up. Street drainage grates become fountains of soupy, foul-smelling liquid.

Cold light filters through the towering canyons of concrete and glass. Alarms buzz and beep, waking sleeping citizens from their foggy dreams.

Traffic stirs. A cross-town maglev rumbles through its underground burrow. Arising, the city gasps once, twice, then holding its collective nose begins an oblivious day.

Choices

He heard the din of shouts and frenzied clanging from a block away. Quickening his pace, Luis jogged up the street, hopping every few steps to avoid the potholes. Bursting through the garage door, he encountered a frantic, bustling scene.

Rod darted about the garage bay tossing gear aboard the transport and feverishly strapping last minute additions to vehicle sides. Manny and Juliana busied themselves with a hurried inspection of the mobile AT observation post.

"This is it," Juliana shouted, checking entries on her E-pad. "The first waves hit early this morning. Grab your gear and hop into the truck."

"About time you showed up," Rod roared. "Thought we'd have to leave without you." He heaved a heavy bundle over the truck tailgate.

"What do ya mean?" Luis struggled into his overalls. He thrust his feet into the boots and yanked the hood over his head before sealing the suit. "It's only 4:45. I'm fifteen minutes early." Quickly he crammed his P-bag with equipment.

"Ah-h-h," Manny sighed from behind the steering wheel. "A lovely day at the beach. The bracing tang of salty sea air."

"What's with him?" Luis hooked a thumb in Manny's direction.

"Him? Oh, he loves this." Rod heaved Luis' bag onto the truck bed. "Here," he flipped him one end of a web strap. "Gimme a hand lashing this down."

"It suits his disposition," Juliana added. "Beautiful day—rotten temper. Rank garbage—he's happy. See?"

"Hey!" She pointed at the thin racers poking from Luis' side pocket. "Be sure to wear those gloves. We'll be traveling through some affiliated territories and there'll likely be some folks who'll take an interest in that beautiful red design on your hand. We don't need to be drawing their attention."

Nodding, Luis climbed into the cab beside a grinning Manny.

"Hiya kid. Hope you got a strong stomach. Gonna be nasty today. Don't be surprised if you run across body parts."

Luis frowned and cinched the gloves tight at the wrist. "I've seen it before."

"I'll bet you have and fresh too." Manny leaned close, almost whispering. "But this stuff's been sitting a while and had a chance to stew in its own juices." He wriggled his eyebrows seductively. "Believe me kid, it's like nothing you've ever seen before. Here's a hint. If you run across a heavy plastic bag, don't open it. Call one of us. We'll check it out. We've found stuff in the past that's required a CitySec investigation." At this he cackled and nudged Luis with an elbow.

"Move 'em out," Juliana's voice rasped over the Com.

"And we're off." Manny rumbled the truck to life and purred it into gear. They bounced and lurched over the yard's protective grating and into the street. Between each bump Luis frantically attempted to buckle his safety belt. He had nearly succeeded when a sudden braking sent him thudding painfully against the dash.

"Asshole!" Manny screamed as a Nica Tempest cut in front of the transport. "They get a fancy car and think they own the road. Hey dickhead!" he yelled from the cab window. "Where'd you learn to drive?"

Eyes springing wide, Manny pointed a quivering finger across the dash. "Why the… Did you see that? Tell me you saw that. That son of a bitch flipped me off. Well, I'll teach him to disrespect City Sanitation." Manny hit the accelerator and ground the truck into a higher gear. "Watch the putz jump when he sees our bumper in his mirror."

Luis covered his eyes and groaned. Bad enough being nervous about seeing action for the first time, but this… It's going to be a long day.

……..

Sunbeams slipped through narrow fractures in a gray ceiling swept clean by steady breezes. The brilliant shafts turned the beach into a playground of light and shadow. Three vehicles rumbled across the mottled sand, gouging the surface with rim-deep ruts. With low groans and a hiss of air brakes, the transports shuddered to a halt.

Climbing from the cab, Luis stepped onto a beach drenched with a thick, mercuric soup. He'd been here before, but never during a tide. He slopped forward, staring with dismay at the tangles of spent Christmas lights and garland seaweed. The coastline was littered for miles with crumpled bows, plastic mistletoe, frayed holly wreaths, and the twisted remnants of artificial pine trees denuded of their lifelike needles. The syrupy air reeked of sulfur and dead fish. He was fumbling his hood into place when Manny called from the truck.

"Stinks, don't it?" Luis nodded and yanked the suit mask over his nose. "Didn't think we put out this much shit, didja? Well, here it is kid. Mine, yours, even your grandparents." Manny snickered and gestured along the beach. "Mind you this is Christmas. The rest of the year it's not nearly as bad."

"Come on." He jerked his head towards the vehicles. "Let's get unloaded."

Slipping through the mire, they climbed onto the truck bed. "Remember." Manny uncinched a strap. "Scoops first, then rakes. Set the guide poles last. Leave your P-bag in the cab. Take only the gear you need. It's one less thing to load up when we head back tonight."

"Wouldn't it be easier to leave everything here till we're done with the job?"

"Are you nuts? The dinges and rummage rats 'll steal us blind if we leave it here."

Juliana appeared at the tailgate. "If we had our regular seasonal force there would be 24 hour shifts and we'd do just that. But since we don't, we'll take everything back with us."

"Everything?" Luis asked in disbelief.

"Everything," she answered slogging off through the muck. "Now get a move on. I've got to set up the Oby."

Luis glanced at Manny.

"The observation post needs to be set up out there." Manny pointed towards the surf.

"Why out there? Wouldn't the beach do just as well?"

"What is this? Twenty questions! Because she needs to monitor the swells and the water chemistry. It gives us a little extra warning should anything show up." He tugged at Luis' sleeve. "You don't think these suits are caustic retardant for nothing."

Juliana slowly maneuvered her rig through the spindrift and crashing surf. Just before the breaker line, she stopped and anchored it into position. From Luis' vantage, it appeared some huge creature had hauled itself from the ocean and was resting a moment before deciding to come ashore. A series of rotating antenna sprouted from its top and automatically aligned themselves with unseen CoSat and City communications beacons. Sapor nodes snaked from the Oby's sides and slithered into the water. Suspended at different levels, each node continuously monitored the water chemistry for dangerous levels of natural and artificial compounds.

With rough shouts the crew arranged their scoops in a staggered formation parallel to the surf edge and began inching along the beach. For hours roaring machines and grinding sand overwhelmed the ocean's voice. Rasping burrs heralded the demise of plastic effigies and ornaments. As the air warmed to a brisk 40 degrees, they halted to clear sieves and check load levels.

"Hey!" Rod yelled to Manny. "How can you stand the smell? With that honker of yours, it must really be tough."

Manny pulled the hood mask from his face and struck a regal pose. "This," he waved towards his face, "is the proboscis of Emperors and Kings. Solomon himself would be proud of such an appendage."

Rod grabbed his crotch and snorted. "I got your appendage right here."

"Bite me!" Manny shouted.

"And the head boss," Rod continued malevolently, "has got your proboscis right here." He jammed a thumb between his butt cheeks.

"That's right." Manny sandwiched his nose between open palms. "Fighting for air right next to yours."

Rod shook a muck spattered orange fist. "Up yours!"

"Shtik drek," Manny snickered and winked surreptitiously at Luis.

The skin above Rod's mask flushed bright red, and his eyes glittered. "Don't think I don't know what you're saying. Just keep it up and you'll be laughing out the other side of your face," he threatened.

"Back at ya!" Manny let loose a blatting raspberry.

Luis stared uneasily between the two. "You guys always go at it like this?"

Rumbling deep in his chest, Rod dragged his filter to one side and hawked a lugie into the air. It arced gracefully across the ridges of muck and splattered in the plastic, green mitten of a waving Santa. Rod stood a moment admiring the distance. "What a catch. The Majors fer sure." He grinned over his shoulder and caught Luis' furrowed brow. "Hey, don't worry none about it kid. It's just joshing."

"Yeah," replied Manny. "We're always razzing each other. It passes the time."

"And time we got." Rod's machine engaged with a bellowing roar. "Come on," he called over the link. "Let's hit it or we'll be here forever."

....

Backs straining, they scooped and raked refuse from the sandy shore. The labor seemed endless. Headway achieved during the day disappeared overnight as the relentless tides discharged new deposits onto the beach. Each morning the mountains of sludge appeared larger and more formidable, their detritus older and ranker.

Protesting muscles grew numb. Luis' mind, overwhelmed by the seeming immensity of the job, retreated behind a veneer of dazed indifference. The days blended into a hazy routine, with waking, eating, and sleeping the only notable events. Up at 4:00. Eat a hasty breakfast of leftovers. Be at the garage by 5:00 and on-site by 6:30. Eat a 30-minute lunch at noon—courtesy of the city. Eat dinner at 5:30, also on the city. Pack up at 10:00. Grab a quick shower at the garage, and back to Alice. Luis groaned each time he climbed into bed, remembering that in five hours he'd do it all again.

His journey home became a blank wall of exhaustion, a zombie state where little entered his awareness except what was necessary, the train, his stop, the apartment complex, his apartment door. Christmas music, animated decorations, and advertising barkers were reduced to myopic rumbles. Rebounding through the growing crowds of late-night shoppers, he plodded into the subway and climbed aboard the Cross-town.

The ride was a steady pressure of acceleration, a jumble of quickly forgotten faces, and the wheeze of opening and closing doors. Even Rico and Dinky-D had become unimportant, just another part of the mass. They threatened him twice more, but each time he failed to respond and instead stared through them with glazed eyes. Rico spit at Luis and Dinky shook a plasti-cast fist in his face. "Your nothing! You're nobody without us!" they screamed. Even that didn't rouse him; he was too tired. At the last confrontation, he spotted Nik grinning from the opposite end of the car.

Night—day. Dark—light. During a particularly bright period Luis stopped and looked around. The sky was a crisp pale blue, the sun brilliant white, and the beach… He blinked several times unbelieving. The beach was clearing.

Four weeks. His mind groped at the thought. *It's been four weeks.* He stared at the grim features of Manny and Rod. Their banter, though somewhat strained, had continued through it all. *How do these guys do this day after day, season after season*?

"Anyone ever think how stupid this is?" Luis leaned against his power rake. "We make it, pick it up, and dump it out there. It floats back in, we pick it up again, and take it to an incinerator. What's the point?"

"The point," Rod jabbed a finger at the sky, "is job security. All this," he spread his arms, "is our bread and butter."

"Check out the markers." Manny jerked his chin at the fluorescent yellow guide poles they had set the first day. The sludge had receded to one quarter of their height. "Looks like we're getting the best of it."

"About time," Rod growled. "This went smoother than I thought. I'm just glad there weren't any fragments."

"Hey Julie girl," Manny called. "How are the eyes? See anything?"

"Nothing so far. CoSat imaging indicates a Beaufort 5 weather system 75 miles south by southeast. We'll catch a faster current and higher tide, but that's about all."

"Alright." Rod minced a quick-footed jig. "If this keeps up, we'll be able to cut down to ten hours. And next week when the rest of the seasonal grunts get here, we'll be down to eight."

"And Louie here will be able to get some beauty rest. Ain't that right Louie?" Manny tossed him a kiss.

"Screw you!" Luis flipped a series of three fingered signs.

"What's that supposed to be?" Rod jeered. "Some sort of secret signal."

"No. It's a warning not to be messing with me."

"O-o-o-o I'm scared." Manny covered his head with his arms. "Whatcha gonna do if I don't, banger? Huh? Gonna jump me on my way home."

"That's it! You're gone!" Luis leapt from his rake and started across the beach.

Manny jumped from his rig into calf-deep runnels of gray-black ooze. Immediately, he began capering around, slipping and sliding through the slurry, his fists cocked, arms milling. "Come on. Put em up. Put em up."

Rod's voice crackled over the comlink. "Alright, you two!" The words blared painfully at full volume and made both men clutch their earphones. "Knock it off and get back to work. This stuff isn't going to go away on its own."

Stomping back to his machine, Luis slammed a fist against the engine housing before engaging its control grip. As it lurched forward, he hunched deep into his Kevlar P-suit. "Watch your back with these assholes. They got it in for you." From the corners of his eyes, he watched as Manny and Rod hollered and gestured over the mechanical din. Engaged in an endless battle of sarcasm and insults, they appeared oblivious to his sulk.

The work flowed smoothly. By dusk they had reached a steady state with incoming tidal surges. The setting sun stretched their shadows into the ocean. In its dim light, the Oby seemed a hulking shapeless mass poised in the surf. Windows lit from within by telemetry screens lent the appearance of brooding sentience.

As darkness crept across the sand, the Kleig lamps mounted on vehicle roofs clashed into stark blue-white brilliance. Men, equipment, and landscape were instantly thrown into ghostly wintertime relief. Sludge mounds became glistening snow drifts. From the inky blackness, frost-crested waves rolled and dashed against the beach.

Juliana's voice rang over their headsets. "Switching to night mode. Scanning vectors set at 500 yards. Starlight sweep negative. Sea level crest has increased two feet. Current plus 5 knots. Chem-comp factors within normal ranges. But…," she added, "I wouldn't drink the stuff."

Luis banked his machine for another pass when a hesitation in the water's motion caught his attention—a fleeting dip and bob of something large and heavy. He squinted his eyes. There it was again among the breakers, an object moving slower than the water. "Hey Rod. What's that?"

"What's what?"

"That." Luis pointed over the water. "There, just beyond the Oby."

Braking his machine, Rod turned to follow Luis' pointing finger. He swung his head from side-to-side, trying to catch a glimpse through the reflecting light. After a moment he froze. "Hey Julie?" His voice strained to remain calm.

A stifled yawn echoed over the com. "Yeah, what's up?"

"Better check it out. Looks like a rider at eleven o'clock. About 50 yards. The faster current and rising tide must've slipped it past Telemetry when you switched over to starlight mode."

"Just a minute." Equipment rattled and beeped over the com. "Damn this glare. I can't see a thing. Hold on," she grunted. "Let me get these optical filters in place."

Caught among high running breakers, the mass tilted from the sea. Swelling to the size of a Maglev engine, it lumbered over the shoals towards the Oby.

"Oh shit!" Juliana screamed. "A fragment! Everybody-."

The groan of tearing plastic and metal smothered her voice as the heavy clay-like mass slammed into the Oby. Dura-plastic walls designed to resist the pounding of waves, buckled and tore open under the fragment's relentless assault. The rent erupted with showers of yellow sparks and arcing blue-white electrical discharges as ruptured power leads shorted out in the surging seawater.

"Julie!" Rod shouted and tore off his facemask. "Julie!"

Stumbling from his scoop, Manny grabbed Rod's shoulder and yelled into his ear. "No response! She must be down! We got to get out there!"

Nodding curtly, they started off. Rod advanced several steps before turning. Luis hadn't moved. "You coming, or what?"

Eyes round in disbelief, Luis waved spastically at the wrecked Oby. "Out there? Are you nuts! We'll get killed! She's probably already dead."

Charging back, Manny jabbed his face at Luis. "She's put herself on the line for us plenty of times. We owe her."

"I don't owe her nothing," Luis growled towards the sputtering observation post.

Rod poked a gloved finger into his chest. "If it wasn't for her greaseball, you'd be hustling your ass on the street." He spit to one side. "But I guess you don't care about that."

"Forget the little asshole," Manny hissed. "He's just a nowhere Johnny. Don't care about nuthin."

Dead eyes fell on Luis. "Call it in. Then stand by the com." Rod grabbed Manny's arm. "Come on." They stomped off through the clinging mud.

Their squelching footsteps faded as Luis keyed the report to Sector HQ. "Rim licking assholes," he sputtered and signed off. "Go ahead and get killed. See if I care." Kicking at a clod of muck, he dislodged a bearded, plastic face. Its faded, blue eyes winked at him.

"Just who do they think they are. I mean, so what they give me a job. I don't owe them nothing." Over the comlink he could hear Rod and Manny cursing as they struggled into the wrecked Oby.

Scarecrow silhouettes blotted the exposed rent. "Oh Christ!" He heard Rod holler. "She's in the section that ripped away."

"What'll we do?" Manny yelped. "What'll we do?"

"Got to climb out there and get her."

"We won't make it. The fragments snagged on the superstructure. It'll tear away any second. We'll be crushed."

"Got to try," Rod bawled. "See she's moving." Faint moans whispered over the headset.

A string of sharp nasal profanity cut over the com. "All right. All right," Manny growled. "Let's do it."

Listening intently, Luis tried to separate their progress from the din of crashing waves and rending metal. With each surge, portions of the Oby tore away.

"She's stuck. The console collapsed on her legs."

The link filled with a series of prolonged grunts and colorful invectives. "Can't move it! We'll have to pry her loose."

Luis searched his feet. Gray muck smothered his toes and golden garland wound about his ankles. "Man, what am I doing. Hold on!" he yelled into his throat mike. "I'll give you a hand!"

Splashing through chest high water, he reached the Oby and dragged himself aboard. The decking rocked and flexed with each surge, forcing him to crawl on hands and knees to the fore section. The entire compartment clung by a few ribbons of twisted metal. In the glare from the beach lights, he could see Rod and Manny attempting to free Juliana's limp form from a crumpled console bench. Sparks flickering from sheared power leads imparted a strobe-like motion to their efforts.

"What can I do?" he shouted.

Neither Rod nor Manny looked up. "Glad to have you with us kid," Rod gasped. "This section is ready to tear away. No way we can get across. We need you to toss us a line."

"What? Where?"

"Anything!" Manny screamed. "Just get it to us!"

Luis desperately cast around. Sputtering wires dangled from the walls. Too much juice. He'd fry. Brackets anchoring the frayed opti-cables proved too strong for his maniacal tugs. Spying a coil of braided, moly-steel cable strapped to the bulkhead, he staggered across the buckled floor and yanked it from the wall.

His first toss splashed yards shy of the trio. Knees quivering, he inched across to where the platform dipped into the ocean. Waist deep in watery sludge that sucked and tugged at his legs, he tried again.

This time the coil splashed near their feet. With a deft motion, Manny snagged it from the water and clipped it to Juliana's utility belt. Attaching himself, he passed it to Rod who, with several quick jerks, hooked the cable to his waist.

They had begun prying at the bench when the compartment, still lodged on the fragment, shrieked loose of its moorings, and tumbled towards shore. The sudden shift in weight yanked Luis to his knees. Gasping for air, he clawed back to the surface still clutching the cable. Wiping gray slime from his eyes, he glimpsed Rod and Manny wrestling Juliana from the rolling compartment.

Breakers, no longer dampened by the fragment or compartment wall, seethed through the breach. Leaden spray clouded Luis' vision. Loose equipment tumbled about the Oby. Sharp plastic and metallic edges slashed at his suit and gouged furrows along his legs. A large object slammed him to the floor. Knife-sharp pains stabbed his legs as he struggled to his feet. In the growing battle to maintain footing, Luis lost sight of the trio. He could feel their weight on the cable as it sliced through the water. With his head back and the greasy line clenched tight in his fists, he braced himself against a ruined wall.

Waves submerged his position, knocking his facemask aside. Luis choked as flaming liquid pushed past his gritted teeth and into his throat. His nose and eyes burned. He tried to spit, but his tongue, swollen by caustic chemicals, refused to obey.

His arms ached; his shoulders throbbed. He wanted desperately to let go, to run for shore, but if he did… Luis felt the cable slip and squeezed tighter. Gagging, suffocating, he focused his entire awareness on maintaining his grip.

A vibro-knife floated out of the darkness followed by Dinky's screaming face. "You ain't nothing without us! Nothing!" From across a long hall Rod's eyes bored into his. "Look kid we need your help, but it's up to you." Sirens wailed in the night as he gazed helplessly into Fuerto's dying eyes. Red bubbles frothed from a deep gash across his brother's throat. "Leave him," Terrance snarled. Alice's stomach swelled before him. "Blood's thick," he murmured. "We got something between us and that means a lot to me." Nik smiled gently from behind his white beard. "Now if I had me a kid, damn straight I wouldn't want to bring him up here." Juliana caressed the tattooed tear on her cheek. "You'll do just fine, but it's up to you."

"It's up to you…" His fist smashed into the wall mirror. A crack ran its length, spreading into a fissure, then a chasm. Luis split in half as an entire section fell away and shattered to the floor.

He felt himself lifted and slammed hard against an unyielding surface. His arms went slack, and the cable slithered from his grasp. "I tried," he gurgled. "I tried."

Something wrapped itself roughly about his throat and dragged him backwards. Shadowy forms loomed over him, wailing incoherently. He spied Santa Claus waving from atop a hill of silver mud; clearly saw him lay a green mittened finger alongside his nose and wink.

Reindeer churned a dirty froth across the waves. Laughing maniacally, Santa surfed his sleigh along endless crests of knotted garland, discarded bows, denuded pine trees, and reams upon reams of shredded and torn wrapping paper. For a moment everything glittered with a festive air, then all the hues and colors blended into a great gray towering wave that crashed to the ground, burying him. Luis struggled for air, for freedom, but his feet remained anchored to the spot. In his hand appeared a shovel, but the muck grew deeper no matter how fast he scooped and heaved.

He woke screaming, cold sweat trickling down his face.

"It's all right," a soft voice murmured. "Everything is OK." Arms cradled him and he clung to them with desperate strength.

Alice nuzzled his ear. The pressure of her lips and the soft caress of her breath felt warm and comforting. "The doctor says you'll be fine. They got to you early. You have a few chemical burns, some torn muscles and ligaments, and a few lacerations, but nothing serious. The gro-packs will have you up and around in no time."

"Yeah," Luis rasped. "Yeah." With a shaky hand he massaged his throat. It hurt.

"There're a few people here to see you. They've been waiting since the doctor said it was Ok."

"Who?" he managed as a bald, orange suited figure burst into the room. Behind it trailed two others. One, equally orange but with a shock of unruly black hair, shuffled across the floor. The other in a white hospital dickey hobbled along with a cane.

"Hells bells kid, you're looking good," boomed Rod. Grabbing Luis' hand in a crushing grip, he gave it several hearty pumps. "You done us proud. I owe you. Hell, we all owe you." He beamed affectionately, then added in a low voice. "Just name it."

Luis wheezed, not knowing what to say.

"Quit pestering the man and let him heal." Limping closer, Juliana took Luis' hand and looked severely into his eyes. "The fat man here says you saved our lives by anchoring the cable and nearly drowned holding on." Nodding slowly, her face softened, and the blue tattoo glistened as a tear trickled down her cheek. "I just wanted to say thank you."

Manny slapped his forehead. "Oh, fer Christ's sake, quit with the blubbering will ya. This ain't no funeral. We're all alive and glad to be here." He stumped to Luis' side and gave his hand a brief tug. Quickly stuffing his hands back into his overall pockets, he stood there shifting uneasily from one foot to another.

"The three of us been talking and… well we want you to know that you got a permanent job if you want. It's fixed see, with full bennies that'll take care of the kid when it comes along." He gestured at Alice's obvious pregnancy. "Of course, you'll have to work with us." Manny circled his thumb at Rod and Juliana. "But… ah-h-h… we'd be glad to have you on our team. And… well… I just wanted to say… for myself that is… ah-h-h… thanks. I… um-m-m… I… thanks." Flustered, Manny plunged his hands repeatedly into his pockets. He turned back several times as if to say something more than mumbling a nearly incoherent "Thanks," before joining the others at the foot of the bed.

Luis closed his eyes. A permanent job. Not seasonal, but one of the regular crew. Steady year-round work with the city. No more street hustles or take what you can get. It would mean a lot. Alice could go back to school. Hell, even he could. They could move, would have to move. Luis fingered the tattoo between his left thumb and forefinger. Maybe a different life for their kid. He watched Alice chewing her lower lip, a habit he'd always found endearing.

Yeah," he croaked. "Hell yeah."

Selling Point

"Here it is!" With a flourish, Janet Dyson threw open the door and stepped inside. Dust rained from the ceiling, frosting her hair and shoulders. Holding a hand delicately to her nose, she sneezed once, then smiled apologetically.

Tom Wyman poked his head around the jam and squinted into the darkness. His shadow cast a pointed silhouette in the bright orange square of hall light that extending through the doorway. Gray blobs resolved themselves into a scattering of dilapidated furniture. Cobwebs shrouded the walls, and a strong unpleasant odor filled the air.

"Sorry about the overhead lights." Janet shrugged the padded shoulders of her red, amazon jacket nearly to her ears. "The previous owner never replaced the filaments. Our original write-up says there's a working floor lamp. The heat's been turned up, so at least it's comfortable. You're the first to see the apartment since it came out of probate."

"Who the hell lived here? A pack of dinges." Tom cupped a hand over his nose. The sour odor made it difficult to breathe.

"Can we open the windows? The air seems a bit thick."

"Certainly." Cautiously picking her way across the room, Janet angled toward piebald patches of sunlight streaming from the front windows. Tom remained at the doorway admiring her swaying figure as she faded into the half-light. He winced at the wet crack of flesh against wood.

Muffled curses erupted from the darkness. Leaning into the room, Tom tried to make out what had happened. "Are you Ok?"

"Yeah. I'm fine. I just barked my shin against an end table. Stay where you are until I get some light in here."

Swearing softly, Janet reached the sill and after several grunting tries managed to wrench open its lock handle. Glazing snapped and crackled as the windows butterflied open. Bronze sunlight flooded the room.

Noises echoed from the street below: the grinding honk and rumble of traffic, the muted rustling of pedestrians, and faintly in the background, a high thin warbling.

Tom tilted an ear as he carefully navigated the threshold. "This neighborhood seems remarkably quiet for a No-Bar. I guess that means the crime level is pretty low." Moving slowly, he skirted the room and joined Janet beside the window. "Security must be tight," he added hopefully.

"This area is in the process of being revitalized, but it's not a restricted enclave, if that's what you're expecting." Janet tucked an errant lock of auburn hair behind her ear. "It's a protected subdivision open to the city. The building has its own security lockout, and the neighborhood is patrolled by a citizen watch group. Still," she continued blandly, "it's not a good idea to travel alone or without a weapon, even during the day."

Tom's hand automatically crept toward his breast pocket. Janet watched the movement with amusement. *He's a hermie.*

She appraised him with a cold, unobtrusive eye. All-fit styrene clothes, pseudo-leather brogans, Jr. cut hair. Wonder what he's doing here? Usually, enclavers live and die within their walls. If he's slumming like this, they probably drove him out.

Such friendly communities, Janet sneered. They have their ways of letting you know when you're not welcome. There's the social censure when friends and colleagues turn their backs or avert their eyes as you walk by. The overnight cessation of invitations to group functions. The, at first gentle, then forcible insistence by the neighborhood steering committee that their community isn't right for you. The loss of self-esteem as professional contacts dry up and company officials suggest that you might wish to seek employment elsewhere.

Her eyes narrowed slightly. But most of all, there's the terror of suddenly being thrown into an entirely new world with different rules and different goads.

Tough luck. She forced a smile. He'll have to drag himself out of it 'cause nobody will do it for him.

Gentle breezes stirred a sharp, tangy scent through the room. "What's that smell?" Tom took several shuffling steps, sniffing the air. "Can't be from outside, it's a blue day today and the air index is only 200." Head casting, he let his nostrils quarter the room. "I swear it smells like…"

Sighing heavily, Janet bent over, stretching her legs for effect. Mauve-tinted, auburn tresses veiled her face as she rubbed her shin. "That's a tragic story."

Tom's eyes followed the undulating line that stretched from her red spike heels, up her calf, to the rounded curve of her tight-fitting lycra short-sweep. "I'm sorry." He shook his head. "What did you just say?"

"I said it's a tragic story. O-o-o-f." Standing straight, Janet tugged her skirt back into position and gazed sadly out the window. The siren had increased in volume. *It's no doubt a prowler*, she searched the street, *but nothing in view.*

"ApCo appropriated this apartment under an AFC contract. Last month the previous owner died from an overdose of painkiller. She was a gerrie with terminal cancer who decided to take the short road. Somehow, she figured out how to reset the dosage on her syringe."

She pointed at a decrepit Zero-G lounger. "Our service personnel found her in that chair."

A blotchy brown stain discolored the lounger's tan seat cushion. Bending close, Tom sniffed and made a face. The smell emanated from there. Coughing lightly, he pulled a kerchief from his pocket and dabbed his nose. "I hope this means you'll be knocking a few points off the price Ms. Dyson."

"To be sure," she admitted. "A domicile of this standing and in this location normally goes for 275,000 Cr, but we at ApCo are offering it for 265,000 Cr—as is."

"Of course." Tom glanced around the apartment. The persistent wailing seemed just outside. Stepping to the window, he leaned over the sill to see if he could spot its source. Only the regular, late morning assortment of trams and pedestrians were visible. Across the street, foot and wheeled traffic avoided a large greenish lump that partially obstructed the alley entrance. From this distance he couldn't tell what it was, but it spilled across the street and sidewalk in a symmetrical oval.

"Mr. Wyman," Janet Dyson tapped her foot impatiently, "if you would, please."

"Huh? What? Oh yes." Dragging his attention from the window, Tom turned and was handed a folder.

"This is a list of the apartment accessories. As we discussed at the office, nothing's been touched since its acquisition. Our records indicate everything is in working order. It's up to you to update the appliances."

Tom rustled through the papers and began a swift inventory. The com units blue-lighted at a touch. Only the security-com, as noted, failed to produce a viable image. He stepped carefully around stacks of news sheets and advanced to the kitchenette. The microven, its inside crusted with molten who-knows-what, hummed when he set its timer. In seconds the fumes of burning grease stung his eyes. Blinking rapidly, he shut it off. Still staring at the oven, Tom moved to the fridge and opened the door. A near tangible wall of cold, putrid air sent him reeling backwards. Inside, fuzzy lumps of rainbow-colored mold crusted the shelf grates and climbed the unit's plasticene sides. Gagging, he slammed the door and cast a baleful glance in Janet Dyson's direction.

Circling the living room, Tom tugged a loose fragment of flowered sheathing from the center wall. It peeled away revealing smooth, off-white fiberboard underneath. Tom gave a light snort, then turned and shuffled across the carpet into the bedroom.

"Jesus," he snarled in disgust. The air reeked of stale urine and sweat. "How could anyone live this way?"

In the dim light from the living room, he could make out an unmade mattress crammed in the far corner. The blankets and top sheet were thrown back as if its occupant had just risen. Hard, white puffs dotted the floor. He kicked one and it rolled several feet before stopping. The walls, as in the outer room, were bare. Other than the mattress, there were no other furnishings in sight.

Tom nudged objects aside with his feet as he moved gingerly about the room. The mattress sheets appeared stiff and waxy. The crumpled balls, now recognizable as discarded tissues, crunched underfoot as he edged his way to the closet. He quickly flipped through the few outfits hanging on the cross bar. *Well*, Tom wiped his hands against his pants, *at least there's not much to throw away*. "You said there's an attached bathroom?" he yelled.

"Yes," Janet Dyson called from the living room. "To the left of the closet. The lock panel is on the right."

The siren stopped. Janet peeped out the window as a black and white CitySec prowler swung in across the street, alongside the alley entrance. Two black-clad figures climbed from its cockpit and entered the alleyway.

Tom jerked his eyes over the recessed panel he'd missed in the gloom. "Got it," he called, fumbling at the release catch. With a soft rumble, the panel slid open, and a night light flickered to brilliance. He nearly screamed at the yellowish death mask gaping before him. Balding and with a lined face, it fought for breath as he stared back in horror. Tossing his head, Tom blinked madly at his reflection in the medicine cabinet mirror. He loosened his Velcro collar and swallowed hard several times before examining the surroundings.

Low light illuminated a tiled coffin just large enough for the stand-up shower and dry chemical toilet. Careful not to brush against any surface, he inspected the fixtures. Mildew caked the shower stall, and a white rime ran from the wall-mounted soap dispenser to the tile floor. Caustic fumes and the lingering tang of urine indicated an imbalance in the toilet's disinfectant cycle, but its bowl and seat appeared clean.

"Filth and trash," he grumbled, returning to the living room. I'll have to toss it all and do a major scrub down. Still the place doesn't appear too bad. Now if April were here... No. He bit off the thought. She did for you. After all the failed attempts, she couldn't stand it and ran off with that... that... that bastard!

Tom gritted his teeth and angrily scuffed a dusty area of the carpet. He glared at the dark blue nap. "This carpet needs to be torn up and replaced." With her hands clasped behind her back, Janet Dyson nodded politely and smiled.

Glowering, he paused before a narrow wall shelf and poked at a small, faceted object. With big green eyes, a thin ovular body, and pointed ears and legs, he couldn't identify it. It was stupid. Just like the knickknacks April collected. Stupid trash!

"Can you believe this." His lips curled into a sneer. "I mean just look at this junk." He waved a hand at the assemblage of cracked pottery and figurines. "It's just a bunch of worthless crap!"

Janet's smile remained frozen. *It's no different than the crap I put up with every day from jerks like you.*

She nervously twirled a platinum band that circled her right wrist. *God, I hate these clowns. It never fails. Even if they can afford out of pocket like this bar scum, they come in here cutting at a place hoping to knock down its price.* She shifted slightly, keeping herself between Tom Wyman and the doorway. *Dickering bastards. As if I owned the place and had any say as to what it sells for. Besides, I need to make a living too.*

She squeezed her fingers till they ached. *To think I used to sell high-end enclave units. Now look at me – Janet Dyson MiDo Apartment Realtor.* She laughed to herself. The job hadn't been any great shakes so far, but it paid well enough. *If the supply keeps up with demand, I'll do fine. And I need the money if I'm going to get out and back into some sort of respectability.*

The high whine of a turbo tram floated through the window. Brakes screeched and there came the sound of raised voices. Thrusting her chest forward, Janet tugged absently at her jacket lapels as she spoke over the noise outside. "Did you want to talk it over with your spouse Mr. Wyman? We can hold the place for two days with a 25% retainer."

Tom stared hard at the revealed expanse of cleavage, especially the sharp jutting nibs of her nipples. He licked his lips wondering how they looked uncovered. Were they big, brown areolas—the kind that took your whole mouth to cover, or maybe small and pert—ones you could curl your tongue around? *April had...* He blinked and shook himself.

"Sorry," he massaged his eyes. "I got lost there for a moment. I'm single. This place is for me."

"Oh?" The lapels slid back into place as Janet consulted her E-pad. "Our records indicate you are under marriage contract."

"The annulment was finalized two days ago." Tom ignored a sudden ache in his chest. "Your records probably haven't updated."

As part of the cohabitation settlement, he and April sold their Southbridge residence and divided everything 50-50. Ostracized by neighbors, most of whom sided with April, Tom elected to move. So here he was looking for a condo in some unprotected neighborhood. *Imagine*, he fumed, *going from first world to third world overnight. And just because of a genetic predisposition. Sure, we had two aborts, but she didn't have to tell everyone. And she didn't have to take up with that G.I.C. in the next quad.*

Pursing her lips, Janet scraped the E-pad with a long red nail. "I'm afraid that this changes everything Mr. Wyman." She looked up, a serious expression clouding her features. "We based your credit rating on a two-income household. Unless you're able to provide a substantial down payment, I'm afraid we'll be unable to offer you this property."

Tom ground his teeth. He had a certain image to maintain, even if tarnished, and this was the max he could afford without going boho. "How substantial is substantial?"

Janet tapped several entries into her note pad, then patted a finger against her lips, waiting for the display. "Say 60%." She smiled brightly. "With that amount down the rest of the terms will carry."

Tom's gaze darted around the apartment. He needed a place now, and this was the best of the lot he'd seen. "All right, I'll take it, but all this crap," he waved at the furnishings, "has to go."

Janet shrugged. "That's your problem. You buy it. You clean it. As I mentioned earlier, the contract states this domicile is sold as is."

"What!" Tom's eyes bulged and his head thrust forward. "I click over 159,000 Cr and you expect me to clean this place! Let me see that!" He snatched the pad from her hands and glared at the document. "Humph." He sagged visibly. "I suppose… Hey, what's this." His finger traced several lines of fine print along the bottom of the contract. "Nobody said anything about that."

Careful not to brush against him, Janet peeped over his shoulder and followed his sliding finger. Tom found himself transported by her perfume. He leaned closer and she backed quickly away.

"That's the mortality clause." Keeping her voice even, Janet casually dropped a hand into her purse and rested it against a high voltage needler.

She learned long ago that a woman had to protect herself. Sure, the lycra and stilletos were a come on, but they were standard business tools and not to be handled by the clients—at least not without her permission.

"It states that in the advent of your death, if you have not designated a beneficiary, the apartment defaults to its original holder. In this case, ApCo. There's a similar default clause at the beginning. Here," she traced a sharp red nail along several lines, "under payment plan. The apartment defaults to ApCo in the event of your failure to make payments."

Tom grunted and kept reading. The scent of her perfume lingered in his nostrils. It was so heady it overwhelmed the moldering smell that permeated the room. He found himself thinking of April and suddenly felt very lonely.

"We can process the contract right now if you wish." Janet approached the apartment vid-com. "I can link up with the city's real estate database through this terminal and it can be yours today." She rippled her eyelashes slowly, luxuriantly. "We've clients lined up who are very interested in this property, so I can't guarantee it will be available tomorrow."

Tom cleared his throat. Outside the street noises had returned to normal levels. "What's your schedule like today?"

"After this meeting I'm through." She glanced sideways and dropped a hand towards her purse. "Why?"

"Look, I feel like I've been a bit of a dogger. You know carrying on about the apartment and all. And I'd like to… well, you know, apologize." He hunched his shoulders and stared uneasily at his shoes. "I thought, if you weren't busy tonight maybe we could have dinner."

"I'll think about it." She winked and turned back to the view panel. "Now as to the apartment, would you like to finalize?"

"Oh yes. Yes of course." He fumbled a note case from his coat pocket. "What do you need?"

Janet blew a cloud of dust from the touch-keys before jacking her note pad into the terminal. "We'll do a credit authorization first." She winked again. "Got to make sure the funds are there."

"Certainly, they are. I never waste anyone's time." Squaring his shoulders, Tom keyed in his personal finance code. "Least of all yours." He smiled and his heart fluttered as Janet quirked a corner of her mouth.

"Once funds are verified, we'll do thumb and retinal scans," she continued. "Standard stuff." With speed born of long practice, Janet raced through the procedure.

Her expression appeared cold and aloof in the screen's blue glare. Frown lines Tom hadn't noticed were thrown into sharp relief. She reminded him of a marble statue he'd seen in a museum. A Greco/Roman sculpture titled: *Maiden by the Pool.* Beautiful, reserved, distant, she peered into a shimmering pool of water, transfixed by her own reflection.

Fascinated, he followed her prompting without question. He pressed his thumb against pad, then fit the scan cube to his eye.

Light-blind in the scan's afterimage, Tom blinked furiously as flickering pinpoints of light swarmed through the air. For a moment the sparkling currents coalesced into a nearly visible torso. A lean face turned towards him with a look of pity. Fiercely rubbing his eyes, he watched as the image faded into dust moats floating in a sunbeam's path.

"And that's all there is to it," Janet declared, and deftly tucked the E-pad into her satchel. "You are now the proud owner of Apartment 290 in Complex 4 of the East MidDo subdivision."

"Well." Tom rubbed his hands together. "Shall we celebrate?"

"Celebrate?" Janet stepped back, her eyes alert. Her hand remained in her purse.

"You know," he hesitated, "dinner. A few minutes ago, you said you'd think about it."

"Dinner. Oh, I am sorry." Shrugging one shoulder, she leisurely circled to the window. "I can't." On the street below, white-coated Security Technicians were hauling a black and crusted body into a scooper van parked at the alley mouth. "I just remembered I've a date with my steady partner. We're thinking of applying for a nuptial contract." Her eyes glittered and her lips stretched into a thin, frosty line. "Enjoy your new residence Mr. Wyman. And remember what I said about neighborhood precautions."

"Hey wait a minute." Tom reached out and snagged her sleeve. Janet spun out of his grasp. Tom jerked back as her elbow grazed his nose.

"But I didn't…" His voice trailed off as she yanked the needler from her purse. Blue sparks arced across the needler's electrodes as she sidled across the room and backed silently through the door.

Mouth gaping, Tom watched her go. In the sudden gloom, the room closed about him. "I didn't mean anything. I just wanted…" Eyes and cheeks burning, his throat aching, he leaned against the windowsill and tilted his face to the sunlight.

Below, the white CitySec morgue van pulled into traffic and sped off down the street.

Rissa in the Morning

Dado always says if you're going to rummage, it's best to get to the beach before CitySan. 'Cause once in, they bumble ahead on their hidie-horses scooping stuff up regardless its worth. But for me what it really means is, you got to be there before the sun peeps and work fast.

I was on a rummage run along the old Dabny pier, a mile or so down current from a wrecked Oby. It had busted open in the big tide a while back but was too far offshore for me to swim safe.

The waves was really smashing it up, so I had my eyes peeled for wash-ups like opti-fiber bundles and copper wire. A week ago, I found a drum of quik-jel that had ripped loose from somewheres inside. I couldn't get it home by myself, so I got Jojo to help. Ma selled it for 20 credits. She give me five for finders and Jojo two for sweat. He was mad and threatened to beat me up if I didn't fork over another one for protection. So, I did.

The bay wind was cold and all I had was a blanket wrapped around my shoulders to fight the chill. I carried an empty plastic bottle in case I found clean drinking water and my hunting gear was tucked under an opti-fiber belt that I wove myself. It wasn't much, but it was all I needed: an old steak knife, a slingshot (I'm a pretty good shot.), and a footlong club for whacking anything that gets too close. I always try to be ready 'cause Dado says, you never know when you might get a chance at a dog, or a cat, or a rat even.

Anyways, the pier was leaning so far cattycorner it nearly touched the water in places. Old dry-rotted tires was lashed along the sides and its boardwalk was toothless with missing planks. The pier's a dangerous place. You got to step right, feeling ahead with your toes, else you might nudge the wrong thing and get smacked on the noggin with falling stuff. You also got to be out from under before the tides come in. 'Cause if you don't, things get real ishy. Everything wobbles and creaks and groans something fierce when the waves smash against the pilings.

Dado says the pilings are covered with barnacles, or what used to be barnacles. He says they're like the rest of this world now. Things've changed so much and so fast, he can't rightly tell what they are anymore. All I know is their shells are sharp and can cut you and if you brush too close, they'll snake out quick and bite ya. It really hurts.

Anyways, I was down there poking through the wash, not having much luck, when I heard a groan. I scrunched down and scooted into the deeper shadows 'cause it's not keen to be spotted. My ears was tight from straining and my eyes bugged from looking hard when I heard it again, low and mournful like the early morning winds. But it wasn't them. At first, I thought it might be, but the sounds were too uneven and seemed to be coming from inland.

Up near where the pier started, partly hidden by sand and trash, there's an overhang you can crawl under that's real good for shelter. You needn't worry 'bout it fallin down; it's rock solid. You could jump up and down on it without it coming apart. It's not like other parts of the pier where the boards are so rotten, they'd bust in half if you sneezed. It don't look like much from outside, but once you're inside it's snug, dry, and deep. I've hunkered there many times when the storms or night lights caught me out.

Well, I followed the sounds and sure enough there, tucked up under the overhang, lay a dinge. The day was breaking, and a band of yellow stretched across the horizon making it easy to see the rags wrapped round the stiff's feet.

I eased the club from my belt and slid closer, careful like, 'cause as Dado says, you never can tell what an animal will do when it's surprised.

Turns out I needn't have worried. When I got near enough it was plain from the scuff marks and big splotches of blood that he'd crawled there by himself and wasn't likely to be crawling nowheres else.

Backtracking the trail was easy too. There was just two long grooves dragged through the sand. I followed it about a quarter mile or so to the pavement edge and didn't find no other footprints. After dusting our tracks to make sure we couldn't be followed, I returned to eye the dinge some more.

I prodded his foot with the club and got no response. I squinched down and peered into the niche. From the chin whiskers I could see it was a man sure enough, but his face looked wrong. Sorta lopsided.

Ducking my head, I sidled in, club ready. Grit dug into my bare knees, and I held my nose tight, 'cause in that small space he stunk real bad.

I checked him over and the first thing I see was a sharp red crescent cut across his cheek where a boot heel or something like it had landed. His eyes and lips were puffed up while the rest of his face was mashed purple and black. I couldn't tell what his body looked like 'cause he was covered with old ratty clothes.

Right away I figured a pariah pack had ketched him. I knew about the packs 'cause Dado drilled me on them over and over before letting me out on my own. They're mean, and usually hunt at night. That's why it's always best to hole up when it gets dark, even if you are little and know your way around like me.

I stared at the man. He was like a mouse I found once, torn and bleeding, but still alive. Something had ketched it, probably a cat, and somehow the mouse had escaped, or the cat had just got bored. I took care of it, giving it drops of water from off my fingertips and trying to feed it soggy biscuit crumbs I saved from dinner. I really wanted to help, but when Jojo found me with it he threw the mouse out the window. I ran outside, but by the time I found it, it was dead. He laughed and said the mouse would have died anyway and that the best thing to do in those cases is to kill 'em and be done. Maybe he was right, but I wanted a chance to try. I frowned hard and pounded my knee. This time Jojo wouldn't stop me.

I didn't have no food on me 'cept a stale chunk of biscuit bread that was best to soak before eating it was so hard. My plastic bottle was empty 'cause Dado says it's not good to go on a run unless it's all the way full. Carry it part way full and it sloshes around and makes a lot of noise. That's why I count on finding water when I'm out. Then I remembered a puddle of fresh water I'd spotted when following the dinge's tracks.

I kept low and wound my way through patches of dried goldenrod. Their brown leaves scratched and made a lot of noise when I brushed against them. At the pool edge I waited several minutes before creeping out. The pool wasn't big, but it was big enough to attract scritches and other uglies.

I bent down and looked flat across the surface. There was no rainbow shimmers from nasty chemicals that can leak in and make you sick. Then I leaned close for a sniff. Water too old or too dirty has a funny smell and if you drink it your belly twists into knots and really hurts.

The water didn't smell all that bad and since there were things swimming in it, I figured it was passable. Scooping my bottle full, I run back to the pier.

"C'mon drink it." I pressed the bottle edge against the man's lips. When he didn't take any, I tried pouring some into his mouth. I tilted the bottle too far and slopped water across his face. He moaned and coughed a little as it dribbled from his whiskers and pooled beneath his head. Then he started mumbling.

"Forty days. Forty days."

When his eyes cracked open, I could see they was as bright red as his blood. It hurt just looking at them.

"Claire?" he croaked.

"I'm not Claire." I giggled and pulled my hair from my face. "My names Carrissa."

The man's eyes twitched, unable to focus. "Who?"

"Carrissa," I said again.

"Missa?" he sounded uncertain.

"No Carrissa. Car-ris-sa."

"Awright, Carrissa. But you're just— Ah-h-gh!" The man's face twisted, and his body stiffened. He squirmed a lot and his heels dug hollows in the sand. It took a while, but finally he relaxed, and his breathing slowed till he wasn't gasping so much. Blood trickled from the corner of his mouth, and stained his lips all black and red.

The sun had popped all the way up and looked like a bright red ball bearing sitting on a table. Light come in under the overhang, just warming the dinge's feet when he spoke again. "Didn't they teach not to mess with strangers." The words sounded mushy coming through his swollen lips.

"Sure, but I checked you out when I found you. There's nuthin you can do what I wont' be able to smack you first with this." I hefted my club.

"But I mighta been diseased. You coulda caught something real bad."

I shook my head. "You wouldn't have got beat up like that if was you was con... contag... catching."

The dinge studied me for a second. "What if somebody was after me. You mighta gotten shanked." He tensed a little, his face puckering. "The folks that did this to me like little girls like you."

I pulled the blanket tight around my neck and dug a finger into the ground. "Nope. Nobody's following you. I checked. I even wiped out our tracks coming back."

The man nodded and relaxed. "Smart girl," he rasped.

"Dado says I got talent. That's brains, beauty, and ambition."

Those horrible eyes rolled over to look at me. "Your Dado's right," he sighed like he was tired, "you are talented."

"Yep." I smiled.

Waves crashed against the pilings and the pier groaned as if aching with age. It sounded like Dado getting up in the morning, all creaks and pops.

"Still, it wasn't smart."

"My Grandpa Dado's smart. At least Mamma calls him a smart ass."

The man chuckled silently. "You're just a bit of a thing. How old are you?"

"Eight. But I'll be nine come summer."

He stared at me till I got uncomfortable. I grabbed my club and begin edging back. "Young, young, and younger," he muttered, turning away. "How come they haveta be so young?"

"I'm not young. I'm eight." I thumped my club against the ground. "I can hunt just as good as my brother and dodge bettern him too."

"I'm sure you can." His lips twitched upwards, and he glanced back at me. "Where'd you learn to speak so good. Most kids I hear your age talk gibberish."

"Dado teached me. He useta teach a lot when he was younger. He says learning to talk right will get me more chances than not. 'Sides," I twirled a finger in my hair, "it's part of being talented."

"I suppose." The man closed his eyes. "How 'bout some more water."

"Sure. Got some food here too." I pushed a few soaked pieces into his mouth.

Turning his head, he slowly spit out the biscuit and several hard looking lumps of bone. "Can't eat," he managed. "Teeth are all busted. Water's 'bout all I can handle."

The man laid there, taking slow shuddering breaths. Every so often he'd stop, and his face would twist into the most awful expression. Then he'd relax, careful, like he wasn't sure if it was going to hurt or not and start breathing again. I noticed that blood was trickling outta his mouth in a steady stream.

"You're not going to live, are you?" I asked.

His head shook back and forth, barely moving. "No."

"But why?" I was angry. How could he die after I just tried to save him? "I gave you water and food."

A smiled crawled up one side of his bruised face. "Sorry," he wheezed. "Guess I've had one too many kicks in the ass."

A low groan slipped from his lips, and he closed his eyes. "Not to worry. It's best this way."

"But I don't want you to!" I slapped the ground hard.

"Sorry," was all he said.

"Well then go ahead and die! See if I care!" I got up to stomp away when he called me back.

"Wait. I got something for ya." He tried lifting a hand to his chest but stopped when the effort became too great. "You'll have to get it. It's there in my right pocket. I can still feel the lump. Hope it's not broke."

The sun was shining all the way to the dinge's face, and he squinted in the glare. I slid close, ready to jump away should he move too fast. Then careful, so's no to hurt him any, I reached over and pulled a smooth object from his old, ragged coat pocket. At first all I could see was something bright, glinting like sun on water. It was clear same as glass, but shaped funny like an animal with two big, shiny green eyes. I knew as soon as I see it, it was special. "What is it? I never see nothing like this before."

"I don't suppose you have," he groaned. "It's a keepsake owl. I found it in the trash outside a mid-city apartment. It… it…"

The spasm started low, growing steadily into a bloody ragged cough that doubled him up. I dropped to his side to see was there anything I could do. His body jerked and trembled beneath my hands. Panting, he waved me away and began a long slow unfolding that took several minutes.

"Owls are supposed to represent wisdom." His words came soft as a faint breeze, rising and falling like the waves. "Probably all that's left in this town… besides your grandpa that is. It's all I have to…" He paused and I thought he was gonna break into another fit. "To thank you for trying. Not many would. Not many did." His eyelids fluttered and his forehead twisted into knots.

It took a while before he calmed down and got to breathing good again. "Now go away." He waved a stiff swollen hand. "Leave me to the sun."

Tucking my prize away, I peeked out from under the overhang to make sure there was nobody around before sneaking off. As I pulled down the beach, I thought I heard his voice muttering "Forty Days," but the wind carried it off, so I wasn't sure.

When I got home Jojo knowed right away I had something special. He asked to see it and when I showed it to him, he reached out his hand. "Gimme."

"No." I stuck out my lower lip.

"Fork it over rag doll or I'll hurt you bad." He knowed I hated the name rag doll.

"Leave me alone. It's mine. And don't call me rag doll. My name's Carrissa."

"I said gimme rag doll." When he grabbed for it, I swung my club up and conked him good alongside of his head. He went down all goggley-eyed and begun to cry.

I yelled real loud and told him if he was to ever try that again I'd really let him have it. He just cringed back and kept blubbering. I also let him know I wasn't going to let him bully me no more. And to make my point, I wonked him again with my club. He howled louder.

I watched him sobbing with his face all scrunched up and smiled. Not again. Never again.

He scooted away, giving me lots of space, as I marched from the room. Dado would be out on the back porch, and I wanted to show him my pretty thing.

Reverto Domus

The shuttle swerved across the empty commuter lane, narrowly avoiding a mound of bloody fabric wadded in the median. Taking the Brighton Boulevard exit, it wove through the Banyon Reclamation District, turning onto Waverly Avenue just after the Pelmont intersection. Halfway down the block it ground to a halt in front of *Babouc's Service & Repair*.

"That will be 35 credits," chimed the wire drone's automated pilot. "Discount Zone vouchers and Omni cards are accepted."

Harl Babouc groaned and rolled to one side. He dug an Omni card from his pants pocket and swiped it through the credit slot beside the duty hopper. The cab meter recorded the payment with a soft, tinkling gong.

"Take advantage of discounted travel rates through prepaid Zone vouchers," it announced.

Harl stared glumly at the meter display. He was tired and wanted to be home. "I don't have time for this," he muttered.

"Beginning this month," the voice continued, "Zone Services is offering discounted rates of up to 40%. If your plans include frequent intra-city travel—"

"No thank you," Harl spat. If he didn't interrupt it with the accepted phrase, the machine would keep him confined until its advertising spiel concluded.

"Thank you for using Zone Services," the tinny voice sang. "Have a nice day."

"Come on." He scratched vigorously at the black stubble on his chin. "Just let me out of here."

The cage lock disengaged and Harl climbed wearily from the basket. The drone waited until he had extricated himself before slamming the gate closed. With a steady whine, it pulled from the curb and hummed briskly down the street.

Harl stood silently, watching it disappear around the corner. "Good thing I bagged that Omni card before I left, or I'd still be walking." Somewhere down on the beach he had shifted from a bodiless presence back to solid form. Ithuriel must have had a good laugh making him walk, instead of transporting him home. It had taken nearly the card's entire balance to cover the thirty-mile shuttle ride to his shop.

Harl grimaced as he massaged his cramped leg muscles. This was it; no more heaven-sent assignments—no matter what the threats. "If I'd known what I'd see," he mumbled, "I'd have stood the audit."

Sunlight edged over the distant mountain peaks—enough to illuminate the world, but too early to warm the air. Harl glanced along the vacant streets and sidewalks, examining the shadows with newfound apprehension.

Nothing. It was too early—even for them.

With a relieved sigh, he stumped across the sidewalk to his storefront. The shop door unlocked at his palm press, and he pushed inside.

Tossing his jacket atop the service counter, Harl brushed through the curtains and into the back room. Angling across the floor, he jerked open the box fridge and helped himself to an icy beer. Popping the tab, he took a long pull, belched loudly, then shuffled slowly to his lounger. He plopped into its seat and wedged the sweaty can between his legs.

"Shit." The word rang hollowly through the air.

The can rattled against his teeth as Harl took another gulp. Foaming liquid burned its way to his stomach where it pooled in an icy lump. He slouched deeper in the chair.

"Too much," Harl murmured, finishing off the beer.

He stared blankly out the high, narrow windows lining the west wall. A black squall line flashed and flickered in the slices of visible sky. After long seconds, low rumbles rattled the windows and throbbed lightly through the room. *There'll be rain soon. We always need rain.*

With a soft burp, Harl climbed painfully his feet. Swaying slightly, he glanced at the can still clenched in his right hand then shuffled across the floor to the refrigerator. Returning to his chair with the remaining six pack, he yanked a can free, popped the tab, and took a long slow pull. Beer dribbled from the corners of his mouth and down his shirtfront. After catching what he could with his tongue, Harl drew a sleeve across his mouth. Thoughtfully, he examined the can's laser etched label. It flickered with an ever-changing mosaic of rainbow patterns and tiny dancing figures.

Carib's. The name glowed in flamboyant, cursive gold lettering. The legend read that it was brewed with distilled water, synthetic hops, and cultured barley flakes. *Cheap*, Harl sniffed, *but tasty*.

He took a small sip and looked around. The workroom benches and racks were comfortably cluttered, their dull metal finish glowing warm and friendly.

The lounger hugged him with the familiarity of an old friend. The room held a hushed welcome-back feel. He was glad to be home. He belonged here, was safe here.

Rain rattled against the windowpanes. Harl glanced up at the sudden sound—thankful to have made it home before the storm broke. "I'd hate walking in this." He took another drink, watching oily blobs of rain explode against the shatterproof glass. As the storm increased the drops melded into rivulets that meandered down the window's clear surface. Their steady coursing settled him deeper into the shop's embrace.

His lips quivered and a sharp pain lanced through his breast. Tears burned from his eyes. Wedging the can between his thighs, he buried his face in his hands. A thin, ragged sigh whistled between his fingers; a shudder rippled his shoulders.

He genuinely feared the report he was to give.

"Enough." Harl slapped a hand against the lounger arm. "Got no time for this." His face began to pucker and twist, but with a valiant effort he managed to bring it under control. "What are you going to say?" He pounded his fists on his knees. "Think man! Think!"

Two hastily gulped beers blunted the raw edge of hysteria. Harl leaned back and closed his eyes.

A shrieking, flaming scarecrow stumbled towards him. Darkness echoed with the sounds of bloody fists and guttural curses. A herd of pedestrians rushed past; their heads down; their eyes averted. Muffs were clapped tightly over their ears and scarves swaddled their mouths. A sea of resigned faces spun by. An infinite wall of view panels flickered to life and bathed the scene with a ghostly blue light. From each display shown a silent, brilliant white, predatory grin.

Harl rolled the beer can against his cheek. It felt wonderfully cool against his skin. If any place deserves destruction, it's this armpit of a city. Most of the people would be better off dead; they're already half gone as it is. Besides, he pressed the can to his forehead, what do I care what happens to them.

He tossed back another mouthful of beer. *Better them than me.*

And yet…

He saw again the wonder and strength that transfigured a child's face. He floated, warm and secure, as a grandfather's love washed over him. The loud drunken banter of friendship echoed in his ears. He recalled the bonds of shared adversity and the reluctant willingness of self-sacrifice. A man's breath dribbled away, caressing his cheek with a final benediction. In his mind's eye, he received a dazzling gift for unselfish aide.

Harl squeezed himself tight, trying to contain the cold current that knotted his insides. He was safe regardless his report. Ithuriel had promised. But what of the others. A negative report meant taking away everything—all they were, all they might become. He found it difficult to reconcile the despair and empty resignation he had witnessed with the blinding glimpses of hope that had passed his way.

"I can't do it. I just can't do it," he moaned, rocking back and forth. "There's got to be some other way." Thunder crashed through the room. Menacing, blue lit shadows scarred the walls. A hard, pelting rain rattled the windowpanes. The shop roared with the force of the deluge. Another flash illuminated the beer can nestled in his lap. The world shattered into a thousand million pieces of multi-colored light. Harl stared at the can's laser etched label, dazzled by the vision.

Laughter began low in his chest, a muted chuckle that grew louder and louder, until tears streamed from his eyes and down his cheeks. Enraged elements screamed and shook the shop, but Harl's laughter brushed them aside.

Lifting the can, he toasted the raging storm.

That morning Harl set to work. He scoured every square inch of his shop for parts. He ransacked shelves and even scavenged items from repaired units. His workbench became a frenzy of soldering, circuit tracing, cutting, and crimping. Chips, V-boards, plastic and metal casings tumbled from the bench. Silken snarls of opti-fiber threads swept the floor.

A frantic hammering at the shop's front door was ignored. The project was too important to brook any interruption. He worked all through the day, that night, and late into the next day.

Numbed with exhaustion, Harl sat back and stared at what he had accomplished.

A shiny, gold and obsidian saucer rested within an opti-fiber nest on the workbench. Small, of a size to fill one's palm, its nondescript surface mirrored the surroundings.

Harl chewed worriedly at his lip. Would it be enough? Would it be understood? There was only one way to find out. He took a deep breath and with a loud clear voice, summoned Ithuriel.

Storm clouds parted, allowing a shaft of sunlight to pierce their ranks. The beam slanted through the windows and into the room. The angel stood before Harl.

"You have a report?" Ithuriel folded his arms and slipped his hands into the sleeves of his long robe.

"Yes, I do," Harl nodded, "but before I give it, I have a question. Why, after your guarantee of safety and providing for my needs, did I have to pay for a cab to bring me home?"

The angel raised an eyebrow. "You're safe, are you not?"

"Of course, I am," Harl groused, "but that's not the issue. You had no problem turning me into a spook and flicking me around the city. Why didn't you bring me home the same way?"

Ithuriel chuckled. "You carried money." It was a candid statement.

Harl gritted his teeth and said nothing, after all, his paranoid precaution had cinched the angel's promise of a safe return. He had taken the Omni card in case Ithuriel forgot and left him stranded.

"Now then," Ithuriel's face remained serene, "your report."

Nodding abruptly, Harl snatched the device from the bench and thrust it into the angel's hands. Ithuriel lifted the compact saucer and peered deep into its mirrored depths. The polished surface offered a warped reflection of Ithuriel's own cherubic face and curls. His eyebrows lifted in question.

Solemnly, Harl pulled a remote from his coverall pocket and keyed a switch. The device shuddered to life. Rows of pinpoint opti-fiber lights flared, then settled into a sequence of repeating colors and geometric patterns—orange stars, blue diamonds, yellow squares, red triangles, and green circles. A touch pad, recessed into the saucer's top, became visible, its input keys glowed violet beneath the surface.

A breathed Oh-h-h escaped the angel's lips. Delighted, he turned the device from side-to-side, examining it with childlike curiosity. The saucer was warm, almost body temperature, and it hummed like a thing alive.

"Marvelous." Ithuriel's fingers lingered over a row of shifting amber and emerald lights. "Did you make this?"

"Of course!" Harl spat. "Who else?" He bowed his head, biting back his anger. Taking affront wouldn't do under the circumstances. He took a deep breath and started again.

"I spent the last two days building it from recycled parts." He waved a hand at the rubble strewn about the work area. "Some expensive. Some cheap. All serviceable."

Ithuriel turned a clear eye. "What does it do?"

"Do?" Harl frowned and stared at his feet. They seemed a long way off. He moved them, just to be certain they were still connected. "It hums. It whirs. The lights wink and change pattern. Sometimes it rattles and shakes, but eventually calms down to a low purr. "

"And..." Ithuriel smiled.

"And it's programmed to randomly alter its programming. The patterns and sequences change spontaneously over time."

"And..."

"And nothing." Harl shook his head and shrugged. "That's all it does."

"I see." Ithuriel smiled indulgently. "I'll cherish the gift, but I came for your report."

Harl glared woodenly at the angel. "You're holding my report."

"What!" Ithuriel stared at the device in disbelief. "This bauble? Why it's nothing but..."

Harl raised a hand for silence. Ithuriel quieted, astonished at his audacity. "Bauble? Perhaps. But will you destroy this bauble because it is created of random materials and components, and holds no obvious purpose?"

Frowning, Ithuriel tilted the device to one side. He nearly dropped it as a high frequency oscillation vibrated through the casing.

"Careful," Harl cautioned. "It likes to be kept upright."

"Likes?" Ithuriel gawked at the saucer. "The machine likes?" Imperiously, he stood it on edge. The hum rose to a scream, painful to hear. Quickly he righted the device. The sound dropped and the vibrations resumed a contented purr.

He cocked an uncertain eye. "Can this be shut off?"

"Its programming may be altered through the touch pad on its top, but once started the device cannot be shut off without destroying it entirely."

"So?" Carefully, Ithuriel tilted the device, letting the whine build just a little, before quickly righting it. He dared an experimental tap at the keypad. The hum changed pitch and the lights shifted to a new rhythm.

"So." The angel nodded. "Such a little thing to convey so much meaning."

Turning, he bowed to Harl. "Your sagacity, tinker, is great. From our vantage we would have missed the subtleties that your report so eloquently captures."

Harl fought to keep his exaltation from showing. *It worked! It worked!* "Thank you," he murmured. Inside his shoes, his toes performed a tiny jig.

"Such a well-crafted report." Ithuriel lifted the saucer until he could see its bottom. "It's a shame we can do nothing with it." He lowered it back to eye level. "Mores the pity."

"What?" Harl fell back against the lounger's arms. "Why not?"

Ithuriel lifted his gaze from the device. Its lights began flashing chaotically and the hum became violent pulses that jarred the fingers. "Because your report is moot."

"Moot!" A vein throbbed along Harl's temple, and his face burned a deep, wet crimson. "Why moot unless you already made your decision. And if so, then why did you send me at all?"

"Because we desired the guise of objectivity. Nothing more." The device began jerking from side-to-side. Ithuriel laughed. It was all he could do to maintain his grip.

"Nothing?" Harl stomped his feet. Helpless frustration coursed through him. He wanted to grab the angel and shake him, to make him reconsider.

"Nothing!" Ithuriel's snapped. He clutched the device to his chest to prevent its frisking from his grasp.

Harl sagged loosely into his chair—spare bones in rumpled clothes. "Then it was all for nothing." He stared blankly at the now calm device purring in the angel's arms. He had hoped… but now… Harl buried his face in his hands.

Ithuriel relaxed his arms but remained ready to enfold the device should it decide to suddenly leap away. "You do not understand, tinker. Your report is not a waste. The need for it has just been…" he searched the ceiling, "postponed. Issues of greater import have claimed our attention. For now, your city and its people will be left to themselves."

"Why?" Harl choked, barely able to speak. "Why such mercy?"

The angel nudged him with a sandaled toe. "Who knows? Perhaps by the time we are ready to reexamine this issue, the situation will have decided itself." He held the now quiescent device before Harl's eyes. "You see tinker, even we cannot predict the spontaneous alchemy of the human soul."

Ithuriel grinned and Harl, mesmerized by the device's flickering lights, grinned too. His grin became a huge yawn.

"Tired?" inquired Ithuriel.

Harl's jaws stretched wide with another yawn. "Feels like I've been up for months."

"Then you should sleep."

"But my shop?"

"You're shop will care for itself." Ithuriel drew a tingling finger across Harl's forehead, and his eyelids fluttered closed. "Now sleep."

There was a faint rustle of cloth, then silence.

Epilogue: Customer Service

The snooze alarm buzzed Harl to wakefulness. He stretched luxuriantly and knuckled the sleep from his eyes. His feet basked in a pool of sunshine. He wriggled his happy toes. It had been a wonderful nap. The summer sunshine so relaxing.

Summer! He jerked upright in the lounger. *But it's spring and...*

He stared around the room. The windows were closed and locked from the inside. Mr. Rossy's sump cam was clamped to the work bench. A flux rod leaned against the vise. The laser torch dangled from its mount beside the needle punch. Repair projects were arranged in neat rows along wall and floor. Everything was in order, even the dust lay undisturbed. There was no sign anyone other than himself had been in the room or that any time had passed except for his nap.

Harl shoved his hand out to arm's length and turned it slowly from side-to-side. He flexed the fingers. There was no pain, no scar, no evidence of a wound of any kind.

He climbed unsteadily to his feet, stumbled to the fridge, and yanked open its door. The six pack was still there, untouched.

"It was a dream." Harl sagged against the door. "Just a dream."

He drew shaking fingers across his face and chuckled softly. Of all the things to dream. Angels threatening city-wide destruction. And all those people. Christ, where did that stuff come from. He chuckled again. Already the images were fading. Imagine my opinion meaning anything.

A violent pounding on the shop's front shook him from his revere. *The shop!* He slapped his forehead. *I gotta open up!* Scrambling through the curtains, Harl pressed the lock release to the front door.

"About time!" Cal Tremont lurched through the shop door lugging a Tri-D. The viewer's weight curved his already crooked spine until he looked like a question mark mounted on bowed legs.

"Where the hell you been," Cal wheezed. "I been waiting out there for god knows how long." He hiked a stiff leg over a coil of coaxial cable and continued stumping his way to the counter.

"I was taking a nap." Harl gave his face a brisk chafing, trying to rub away the vestiges of his dream.

"What're you doing sleeping in the middle of the day?" the old man shouted. "Time enough for that when you're dead." Cal set the Tri-D down and braced his hands against his knees. "Damn thing's heavier than I remember," he gasped.

Harl hurried around the counter. "Here let me help you with that."

"I can do it." Cal placed a possessive hand on the Tri-D. There was a brief tug-of-war before he relinquished his grip with all the grace of an oyster giving up a pearl.

"It's no problem," Harl grunted, lifting the set. *It is heavier than it looks.* He glanced again at Cal Tremont. The man was 90 odd pounds of bone wrapped in loose folds of withered, brown skin. Though bent and old, he still had his original teeth, a head of thick, white hair, and clear, sea-green eyes that cut to the bottom line.

Harl set the viewer beside the counter. "What can I do for you?"

"Thought that was obvious." Cal slapped the viewer housing. "Brought in my TD. Thought you might look it over. It's all bunged up. Everything's wibble-wobby."

"Are those the technical terms?"

Cal Tremont grinned. "Yeah! Got them from the owner's manual. Wibble-wobby comes right after hokum-pokum and thing-a-ma-bob."

Harl laughed and dragged the set behind the counter. "I'll get to it. How does next week sound?"

"Well," Cal hesitated, "I'll be missing my favorite shows…"

"I'll get to this afternoon and post you soon as it's fixed. How's that?"

"Wel-l-l, I guess," Cal drawled. "If it's the best you can do."

Harl printed a double receipt and handed one portion to the old man, then pasted the other onto the TD drum.

Cal folded the chit a tucked into his shirt pocket. He cleared his throat with a rattling cough. "Hear about Earl Caffree?"

"Hum?" Harl glanced up from his bent position.

"Earl Caffree," Cal offered again. "Didja here what happened to him?"

"Nope," Harl looked up from his work. "Can't say as I have." He examined Cal's face. The old man's expression hadn't changed, it held the same sour look, but his eyes sparkled with the obvious excitement of fresh gossip.

"He's dead."

"Dead?" A tingle of fear arced through Harl's groin as he dragged the TD into the back room. When he returned, he leaned forward and folded his arms on the countertop. "Did you say dead?"

Cal nodded. "I just come from his street. There was a CitySec patroller, and a scoop wagon pulled up. You know, one of the big white ones?"

Harl nodded that he did.

"A couple of boys in white coats hauled him out in a full-body trash bag. It's just as well." Cal's lips twisted into a sneer. "He was a miserable S.O.B."

"D-d-do they know how he died?"

"Sure," Cal continued. He seemed not to notice Harl's stammer. "Seems the idiot fried himself on that Tingler of his. Wanged it up to max and cooked himself."

"So, it was an accident then?" Harl felt relief wash over him.

"Nope," Cal Tremont shook his head. His loose jowls swayed back-and-forth. "More like suicide."

Harl closed his eyes and a leering death's head swam into view. "Sure, it's got to look natural?" the death's head asked. "You know suicides are nice too." Harl jerked a hand to his face, knocking a stack of wafer chips from the countertop. They crashed to the floor and the specter vanished. "Suicide?" The question dribbled from his lips.

"Unintentional of course." Cal winked, delighted at the response. "Seems the idiot took his Tingler apart and hopped it up. He must've done a good job too, because it was still running when they found him."

"You know," he added almost as an afterthought, "Earl used to be a senior hardware engineer down at Pantheon. That was what," Cal searched his memory, "maybe twenty years back."

Harl's head wobbled on his neck. The world seemed very far away. He stared at a cobweb hanging in the ceiling corner. Once anchored by three points, it now dangled by two. "No, I didn't know."

I gave the man a Magnum when he was expecting a .22. I should have known that the first thing he'd do was set the pulse to maximum. Didn't I know that? I must have known that. Didn't I?

"Well, the cops I talked to seemed to think that's how it was. At least they said that's how they're writing it up."

"The security patrol spoke with you?" Harl stared at Cal in disbelief.

"Oh yeah." He waved his hand. "They were real talkative. Seems they've been getting mighty tired of handling all the complaints about him."

He leaned closer and whispered confidentially. "I got the feeling they didn't care much one way or the other. They were just glad to see him dead. Them and a whole lot of others," he added under his breath.

"And Murial?" Harl's fingers clenched white against the counter.

"Oh, she'll be all right. You'd a thought she'd be happy, what with that scoundrel checking out. But there she was, wailing fit to beat the band. I tried to calm her down, but—" Cal shrugged.

He peered timidly from under his thick bushy eyebrows and touched trembling fingers to Harl's sleeve. "You know he used to beat her."

Harl turned his face aside and nodded briefly.

"Yep." Cal Tremont stared sadly at his hands. Blue veined ridges covered their backs and beneath the translucent skin, the bones shown a brittle white. "Yep, he did."

"You know if I was younger man, I'd a done something about it. Lord knows something needed doing." He shook his head.

"Oh, by the way," Cal dug a receipt from his pants pocket and laid it on the counter, "Murial said for me to give you this. Said she didn't need it no more and that you'd know what to do with it."

Harl glanced at the wrinkled invoice. It was dated today.

Well," the old man slapped his palm against the countertop, "got to be going."

Harl started to speak, but Cal waved him to silence. "See you next week," he winked and pushed through the door. Outside, he glanced in both directions, tucked his hands into his pockets, and shuffled off up the sidewalk.

Also from Glenn Searfoss...

About the Author

Glenn Searfoss is an American author of fiction and non-fiction works in computer science, natural history, science fiction, and mythology. He lives in Englewood, Colorado, USA.

CPSIA information can be obtained
at www.ICGtesting.com
Printed in the USA
LVHW051159141221
706147LV00003B/165

9 781789 828399